VALENTINA'S WAY

A SPIRITUAL DISCOVERY

Manny Fiteni

ISBN: 978-0-646-85044-3
Version 1.0
Valentina's Way
 2021

"If you want to find the secrets of the universe, think in terms of energy, frequency and vibration."
— **Nikola Tesla**

CONTENTS

Lost

The world was now spinning as the woman could hear voices, as she lay there in a state of confusion.

Voices inside and outside of her head were talking around her. Like a dream. A bad one.

'God, I feel sick,' she thought to herself.

'Just let my life end. It was never worth living in the first place.'

'Where are you, Jacob? Why did you leave me?'

Her thoughts were now scattered, from this world to the next as she became aware of people around her. She was fading slowly.

The woman turned and looked up at the wall clock to the left of her. It was 9pm. It seemed that every time she now looked at a clock in the evening, that time would appear. As if time had stood still for her. What a co-incidence she used to think to herself.

"It's ok miss, you are in good hands," advised the young paramedic. "We will take good care of you. You are going to be fine. Just lay there calmly as we prepare you for the ambulance."

Valentina looked up and saw a young woman of no more than twenty-three years old standing over her. To the left of the paramedic, she saw another figure that seemed familiar to her, but she couldn't quite make out who it was. She assumed it was the paramedic's work colleague who was assisting.

The figure now touched her forehead as she was going in and out of consciousness, until everything went black.

A couple of days later...

As Valentina's eyes gradually became accustomed to the light, she noticed the outlines of people sitting near her. She knew that she was in a hospital bed, as she had seen enough of them in her lifetime.

The light seemed bright, and she could hear her mother talking to her sister Olivia. At first, she couldn't make out the conversation. It was like everyone was mumbling or keeping their voices down.

Valentina reached out, touching her sister's hand.

"Valentina," cried out Olivia. "We have been so worried about you. You gave us such a scare."

Both Olivia and her mother came closer to the bed to acknowledge and comfort her.

Finding it hard to talk, Valentina got out what few words she could.

"Where am I? What happened? How did I get here?"

She had forgotten the events that had taken place only a couple of days earlier in her apartment.

Valentina's mother took her hand and told her that she had been in an accident and that she needed to take it easy and get some rest. All would be explained in good time, she advised her, as she bent down to kiss her daughter's forehead.

"Let me call a doctor and tell them that you are awake" her sister Oliva said, pressing the button that was hanging off the back of Valentina's bed.

As the days passed, Valentina slowly began to recover. She was visited by nurses and doctors of all descriptions. Many of them, she had met before in the past for various reasons on different occasions.

Finally, Valentina got the strength back in her voice and asked if she could speak to her old friend, Doctor Fields, who was a resident at the hospital. She had known him for many years since her university days. He was a straight shooter, and he would give her an unfiltered view of her condition.

"What has happened to me?" Valentina asked her old university colleague, as he took a seat at her bedside.

"All I remember is watching TV in my apartment, and now I'm lying here" she said.

Doctor Byron Fields was known for calling a spade a spade, when he spoke to people. Even in their university days in the debating club, he was feared for being able to bring a point so succinctly to the table in a debate within a short period.

He was not tall in stature but had a massive mental capacity that was matched by his quick wit and command of the English language. A mental giant some would say.

"Valentina, he said, you attempted to take your own

life. You were lucky someone found you before it was too late and called 911. If it had been maybe 10 minutes later, well we may not have you here today."

She looked at him, somewhat bewildered.

"Why would I commit suicide? I'm a little confused. I don't remember any of this" she said concerned by the news that she had just received from her dear friend.

Before he could answer her question, her mother and sister had arrived for their daily visit.

"Get some rest Val, I am sure it will come back to you in due time. In the meantime, it looks like you have some visitors. I will visit with you again, time permitting. If you need anything, just call for a nurse, they will know how to find me."

"Of course, you already knew that didn't you?" he said with a chuckle. "I'll check in on you again before you are discharged. Take care my friend."

Doctor Fields nodded to Valentina's family as they entered the room and quickly went back to his duties.

Valentina greeted her family and then looked out the window, looking into the distance at a couple sitting on a bench holding hands.

A small tear gently ran down her face.

"Everything will be fine my dear," her mother said in a calming voice. "Everything will be fine."

Valentina stayed at the hospital for some time until she was released to stay in her mother's care. She would remain with her mother until it was felt that she could live on her own once again. She was glad to be seeing sunlight once more and relished the breeze on her face, as she left her carers at the hospital.

Although she felt better, her memory of trying to take her life seemed to be buried somewhere in her subconscious. She had been told by her psychologist that sometimes the mind does that to protect itself.

Valentina accepted the prognosis for the time being, but found it hard to come to terms with the fact that she would have got to this point in attempting to end her own life.

"I know that you have struggled since the death of Jacob, but you do need to move on from this position", her mother blurted out one day.

"We all lose someone that we love. I lost your father early in my marriage. It was hard for me, but somehow, I found a way to survive. We all do. Time to snap out of it my love" her mother said.

"You are successful, you need to let the past go and just get on with it."

Valentina was not ready to have this conversation about her boyfriend, now or maybe never. It was still too raw.

She just wanted to move on with her life and forget any pain associated with the past. No matter what her mother was saying, she was not trying to dwell on the last year of her life.

Yes, there were times, that she would think about the death of Jacob, but it was like everybody was heaping this on her for something she doesn't even remember happening.

Repressed memory or not, she couldn't understand why she would try to take her own life. She had so much to live for.

Before another word could be said, there was a knock at the front door.

It was Valentina's boss, Mr Riley, who wanted to see how she was travelling and discuss her employment future.

Mr Riley was a man in his fifties, a kind man who was respected by all in their workplace. He wore black rimmed glasses and due to a motorbike accident, many years earlier, walked around with a cane to steady himself.

Valentina had never had the big boss come to visit her before, even though she had spoken to him several times in the past as he made his rounds in the workplace.

Valentina offered him a seat in the loungeroom on the old recliner chair that had once been her father's and was now reserved for their uncle Tony, who had become the guardian to the three women.

Mr Riley sat down, putting his walking stick to the side of the chair, and apologised for coming unannounced, but he had another appointment in the area and thought he would kill two birds with the one stone.

"Valentina, I would like you to take another couple of months off before you come back to work. You are one of my best employees, but you have been through enough and I need to know you are mentally fit for such a demanding role. Now before you say another word, we will cover you as best we can while you are away with full pay, but what you do need to do is to take a vacation. Clear your mind, so you are refreshed."

"We place your wellbeing above the organisation, and it has been decided that you can take some leave, so that you may recover."

"But" Valentina interrupted.

"No buts Valentina, Doctors orders, I need my best at their peak. It is hard to get quality people and I do consider you someone of quality."

Valentina smiled and decided not to argue with her employer. A long rest, she thought would do her good. She had been working incredible hours in more recent times. Partly because the work was there and partly because it was a good distraction from thinking about the events of the past.

Valentina offered him a coffee and cookies, which he gladly accepted as they made some small talk.

He never once asked about her suicide attempt.

Mr Riley stayed for around 45 minutes and then waved goodbye from the door. As he departed, he turned back to Valentina as she sat quietly in her chair. Her mother closed the front door behind Mr Riley and sat next to her.

"We will be fine my dear. See even the big boss has come to see how you are doing."

Val smiled almost embarrassed that such fuss had been made about her. She was an independent and confident young woman that never tried to stand out and now it was like she had become centre of attention.

As the days passed Valentina was ready to move back into her apartment. Although there was always a dark cloud over her, she felt she was ready be on her own again and get back to some normality.

Her friend, Mia was driving her there and today was a good day. Valentina experienced some bad ones since that fateful episode, but today seemed different. Mia always lifted her spirits and today was no different.

Mia and Valentina had known each other since they were young. Mia was the "happy go lucky" out of the two girls and Valentina was the more studious and serious one. Somehow, they remained friends through all the years. Sometimes she wondered how they remained so close over so much time. In many ways they were so different and in other ways they were similar in background. They both had immigrant upbringings. Mia was of Spanish descent and was brought up nearby, only two streets away. Valentina was of Italian heritage, but the two felt a kinship due to their similar circumstances.

They arrived at her apartment after a stop midway for some Krispy Kreme doughnuts, which the girls always loved to eat, even though they felt guilty afterwards.

Mia helped with Val's suitcase as the two made their way up the stairs at the front of her apartment building.

"I have an idea," blurted out Mia as the two of them took a seat on the couch.

"Why don't we go on an overseas vacation? We have talked about it since high school, and I know I need a break from my job, and it would be good for you too."

"Didn't your boss tell you to take a vacation? I think he is onto something."

Valentina nodded, "Well yes, but."

Before Valentina's sentence could even be finished, Mia interrupted her.

"So, its settled, we are going on our first big adventure together. Where shall we go?"

"How about South America? We could go to the carnival in Rio?" Mia said.

"Or Paris would be fun, we always talked about meeting a French man."

"I know where." Mia's mouth always moved faster than her mind.

"I have been reading all about the land down under, Australia. You know where they have all the sharks in the ocean. I was reading this article on this guy who lives in the outback, who is some type of Sharman who lives alone. He is said to be able to look at a person and know everything about them and then proceed to dig into their soul and tell them what their life's purpose is. We can't pass up an opportunity like that, can we? That sounds pretty cool, don't you think?"

"Let me guess, Valentina butted in, it's Crocodile Dundee and he has a great big knife."

The girls laughed.

"Maybe Australia would be a good way to leave a few troubles behind and if the guys look anything like Hugh Jackman or Chris Hemsworth, then it would be worth the trip."

Valentina felt that she needed to gain new perspective on life and what better way to do that than going as far away from everything and everyone. This maybe the answer to her prayers. Afterall, she did have a couple of months leave up her sleeve and she had always wanted to do some travelling, but study and later work duties seemed to get in the way.

The girls ordered pizzas, drank wine and laughed the night away. Searching on the internet all the things that they could see and do in Australia.

Although there was a lot of laughing and teasing, Valentina still felt this darkness inside, that things were not quite right. She never let on to Mia about these feelings.

Leaving LA

"**C**ab waiting Val, grab your things and let's go," shouted out Mia.

"Ok be right there" she shouted back as she was mentally checking off a list, ensuring that she had packed her last-minute things. Toiletries, makeup, phone, charger, passport. I think that's it, she thought to herself. She took a deep breath and looked around her apartment, ensuring all the power had been turned off. They were going to be away for a while. No need to pay any more than she needed to.

Just as she was about to close the door, her phone began to ring. She grabbed her phone from her handbag and placed it to her ear.

Valentina didn't recognise the number but answered it anyway.

"Val speaking".

No one answered, but she could hear breathing on the other end of the line. It was subtle, but she could definitely hear low shallow breaths from someone.

"Anyone there?" she said.

"Who is it?" asked Mia.

"I guess it's a wrong number."

"Maybe Chris Hemsworth is making sure I am getting on the plane" she giggled.

"Off to the land down under," they screamed excitedly, as they hopped into the cab after stuffing their numerous bags into the boot and back seat.

They eventually arrived at the airport and headed towards the Qantas airlines check-in desk. As they waited in line, they pulled out their passports and tickets, ensuring that they had everything ready for check-in. They could hear other passengers before them with Australian accents. It took a bit to get used to the twang in their voices, but they both liked what they heard. It was a unique style of English. They didn't understand everything that the people were saying, but they were speaking English, so they were sure they would understand it by the end of their vacation.

They finally made it to the front of the line and were

greeted by a lovely Qantas staff member by the name of Helen, who asked for their passports and paperwork. The girls were now getting excited. It was really happening. They got their tickets, handing over their heavy luggage to the counter staff.

As they made their way to the gates to go through to customs, they presented their passports ready to be stamped. After which they made their way through to the duty-free shopping, which was not far from their departure gate.

"I need something to drink" Mia said, motioning Valentina to a nearby coffee shop.

"Yeah, I think I need something to pick me up. I'll grab a coffee" Valentina replied.

The girls each bought a drink and sat down to chat and kill some time. The plane wasn't boarding for another hour and a half.

Mia took a sip of her coffee and looked at Valentina.

"How are you, Val?" said Mia as she looked back down at her coffee. "I mean how are you really? I know we have a lot of time to chat about life in general over the next month or so, but I just wanted to check in and see how you are feeling? I know it has been a little rough."

Valentina kind of looked away and spoke gently. "I'm doing ok. This year has not been easy on me, but I will survive. I always do."

Valentina chose to change the subject. "Tell me more about our destination and this Aussie Sharman you want us to visit. Let's start with the important facts. Is he good looking?"

"He isn't a Sharman," Mia replied, "but he is some type of spiritual guru or leader. I don't know what they call them down there. I think he hangs out with an aboriginal tribe, but I guess we will find out in a couple of days, wont we? It should be a bit of fun. May even give you a new perspective."

"So, it's a cult type thing?" Valentina jokingly replied.

"No, he doesn't have a flock of people that follow him around or anything like that. From what I can gather he has something to do with the Indigenous people, as I said. I think I read he was taken by them as a child, and then became a spiritual leader and learned their powers.

I don't recall all the facts, but the article I read said that many people go to him for guidance. He can help people move on with their lives and learn their reason for being here. He seems to have some type of insights that other people don't have, and he is gaining a name for his wisdom and accuracy."

"Sounds like we are travelling a long way to meet a psychic" Valentina quipped.

Mia fired back.

"He is only part of the trip, and it will be some fun. We are going to do some of the major cities like Melbourne and Sydney after we have visited this guy. He was hard to get hold of. Apparently, he lives in the bush, but I found his details online and contacted a guy by the name of Steve, who must work for him."

"You know Mia, I think you were right, I do need this break and I am looking forward to this trip, but I am just as happy to hit the big cities and do some sight-seeing and definitely some shopping. To get my mind off things would be wonderful. I am looking forward to this distraction. Thank you for organising it. I hear Melbourne is known for its shopping, food, sports, and coffee. Right up my alley. It's going to be fun and the two of us always have fun together."

"I'll drink to that," said Mia. "Our first destination is Sydney airport, but we will be flying from there, to a city called Alice Springs in the middle of Australia. There we meet this guide called Steve, who will meet us at the airport and fill us in on all the details."

Their flight was eventually called for boarding and the girls gathered their belongings and headed towards the gate. They made their way on board, being greeted by staff as they headed their way down the plane finding their seats and sitting next to each other.

Mia grabbed her allocated window seat as they settled into their new environment.

"I think I will get some shut eye, said Valentina. It's like a 15-hour flight from LA to Sydney. Why is this country so far from civilisation, Mia?"

"Stop complaining, it's going to be an adventure. I bet by the end of it, you will be your old self and don't forget the men down under are hot" Mia said as she touched her armrest as if it was a hotplate. Making a sizzling noise.

It didn't take long for Valentina to doze off shortly after take-off. She was always a good sleeper on planes, unlike Mia who would rather watch movies and play games, which is exactly what she did.

As Valentina entered a deep state of sleep, she began to dream of being in a strange hotel room. It was smallish and had two single beds, one on each side of the room. Spread across both beds were backpacks and clothes. It was a man's room based on the state of the clothes lying around everywhere.

Her view of the room was like that of a fly sitting on a wall, looking down and observing as three men entered this dingy enclosure. They burst in on the two other men, who obviously were not expecting them. Two of the assailants had long hair and the third wore a business-like haircut.

She could hear them but couldn't make out their faces clearly. The shorter of the two original occupants of the room wore a beard and his long hair in a ponytail.

The five of them spoke for a little while as she could feel the tension in the air.

An argument broke out as one of the original occupants remonstrated against something that was being said and stood up to the men. Without a second thought one of the assailants cut open his throat with a sharp blade that he had produced from his back pocket. The other occupant made a run for it and was shot in the back of the head. Valentina noticed another figure in the background crouching low, hoping not to be seen.

As she tried to get a closer look, she noticed the time on the clock. It was 9.00 pm.

All she felt was fear as the three assailants searched the room and then left.

"Excuse me miss," asked the flight attendant for the second time. "Would you be interested in some dinner and beverages?" she asked Valentina, who was in the middle of her dream.

Valentina slowly adjusted her eyes as Mia had been nudging her to wake up and prepare for something to eat.

It was only a dream, but it was so real. It looked all so familiar, but of course it was just a dream. Dreams sometimes feel so real like you are really in them, she thought to herself.

Valentina sat up and thanked the flight attendant, asking if she could have some orange juice with her meal. Mia upgraded to a red wine and then continued to play her games after some initial chit chat with Valentina.

Valentina debated telling Mia of her realistic dream but thought that it could wait until a later date.

After all it *was* only a dream.

The Red Centre

Both girls were exhausted from their long trip and were so relieved to have arrived at Sydney International airport. It was nothing like they had expected.

It was a modern airport, just like home. Maybe not as large in size, but the people dressed the same and at least spoke English. Not the big country town they were expecting, instead a modern society.

Customs was a quick process as the girls used the passport machines that were easy to use. All they had to do was to just walk up to them and scan their passport. Then they were asked to hold their head in a certain position, and it would check their facial features for a match. It was so quick and efficient.

They had about five hours to kill before their connecting flight to Alice Springs was to leave.

"Let's go check out Sydney" Mia insisted.

The girl's baggage was to be transferred to their later flight, so with their hand luggage in hand, they went to the taxi rank to hail a cab.

Their Indian taxi driver by the name of Dhanny was lovely and made conversation with them on their trip into the harbour city, explaining that he had lived in the country for four years now. He had originally come to study to be a chef but was struggling to find a job in his industry. He wanted to become a citizen as so many of his people were already living in the country.

He dropped them off at the Sydney Opera House as requested, where they wanted a photo opportunity. They pulled out their iPhones and took a series of selfies with the Opera House and the Sydney Harbour Bridge in the background. They could see large cruise ships docking in the harbour or preparing to dock. It was a bustling place with tourists and locals everywhere.

The weather was inviting, and they chose to sit at The Opera Bar overlooking the water as the sun shone down upon them. Each ordering a panini and a sparkling champagne to celebrate making it all this way to this fabulous country.

Sydney already seemed amazing, and it lifted her spirits to be basking in the sun, whilst drinking champagne with her best friend.

Mia noticed a man sitting on the next table. He appeared from time-to time to be looking their way and trying not to look too inconspicuous.

He was a stocky man of no older than twenty-five. Dressed in jeans and a white t-shirt, saying 'I love Sydney' on the front. Obviously, he was a tourist as well.

Valentina peered over her sunglasses to get a better look.

"Hey that guy looks familiar, I have seen him somewhere before" Valentina quietly said to Mia.

Mia agreed. "Wasn't he on the plane?" as she turned her head down to not be so conspicuous.

"I'm not sure, but he sure looks like that guy that kept walking up and down the aisles. You know the one who was wearing the Yankees baseball cap."

"I think you are right. He must have the same idea as us. What a coincidence."

The girls ate their paninis and drank a couple of glasses of wine each. They decided to explore the city with the time they had left before their departure. They were coming back to Sydney in some weeks from now, but why waste some good shopping time.

They marvelled at the beauty of this city. A modern city with a blend of new and old-world architecture within its centre. An old architecture that resembled London. The people were so friendly. Everyone was happy to give directions, once they heard their American accents. People would stop when they noticed that they were lost and gave pointers as to what they should see in the city or how to find various sites or stores.

'Go to Pitt St and try the shopping,' one said.

'You need to go to Darling Harbour and check out the food down there' another commented.

'Don't forget to get down to Bondi beach and have a swim.'

The Australian accent took a little getting used to, but the girls had already fallen in love with this city. It was a modern city just like back home and the people were friendly.

Time passed quickly, and they eventually made their way back to the airport.

Their next leg was to be Alice Springs, right in the heart of Australia.

"Hey, check this out," said Mia, holding her copy of Lonely Planet on Australia on the tray table in front of her as they flew to Alice Springs.

"This Alice Springs place sounds interesting."

She began to read out loud from the book in front of her.

"Alice Springs wouldn't win a beauty contest, but there's more going on here than first meets the eye, from the inspirational (excellent museums, a fine wildlife park and outstanding galleries of Indigenous art) to the practical (a wide range of accommodation, good dining options and travel connections)."

"It's the gateway to some of central Australia's most stirring landscapes: Uluru-Kata Tjuta National Park is a four-hour drive away, while closer still, the ruggedly beautiful MacDonnell Ranges stretch east and west; you don't have to venture far to find yourself among ochre-red gorges, pastel-hued hills, and ghostly white gum trees."

"Alice is a key touchstone for understanding Indigenous Australia in all its complexity and its present-day challenges. The Indigenous name for Alice Springs is Mparntwe, and the region's traditional owners are the Arrernte, although many different Indigenous communities now call Alice Spring home."

"What do you think?" said Mia closing the book.

Valentina was still a little jet-lagged from their trip to Sydney and so just nodded, as she slumped to one side of her chair.

Mia laughed

"... and it can get hot there too" Mia finished before Valentina fell back into a slumber once again.

After a further three hours of flying, they made it to what the Australians call the Northern Territory. It was only one of two areas in Australian that is known as a territory. The rest of the country were broken up into

17

states. Alice Spring sat towards the bottom of this region. Close to the middle of the country.

The plane hit the tarmac with a thump, and everybody included Valentina woke up suddenly.

Over the speaker system came the voice of the flight attendant, "Welcome to Alice Springs everyone, the time here is now 4.30pm. We hope you enjoyed flying with Virgin airlines and we hope to see you back in the skies again soon."

The girls gathered their hand luggage and headed out to find their contact who was to look after them on this Northern Territory leg.

As they walked out with the other passengers, they saw a very tall man holding a placard with their names on it.

'Valentina Russo and Mia Garcia.'

The man was definitely not height challenged. He had to be at least six foot four. Long goldish hair with a light beard. He was wearing khaki shorts and a khaki shirt and a large well-worn brimmed hat. His mouth opened to a Cheshire grin as the girls began to approach him and pointed to his sign, as if to say, "you're the one."

"G'day ladies" he said. "Welcome to Alice Springs. Hoping you had a good flight from Sydney."

"My name is Steve, as he held out his hand to shake with both of them. I will be your guide over the next few weeks. I also will be putting you in touch with Daniel this coming week once we get you settled in.

"You are both in for a ride. Hopefully you are both ready for a bit of a spiritual journey?"

The girls looked at each other as Steve ushered them towards the baggage carousel.

Steve grabbed their bags as it came out on the conveyor belt and asked them to follow him to the carpark to his four-wheeled drive. They did as per his request, half excited and half exhausted from their journey.

The girls noticed the heat and flies as soon as they stepped outside of the airport.

"I think I am a little overdressed" said Valentina as she realised that she was wearing long black pants and a pullover.

"Yeah, I think you are right" Steve replied. "Sheila's in this part of the world, tend to wear something light, but you can get yourself organised down at the hotel."

"Sheilas?" asked Mia quizzing this obvious Australian slang.

"Yeah, um, Sheilas means girls in Australia, but I don't think they use that term so much in the big cities. Steve replied. The girls don't like it out there much. They probably don't like it here either" he laughed nervously.

"Anyway, when you meet Daniel. I don't think I have ever heard him use that term; he speaks a little different to the rest of us. Well, some of us anyway."

"So, he isn't Australian?" quizzed Valentina.

"Oh yeah, he is an Aussie, but he has worked in the big cities, so I guess he says some things a little different. Each state of Australia can sound slightly different to the other. I guess it's a little more like the north and the south in the states, but generally we sound the same."

"Do tell us more about Daniel" Mia interrupted.

"Well, I may have to do that over a drink later tonight as we are just hitting the hotel, and I think you ladies might like to freshen up a bit. What do you think?"

Both girls nodded and said they need to have a rest and a shower.

Steve parked the truck and helped take their bags to their rooms after they checked in.

"I'll let you guys settle in. It's about 5.30pm now. How about I meet you at the pub next door and we can have a feed and a drink there at say 7.30pm. Does that work for you?"

The girls looked at each other and then agreed.

They opened the door and stepped into a pleasant, but basic room with two beds. They could see a kettle, tea bags and some instant coffee with some milk in the bar fridge under the vanity mirror.

Two hours went quickly, but both were now famished. Time to catch up with Steve next door.

"Hurry up Val, Steve will be waiting." Mia commanded of her friend as she had one foot out the door.

"You go ahead, I'll be another 15 minutes. I'll meet you there" she replied.

Mia stepped out and headed towards the pub to meet Steve.

Valentina had just finished getting dressed when there

was a knock at the door.

What did she forget now? Valentina thought to herself, referring to Mia. Must be her key if she is knocking.

Valentina opened the door and there standing in front of her was an older man of around forty.

Well-dressed, well-groomed, and looking quite serious.

"Valentina Russo?" He asked.

"Yes, has something happened to my friend Mia?" She just walked out of here to go next door."

"No. My name is Detective Paul Squires from the Gold Coast police" as he took out his official badge for her to see.

"Gold Coast. Is that local?" Valentina enquired.

"No Miss Russo, the Gold Coast is in the state of Queensland up north of Australia and I am currently involved in an investigation, which involves you."

"Me?" she asked. "I think you have the wrong person; I have literally just got off the plane from the United States."

"Yes, we know, Detective Squires responded. We have been following your movements for some time now. I don't want to alarm you, but you would be familiar with a man by the name of Jacob Spriggs?"

Valentina looked at the detective in disbelief. She knew perfectly well who Jacob was.

He *was* her boyfriend.

Valentina stepped backwards towards the bed and sat down as she was now feeling a little light-headed.

"Are you ok Miss Russo?" the detective asked.

"Yes, but why bring up Jacob? Do you know that he passed away? He died in Thailand nine months ago. Why would the police be interested in him?"

"I don't think you know the whole story, but this is not the best place to speak," Detective Squires continued. "I know you have a pressing engagement with your friends, so I will let you go for now. Here is my business card in case you need to speak to me."

"I will be in touch shortly, but for your own safety please do not discuss this conversation with anyone. We have more information around this case, which I will reveal in good time. All I ask is that you pay attention to who you speak to, whilst here in Australia."

"I do need to go, but as I said, I will be in touch. My suggestion is to be aware of your environment."

With that Detective Squires closed the door behind him and made his way to a waiting car driven by another man.

Valentina sat on the bed for what seemed like an eternity as memories of Jacob came flooding back. She decided that this would not ruin her vacation. She stood up from the bed, straightened her clothing and proceeded to the pub next door.

When she arrived, Steve and Mia were in deep conversation at the bar and didn't notice her walking in.

"Let's grab a table in the dining room and order some dinner, I'm starving," said Steve.

The three headed to the dining section and grabbed a table.

"What would you like to drink Val," asked Steve, "my shout."

"Just a gin and tonic please" she replied.

After Steve left to go the bar, the girls talked.

"Where have you been? I thought you were right behind me" Mia asked Valentina.

"Yes, I'm sorry I just lost track of the time, you know time differences and all. But I'm here now."

They all had a few drinks and ordered their meals at the counter, returning to their seats.

"So, what do you think of Australia so far?" Steve blurted out.

"Well, we haven't seen that much of Alice Springs, but we loved Sydney. People were very friendly there," said Mia.

"Actually, Australians in general seem friendly. What's in the water over here?" Valentina asked.

"Beer" Steve replied jokingly.

The meals arrived, and were eaten quickly, as everyone was hungry. Steve told a few jokes to break the ice and the girls felt comfortable on their first day. Of course, Valentina wasn't sure what to make of her visitation earlier.

"What's the story with this guru that we are going to see tomorrow?" Mia asked.

"Daniel? Well, he is an interesting character. Not like

anyone I've ever met before." Steve replied.

"It is rumoured that he was found by a river, not too far from here by some Indigenous elders, who took him in. It is said they taught him their ways and he developed these insights. You know like a third eye, like the Indians talk about."

"Oh, I mean Indians in India, not the American ones."

"Of course, there are other stories that he was really a big city guy and is quite wealthy. He worked in some big job or something and then came here to retire. Not too sure the exact story as he rarely tells anyone, even me, and I have known him for some time now."

"Explain insights," said Valentina.

"They say he is different to other people that you will meet in your life. He sees more than just the flesh. He sees your psychology. What stops you from becoming more. You know the demons inside you that hold you back. He just gets into a person's head, but in a good way. I guess it is a gift he has."

"He understands the earth and our connection to something much greater. The aborigines love him."

"When I first met him, he just started talking and talking and telling me things about myself, I guess I never paid that much attention as to how I was operating, but Daniel sees it all. Initially he frightened the crap out of me."

"He also helped me understand the things that were blocking me as a human."

"How did he do that?" asked Mia excitedly.

"It's like he gets into your soul, peers inside and then he does an analysis and then spits out all this stuff that you didn't know about yourself. It's bloody amazing."

"I've never met another person like him, but then I haven't travelled much further than the Northern Territory, so what would I know?"

"He is very well spoken. He is an Australian, but more refined. More city like, with an outback understanding."

"So, he lives in a tent?" Valentina added.

"No, he lives in a regular house with all the amenities. Three bedrooms I believe. He is just a regular guy, with extraordinary ability."

Valentina was intrigued by this person, and she hadn't

even met him yet.

"So, what does he do exactly?"

"You will have to wait, Steve laughed, but he will mend your heart and soul. That's if you have one," he joked out loud.

Valentina then remembered the conversation earlier with the detective about Jacob.

I doubt anyone will ever mend my heart and soul, Valentina thought to herself. It's shattered into a thousand pieces.

The three talked for several hours more, before the girls decided to retire back to their room. It had been a long trip and tomorrow was to be a big day.

They wished Steve a good night and said they would see him in the morning.

The girls talked for a little while before finally falling asleep. It had been a very long day and it didn't take much for them to both doze off into a deep slumber.

After about thirty minutes Valentina felt a hand run their fingers through her hair. Damn Mia, I'm going to kill you, she thought to herself. Bothering me at this time of the night.

She opened her eyes and looked towards Mia's bed. She was fast asleep, snoring away.

Valentina began to close her eyes again, falling deeper into sleep as she felt a gentle brush against her cheek this time.

She opened her eyes and adjusted to the lack of light in the room. There now at the foot of the bed was a figure.

Was she imagining it or was it real? She wanted to scream but felt paralysed.

The figure had now moved to the side of her bed, and it appeared to be a male standing there. Now she feared for her life. It was like her voice box had been severed. Nothing was coming out.

Here she was in a foreign country with a burglar or maybe worse, standing next her bed and she couldn't say a word to defend herself.

Then the man spoke.

"Don't you remember me my beautiful girl?"

Valentina looked again and then it registered. It was

Jacob. But Jacob it couldn't be.

"It's really me babe. You didn't think I would ever really leave you?"

Valentina sat up and hugged Jacob for the first time in a long time. She had missed his touch. The warmness of his hands and the gentleness of his kisses.

Valentina looked over to Mia's bed, gesturing that someone else was here.

"Don't worry babe, she is fast asleep. It's just you and me" Jacob anticipating her thoughts.

With that Jacob bent down, placing his lips on hers. Valentina felt the warmness of Jacob's gentle lips.

...And with that kiss, Jacob was once again, no more.

Valentina fell deeper into sleep, not knowing if her experience was real or just an apparition.

...But it seemed real.

The Bush Guru

The sun came out nice and early through the curtains of their hotel room, as the girls began to arouse.

"How did you sleep?" Mia enquired. "I slept absolutely fabulously."

Valentina stretched out her arms into the air. "Yeah, I slept well too. I think there is something in the air here that makes it special" she said with a smile.

"That's because you are now living on the oldest continent on this earth, and it has special properties that will rejuvenate you." Mia said. "You can't help but feel alive."

Valentina rolled her eyes, got out of bed, and opened the curtains to let some sunlight in.

"I can't wait to see what this guy Daniel or whatever his name is, has to say today. I hope I haven't travelled all this way just to meet some lunatic. People would think I was crazy, if I told them I was meeting some bushman in the outback, just to find out my future." Valentina said as she headed towards the bathroom.

"He's not a psychic. I'm not sure what he is, but people come to him from all over the world to get their "learnings" Mia replied."

"Learnings?" asked Valentina. "I hope this leg of our vacation is not a waste of time. Anyway, we are here to have some fun and we are doing it together. Plus, I need something to take my mind away from the last 12 months. It has been a woeful year."

Mia agreed and walked over to Valentina, giving her a big hug.

'Honey together we will start again. I know I can't take away your past, but I can be there as you rebuild the future."

"You are lucky that you know your job will still be waiting for you. I bet I wouldn't get that from my employer" Mia said. "Luckily I have accumulated some annual leave."

Valentina nodded and grinned.

"So, what's the format for the day? Do we see this guy this morning and then have the afternoon to ourselves?"

Valentina asked.

"If you had come a little earlier to the pub last night, you would have heard what we are doing today."

"First, we go grab some breakfast at the local coffee shop around the corner. Then Steve will be taking me to meet this guy first. Apparently, this guy Daniel lives a little out of town, so I should be back around 1.30pm. Something like that I am told."

"Then Steve will take you to do the same. So, the morning is yours to explore, just be back at the hotel in time for pickup."

"Then tonight we can have some dinner and compare notes. Maybe check out some hunky guys afterwards over drinks."

"Sounds like a plan," said Valentina. "Let me get showered and dressed and we can go when you are ready."

Valentina showered, dressed and both girls applied some make up before heading out and around the corner to a nice coffee shop.

"Welcome ladies," called out the waitress behind the counter. "I will be with you shortly. You will find some menus on the table. Sit anywhere that's available."

The waitress came to their table five minutes after they took a seat.

"What are you thinking girls? Hot breakfast or maybe some cereal?"

"How about a 'Big Breakfast'? Sausages, hash brown, cooked mushrooms, and eggs anyway you want it?" she said as a suggestion.

'Sold', they both replied.

"I could eat a horse right now" Mia blurted out.

"I'm sure I could arrange that for you, if you like" said the waitress winking at Valentina.

They ordered some coffees as a heart starter, as it was both their daily ritual. They weren't going to break it for anyone, even if they were sitting in the middle of outback Australia.

"Ok done deal, I think I have those jotted down," said the waitress.

"Are you girls both from the United States?" enquired the waitress in a very Australian accent. The girls had to listen carefully to catch her every word as it was so different to the people in Sydney.

"Sure are, said Valentina, both from LA in California."

"Well, we love the yanks around here, they make great tourists."

The waitress turned and took a step back. Before walking off, she stopped and looked at Valentina.

"Have you been in here before, you look very familiar?"

Valentina shook her head.

"I have never even been in this country before, until yesterday. This is my first time here. You must be mixing me up with another tourist."

"Maybe so," said the waitress.

"You too look familiar," said Valentina back to the waitress. "Have you ever been to the states?"

"No, I've never left Australia, she said as she turned to walk away. But I know someone who has," she said under her breath.

At that point Steve walked in. "How are my two beautiful American girls today? Are you ready to meet Daniel?"

"I spoke to him earlier and he has been preparing himself for your meeting."

"What does this guru do to prepare for us?" Valentina enquired. "Put pins in Voodoo dolls?"

"He meditates and goes into an altered state that allows him to focus clearly. He finds that when he meets too many people the different energies can cloud his ability to home in on whoever he is working with. It seems to work from all accounts."

"So, are you excited? I mean you travelled all this way to meet him, and he is excited to meet you."

"Why would he be excited to meet us?" said Mia.

"I think the way he explains it is that each person he meets fills in part of a larger puzzle, that brings him closer to his own fulfilment. He explains it better than me, but I believe that is the gist of it."

"Anyway, when you finish your brekkie, I'll be taking Mia first to meet him. He only ever sees one person at a time for these sessions and he doesn't record anything. So, if you want to make notes, you will need to take a pen and paper."

The girls went to the front counter and paid for their "brekkie". Thanking the waitress who initially had served them. They tipped her and told her they will be back.

"I know that face" the waitress said as they walked out.

Mia climbed into Steve's truck, waving Valentina goodbye. "Wish me luck" she yelled out as they pulled out of the driveway.

With time on her hands Valentina headed out for a walk to explore the city of Alice Springs. The day was already warming up, so an early morning exploration was a good idea.

She wandered around this country town, hoping to catch a kangaroo hopping down the street. Instead, she saw groups of the natives that they call Aborigines, as she walked around the town.

Finally, she decided to go into some of the shops. One after the other, she went inside to see what was on offer. Some were tourist's shops with trinkets to buy and others were normal stores you would see in almost any town in the states. She wandered in and out for a while, until she came to one with this big hollow piece of wood, sitting just under the awning.

The shop owner came out to greet her.

"G'day, she's a real beauty, isn't she?" he said.

"I guess so," said Valentina, "maybe you can tell me exactly what it is?"

"Oh, well that's a Didgeridoo. It's a wind instrument that the Indigenous people of Australia have been playing for around 1500 years."

The shop owner placed himself on the ground, behind the long piece of hallowed out wood and began to play it. It made an interesting sound; she had never heard before from any instrument in the past.

Valentina smiled and thanked him, beginning to walk away.

"Watch out for the Drop Bears if you go out in the bush" he yelled out after her.

Valentina turned around to ask more about his statement.

"Are they liking to a grizzly bear?" asked Valentina. Worried that there were wild predators on the loose in the town.

"Nah, they are worse. They look like cute koalas, but they are much bigger, like the size of a large dog. They will hide high up in trees, waiting for their prey, ready to jump on a person at a moment's notice."

"They have these powerful forearms, designed to rip apart their prey. I'm just telling you because I can see you are new to the area."

Before Valentina could say another word, a man who was in ear shot called the shop owner's bluff.

"God, you talk shit Keith. Sorry hon, but he has obviously heard your American accent and he has told you an old urban legend that they like to tell Americans over here."

"It's bullshit isn't Keith?"

"Yeah, ok you got me, but you have to watch out for the crocodiles at night, they come out in their droves after midnight and walk straight down that main street," as he pointed to the road in front of his shop.

The second man looked at Valentina and smiled. "My name is Sean and there are no crocs this far down, so Keith you need to give it up. Don't scare off our tourists. You need them as much as we do."

Sean put his hand out to Valentina to shake it.

"How long are you in town?"

"Well, hi and thanks, she said. My name is Valentina and I'm not sure how long I am in town for to be honest. We are meeting this man called Daniel Switzer."

"Ah the famous Mr Switzer. He is making a name for himself in these parts and obviously around the world."

"He is an interesting character. I guess a little mysterious. You know the type that likes to be mysterious and always appears to be hiding something. He comes across as a good bloke, but you just never know."

"Keeps to himself a lot, but you will see him in town from time-to-time picking up supplies."

"I spoke to him once when he was meeting someone in one of the coffee shops. There is certainly something about him. Like he knows something you don't. I'm not sure if that is good or bad."

"I think he is harmless, but people have mixed feelings about him. He likes the Abo's and tends to hang with them I think."

"Abos?" Valentina enquired.

"You know, Aborigines. That what we call them out here."

Valentina thanked Sean for his time, including informing her about the local wildlife.

She popped into a local eatery and grabbed a toasted ham and cheese sandwich on her way back to the hotel to wait for Mia's return.

It wasn't long after she had arrived back, that Steve's truck pulled up with an excited Mia.

"It was great" she shouted from inside the truck as it pulled up beside her.

Mia hopped out, hugged her friend, and swapped places as Valentina jumped into the front passenger's seat next to Steve.

The trip took over an hour before the truck turned up a dirt path to a house with a long winding driveway. Steve turned down it and drove carefully to the house at the end of the road.

The truck came to a halt and Steve turned to Valentina. "He will be waiting for you. Just go straight in and you will find a large loungeroom to the right as you walk in. Just take a seat, he will be out when he is ready. Just be quiet in case he is meditating. I'll send him a text in five, so he doesn't leave you waiting long."

"I will be back to collect you in around five hours. Daniel will give you something to eat, so you won't starve. Enjoy your experience and be open to what you are about to hear."

Valentina nodded her head and walked up to the front door. She grabbed the handle. It was unlocked and she stepped inside to what appeared to be a very normal dwelling.

There was no incense burning and no pictures of gurus on the walls. It was just a very normal suburban house. It was in good condition, well-furnished just like any other regular house.

She took a seat near the window and waited, staring around the room. It was reasonably sparse. No women's touch here, she thought to herself.

Unbeknown to her, Daniel had walked in and stood

there waiting patiently for her attention to fall upon himself.

Valentina finally turned to lay her eyes upon Daniel for the first time.

He was a tall man. Over six feet, good looking and from her estimates was in his early forties. Dark brown hair with a tinge of grey on the sides. No facial hair, but a hint of a five o'clock shadow. He wore jeans and a shirt and a pair of brown leather work boots.

"Hi, my name is Daniel, you must be Valentina" Daniel said as their eyes met.

With a little nervousness, Valentina reciprocated his greeting with a hello.

Daniel took a seat directly opposite Valentina, making himself comfortable.

He wasn't one to make too much small talk and was wasting no time in his questioning of her visit today.

"So why do you think you are here?" he said quite confidently.

Valentina was taken aback, thinking that this would be more like the psychic reading that she went to see some years ago at a friend's party.

No tarot cards were produced or asking for her palm to be shown. Daniel just wanted to know her motives.

"Well, she said, I want to know my future, I guess. They say you are a teacher of some type and I have travelled along way to learn."

"Yes, I can hear the accent. Canadian or American?" he enquired.

"USA. California."

Valentina did not want to give away too much information as she wanted him to tell her without knowing too much in advance.

Daniel leaned back as if contemplating his next words.

"Let us start this session about how I perceive you if you don't mind. Good or bad, just accept it. It becomes our starting point for discussion. It is how I start all my sessions."

"Depending on your acceptance determines its direction and where work is to be done."

"Does that make sense?" He asked.

Valentina nodded. Not wanting to interrupt his flow.

Daniel began to close his eyes.

Valentina smirked, thinking here we go, but I will be open to whatever is thrown at me.

After all Mia thought it was good, so maybe she should be positive about the experience too.

She picked up her pen and paper to take notes.

Daniel reopened his eyes and began to speak.

"Your heart is grey, and your pain runs deep from many angles. Intelligence is your umbrella that you use to hide behind, but really you are still a child wanting to be held.

Only one man has touched you deeply. He is one of your soul partners, as well as one of your teachers sent to guide your way through this human experience."

"Your life cross paths with many teachers, but you are not yet open or knowledgeable that you are in their presence. They do not take the form of kings or gurus, but instead are normal people that are made available to you."

"You feel that life has not lived up to your expectations, even though many around you think you are very successful."

"Your love from a man starts from childhood and has only manifested into your adult life as a position of lack, rather than a position of completion."

"You compensate this with "distractions". Work, alcohol and personal destruction or self-hate."

"Your choices have been made to please others, not yourself. You lack the wholeness of being content as you surround yourself with those that are also wounded children, so that you feel part of a greater existence. Unknown dangers surround you and you are oblivious to what they might be. The black dog dominates you, yet you hide him well from sight."

Suddenly Daniel stopped and calmy looked at Valentina.

"Did any of that resonate with you?" he said quietly.

Valentina sat back. "To be brutally honest, I don't know. I think some of it did, but it came out like a machine gun. It was so much to take in. I tried to write some of it down, but like I said, it came out so fast."

"The fact is that I am tapping into something from elsewhere. I can hear what I am saying, but it is like someone else is doing the talking, Daniel said. Not possession or anything like that, it comes from my subconscious mind connecting elsewhere."

"Don't worry Valentina, it will unfold in time. You are here to learn and take these learnings to move closer to your True Being State."

"What does that mean? "True Being State" Valentina asked.

Daniel stood up. He liked to walk around sometimes when he was explaining a concept.

He opened his mouth and began to tell her a story.

"Once upon a time, there was a young boy who was abandoned at the gates of an orphanage, that was in the care of the church. The boy was no older than a toddler and over time the nuns brought him up as their own. As there was no note left with the boy at the time, the nuns never had any inkling as to the lineage of the young infant."

"Of course, they tried as best they could to determine who his parents were back in those times, but without the modern technology of today it was a muted effort. You couldn't "Google" people in those days."

"The boy grew to be a fine young man and over time it became evident that he would make something of his life. When he reached around the age of seventeen a letter arrived at the orphanage. It was unstamped with no details or a return address."

"The young man was intrigued as to who could possibly want to send him correspondence as he knew very few people on the outside world. He took the letter back to his room and opened it to find several pages handwritten by someone by the name of Sky P."

"He did not know of a person by the name of Sky P and did not remember anyone from the orphanage having such a name."

"The letter introduced themselves as a long lost relative, who knew his mother and father and wanted to reveal to him, his true identity."

"The man was naturally excited reading with great interest and in anticipation of understanding why he had been left with the nuns as such a young age. His hands were getting sweaty as he turned over to read the next page. Maybe his parents had died in a car accident, and somebody took pity on him and chose to leave him to be brought up by the church? Or maybe he was unwanted pregnancy."

"The letter read that he had been born to two very special people, who loved him dearly. His parents were not from this land but chose to place him elsewhere as they didn't want him to live in their palace back home for fear that he would be corrupted by their enemies."

"The young man's eyes were now opened wide wondering what his real heritage was all about. His parents lived in a palace?"

"As he continued moving his eyes down the page, it talked about how his parents were told by a wise man, that if their son were to stay in the palace with all the servants and courtiers and luxuries of his parents, that he would never discover his 'True Being". That he was not from this earth, but instead that he was chosen to be a future king of their land. His people were an older race and the letter referred to them as the "Sky People". His people were given powers beyond other lands, but his parents had been warned that if everything was just given to him, then he would never truly reach his full potential."

"The boy sat back laying on his small single bed, as he read the letter."

"How could this be? He thought to himself."

"How could I be from somewhere else? I look like all the other kids, and I act the same. I am surely just another human."

"He continued to read as it told him that it was his goal to discover who he really was and to have this earthly experience. Of which it would be both joyous and painful, in order that he would then understand how to relate to his subjects back home. Yes, he was royalty, but earth was the best school for him to learn."

"It was explained that he had chosen earth as his path, as it would give him the fastest route to knowledge that he needed to become a good ruler and once again join his father the king."

"The boy finished the letter and put it down to comprehend. Over time he forgot the letter, thinking it to be a hoax from another student at the orphanage."

"It was not until the young man had reached a far more mature age and it was his time to die and leave this earth, that all was to be revealed to him."

"It was then that Sky P revealed themselves to him on his death bed, explaining his true origins. The man was now almost ninety years of age. No longer a toddler dropped off at the gates of an orphanage."

"Sky P explained that he was sent from his Kingdom, known as the "Sky People" and that he had chosen this journey on this earth prior to be dropped off at the gates all those years ago. His time on earth was long and painful, by earth standards, but his soul had gained many insights into how to be closer to what it was like to be a ruler in his land."

"In his last few minutes of earthly life, he came to know his true identity and his true mission. One that was for his benefit, not his people."

Daniel stopped and sat down.

Valentina said nothing. She was just absorbing the story.

"When most people look at the world, they look through the lens of a human experience.

So, what do I mean when I talk about a human experience? Humans talk in the language of suffering, sex, hate and addiction," Daniel said.

"These are human experiences, but we are not human. The core of the human is the soul, and the soul is not from here. This journey we call human life is something that we chose to have. It's a little like a hologram. Seeing things from a different perspective that is reflected somewhere else."

"An experience?" Valentina asked.

"When you look at life, through a different lens, you get a different experience. If your lens is seen through pain, then life is about pain. Physical or mental pain."

"When you adjust your lens, you understand that this becomes much more. It is more about obtaining a new perspective or a "learning" as I would call it."

Valentina went to speak when Daniel continued.

"Let me go back to the beginning."

"You and I are not from this earth. Even though we think this is where we originated. We are only here

35

because we chose to be here to get this earthly experience. A "learning" comes from working within this vibrational level and so we have an opportunity to evolve due to this exposure to it."

"It all starts with God or the Source or the Universe if that is your preferred language. This Source is the ultimate vibrational energy. An energy that you cannot see. That moves so fast that it cannot be seen by slower moving energies like ours."

"The human body is one of the lowest forms of energy and so it is dense and prone to break down and suffer trauma. You should know that Dr Russo."

Valentina was taken back.

"How did you know I was a doctor? I didn't mention that to you or Steve. Or did my friend Mia tell you?" Valentina then stopped and continued to listen as Daniel was obviously focused on the task at hand.

"No one told me anything. I just know certain things and I can't explain how I have this knowing. It can only be explained when you raise your vibrational energy. I gather you are familiar with the term, soul?"

"Yes of course said Valentina, I was brought up a Catholic, so this is not a new concept to me."

Daniel continued "So a soul, is consciousness that operates at a higher vibrational level. All souls vibrate differently depending on the "learnings" they have received and adopted over many incarnations."

"The goal is to return to the Source that many call God. Or in this story, the man had to learn things in his life journey, so he could return to his people. He became over time more effective, than when he first arrived on earth. He needed to experience things, so that when he returned to his people, he would be an advanced being."

Valentina started writing furiously, trying to at least get down notes that she could review at a later stage.

"So let me get this right" she said. "I am a spiritual being, but I have chosen to suffer in this world? Why would anyone do that? Suffering serves no purpose, other than unhappiness."

"Good question. Why would anyone want to or need a body to learn anything? Especially when life is so much better when you are in the Soul Consciousness form."

"The reason is that when life is easy, no one learns anything unless they are searching for it.

For you to have received your medical degree Doctor, you would have had to put in hours of study. Given up some social outings and focused all your energy to get the desired result that you wanted. In the process of this struggle, you pulled together past resources, to create new ones that gave you skill sets to no longer be Valentina Russo the civilian, but to transform you into Dr Valentina Russo."

"A being that could do what others could not."

"The same happens when you incarnate into the physical. Being physical or dense matter is challenging. It is the most challenging for the soul, as it is foreign to its existence. This incarnation delivers challenges that will stretch the soul. Give it new "learnings" and potentially prepare it for a new level in its development."

"But why would the soul need to be developed? asked Valentina. Is it not at its own highest level?"

"No, there are higher plains to a soul and its development. When we are in soul state, life as we would explain it, is far more pleasant, but not complete. Moving closer to God's vibration is its goal. Remembering that we come from God. We are in God's image."

"The journey we call earthly life, is but many potential journeys a soul may choose to take. There are many different experiences that a soul has at its disposal to develop. Not just the earthly one that you are currently experiencing."

"Then why would anyone want this journey? piped in Valentina. It's bloody hard and painful at times."

"Yes, you are right. It is a little like a battle ground, isn't it? Dodging bullets, trying to stay alive, just to get to the end of the physical plain. A plain that you knew would give you the most challenges, the most benefits and the most growth."

"I certainly didn't choose this," Valentina challenged.

"Yes, you did," Daniel replied.

"You didn't just choose it, you designed it. Before you chose this path, you designed what it would look like. How hard it would be and what lessons you needed to obtain for your development."

"Everything on earth is by design. Look around you, there are patterns in everything. Look at a flower closely. It will have beautiful, sometimes intricate patterns, so perfect that you would wonder how is that possible? The earth did not evolve, it came from a higher frequency."

"God or the universe designed it and everything he does is perfect. No matter how imperfect we think it is presented to us."

"You have placed situations and people in your path to gain greater understandings. These understandings I call "learnings" or "Wisdoms"."

"As you have chosen the path, then your goal is to improve and become closer to what I call the "Fabric". The spiritual fabric that comes from Source."

"The Fabric is made up of all the pieces that need to fall in place to form the whole picture. They are a series of people and events that will come into your life and give you an opportunity to evolve."

"Sometimes you think they are co-incidences."

"There is no such thing as a co-incidence. Everything is by design. The good and the bad."

Valentina just sat quietly taking notes as quick as she could comprehend what Daniel was downloading. It was as if he was tapping into something else that was feeding him this information.

"When a person seriously thinks about killing themselves, and suddenly someone out of the blue rings them, just as they intend putting their end plan into place, it is not a co-incidence that that phone call took place right at that time," Daniel continued without taking a breath. "Or when someone you haven't seen for decades come back into your life for no good reason, when you most need them. All is playing out a much larger story line."

"It is the Fabric at play. The story must play out for someone to either continue the same path or get the learning, by which they have come to obtain. If you end your life at that path, then you will eventually play out another journey to gain that learning."

"If you do not get the learning now, then there will be other opportunities to gain it into the future."

Valentina stopped Daniel and asked if she could grab a

drink as it was still quite hot and she needed to cool down a bit, and this was information overload.

Daniel pointed her to the kitchen and told her to have whatever she liked from the fridge.

Valentina walked into the kitchen, finding the fridge and while she took a sip of the orange juice that was in there, she leaned against the kitchen counter, trying to let everything she had just heard sink in.

If Daniel was right, then everything she had ever experienced in her life was meant to happen. Was life just a video game that she was part of?

At that point Daniel walked in.

"Overload fatigue?" he asked.

"Just a little." She replied. Am I really seeing life from the wrong perspective? Did I really choose to go through the shit I have experienced to date?"

"Yes, you decided on the design before you were born, but you get to choose the response. Just because you chose an experience doesn't mean you are ready to accept it. You choose it, because you believe it will be the most beneficial path to give you your learnings that you have yet to have totally absorbed into your being to this date."

"Your responses will determine cause and effect. It is a little like walking across a busy road. You can do one of two things. Look both ways and then walk safely across or just walk in front of oncoming traffic without looking. Either way your actions will help determine the potential next phase in your life."

"The way you think and the way you interpret is all relevant. It is a culmination of all your experiences that have brought you to this point in time. As you are exposed to each new environment you will either grow, remain stagnant or regress. Your goal of course is to grow."

"To do that you need to learn to remove the obstacles that are in your way."

"How do I do that?" asked Valentina.

"You become open. You make a conscious effort to change unconscious temperament."

"If you wish to create change then you need to remove what is stopping you from adopting and reaching new vibrational levels. Once that change has taken place, it is then reflected in our soul consciousness."

"That conversation Valentina is for another time."

"I don't know about you, but I'm pretty hungry. I do make a pretty mean pizza. The pizza oven is out the back, just tell me what you like, and I will get started on it."

Valentina and Daniel continued to talk more while they ate their dinner.

"How do you know so much Daniel?" Valentina questioned.

"You have these insights into so many things. Not just that, you read people like a book.

I can't make out if this is just mumbo jumbo or science. I have never met another person like you."

Daniel chuckled and then became very serious.

"All I am doing in tapping into a higher source. Every person has the ability to do this, but we are so engaged with this world and the "things" of this world that we are blind."

"Humans are asleep Valentina. They spend their most of their lives asleep and I don't mean lying around in bed all day."

"If the world wants a new positive consciousness, then we collectively need to raise our vibrational energy to new lofts to save the planet, but more so to save our spiritual essence."

"Many of these concepts you will learn were taught a long time ago, but humans replaced these "Wisdoms" with their own search for power and self-gratification."

"So many people are now like that. Beings that have lost their way. We strive for 'things' and have forgotten that we are of spiritual essence and need far deeper connection to a higher being than the construct of these lives."

Valentina contemplated all that was said and digested as much as she could. All of it made sense, but how was she to transform her own consciousness? She didn't dare start that conversation right now as it was now getting dark, and she knew that was a conversation for another day.

Just as Valentina finished up her wine, the lights of a truck were seen pulling up in front of the house.

Footsteps were heard from around the corner and of course it was Steve, ready to take Valentina back to her hotel.

"Hey guys, how did the day go?" Steve asked.

"Overwhelming but good," Valentina replied.

"She is a fine student," said Daniel "and if she so chooses, I will ask that you come back in a couple of days' time, to begin learning about the Wisdoms."

Valentina agreeing that she would love to return in the next couple of days. She felt that something had shifted for her and would love to know more. Daniel was fascinating to listen to.

With that, Steve grabbed a lukewarm slice of pizza and the two of them got in the truck, wishing Daniel a good night.

As they drove down the winding path back out to the main road, Valentina thought about Daniel and what had been shared that day.

Was there more to humanity and were there really secrets that it had been known for maybe for centuries, but forgotten?

How did Daniel get this knowledge? Was he the real deal? Or some crazy guy that loved listening to his own voice.

He sure seemed genuine. If anything, his trance-like state that he took on, and the information that followed was kind of freaky, but accurate, now that she had time to reflect on what he had told her.

Valentina remained quiet as they made their journey back into the Alice. She was still trying to get over her jet lag and integrate all that she had been told.

As they approached Valentina's hotel, Steve reminded her that tomorrow was an early start. They were leaving at 5am to drive to Uluru and spend the night there.

Valentina was too tired to ask what this place was. She would ask Mia in the morning when she was refreshed.

Steve said good night and Valentina retired back to her room to download what had been said to Mia, whilst Mia also gave her version of events. The girls were excited and exhausted and were looking forward to another adventure tomorrow.

They went to bed early as they knew the drive the next morning was going to be approximately five hours.

Dream Time

"Oh my God, I slept so well last night" Mia wearily announced, as she stretched her arms out and open as she sat on the side of her bed, rubbing her eyes.

Valentina pulled the cover over her head. "What time is it?"

"Let me see, it's 3.45am. We are leaving in just over an hour, you may wish to have a nice warm shower, because we are going to be doing some travelling today." Mia replied.

"Don't you just love this trip. Everything is organised and so refreshing."

Valentina wasn't feeling that refreshed yet, but a shower and coffee would help kick start the day.

The girls got themselves ready, packed a bag with enough clothes, makeup, and essentials for a one-night stay as they had been instructed by Steve.

Mia made them both a nice hot instant cup of coffee in their room before Steve pulled up in his dust covered truck. The coffee shop was not yet open, so instant was the best they were going to get.

Steve grabbed their bags, as they jumped into the vehicle, excited to see what Australia had instore today.

"So, what's this Uluru place, you are taking us to? Valentina asked. "Is it a farm or something?"

"Nah not even close, Steve replied. Uluru is like the largest pebble you are ever going to see in your life" chuckling out loud.

Mia leaned forward. "Are you pulling our legs? Who wants to travel five hours to see a pebble in the blistering heat? Maybe you should turn around now."

"We got up at this unearthly hour to see a massive pebble?" Valentina jumped in to support Mia. "I would rather sleep in."

"Trust me ladies, you are going to love it. It's going to be educational. This is a big tourist destination. People come from all over the world to see it."

The girls sat back in their seats looking out to the desert, counting the road signs that informed drivers to watch out for the wildlife.

"Yep, you got to watch for the wildlife here. Especially the roos (kangaroos). Hit one of those beauties and you have written off your truck. We should be fine during the day, but if one of them gets in front of you at night, they get stunned by your headlights and just sit on the road."

"The carnage that it will do to your vehicle is expensive."

Just as Steve said that, in the near distance the girls could see a mob of kangaroos hopping in the distance.

"They are so beautiful" Valentina told Mia. "I can't wait to see the other animals. Will we see koalas and the like?"

"I am making time in your schedule to go to a sanctuary soon, so you can see them up and personal, but I need to work around your times with Daniel, but yes you will see all of that."

Finally, their long morning trip was coming to an end as they arrived at the resort. It was 9.45am and they had made good time.

"Can you see it?" Steve shouted, pointing to an almighty rock in the distance. "That's Uluru or formerly known as Ayers Rock."

"Keep your eye on it during the day, because it's going to look different as the day progresses."

The girls got out of the truck and looked around at the resort. It was essentially a series of different level accommodations, from the expensive to the basic cabin or camping in your own tent.

"Don't worry, you are in a mid-level hotel. No tents for our American visitors."

"What do you say we get a bite to eat? I think brunch would go down well at this time of the morning. I could go some eggs and bacon."

All agreed and after checking into their hotel the girls met Steve for a walk to Gecko's Cafú for a breakfast to keep them going until dinner.

Everyone was dying for a drink and a nice hot breakfast. The smell was enticing as all three breakfasts arrived together. They all took in the aroma of a hot Aussie breakfast.

"So, what did you both think of Daniel? I didn't want to ask too many questions yesterday as most people spend time processing the information, and in all honesty, most people just want to sit and think."

"Well from my perspective, I thought it was interesting. No, it was enlightening," Mia continued. "Do you think he is from this planet?"

They laughed.

"I for one am interested in knowing more. He maybe a charlatan, but I don't see any danger in what he is exposing me to," Valentina said adjusting her sunglasses.

"I think I need another perspective in my life right now, so it is definitely worth exploring further."

Mia grabbed her hand in a comforting manner with a knowing of the pain that Valentina had suffered in the past year.

Everyone enjoyed their meals and sat and chatted taking in their wonderful environment.

The three of them headed to one of the cultural activities available at Uluru to learn more about the local Indigenous culture.

There was already a small crowd waiting for their guide to come out and give their talk.

An older Indigenous women stepped out to welcome everyone.

"We welcome you onto Indigenous land, home of our ancestors. Today we will speak about how our people survived in the bush around these parts, but firstly I want to talk about the "The Dream Time" or "Dreaming" as we call it."

"Now the white man has never actually been able to capture the real word for what I am about to tell you. Dreaming for the Indigenous people of Australia is a form of spirituality."

"Most stories about the Dreaming talk about the Ancestor Spirits who created the earth. These same spirits also transformed into the stars, the trees, rocks, watering holes etc. Therefore, we have across this country sacred places that we want respected, like Uluru."

"We know that these Ancestor Spirits still reside here within these sites."

"These beings were not considered gods, by my people, but were revered."

"They gave us the rules for living. With a moral code,

as well as rules for how we are to work with the natural environment."

"We believe everything in this world is alive. Naturally we have the animals and the plants that we consider to be living. All are energised by a spirit. Us humans are on the same footing with nature, and we are part of that nature. This moral code I talked about, relates to how we treat our plants, animals, and the land itself with respect."

"Imagine if we were able to return our planet back to these laws and how it would be very different. Not just for the earth, but humanity as a whole. We would treat each other differently if we saw it through the eyes of the Ancestral Spirits."

"After the death of a person, we believe their spirit returns to the Dreamtime from where it will return through another birth as a human, an animal, a rock, or a plant."

"Although the Indigenous people are unique in many ways, you will find many similar beliefs across the world."

"See, the woman said, the modern world thinks we are in some way primitive, because our old ways do not conform with so-called present-day advancements. When white man arrived, they brought their way of living to this land, not taking the time to understand ours. It caused conflict because the two lived life differently. Today we try to live together, but we are grateful that we have not forgotten our beginnings."

"In time, the world will learn that we have always been in sync with reality."

Mia and Valentina looked at each other, nodding their heads.

The rest of the session talked about how Indigenous people survived in the outback, followed by a Q&A session.

They left the session, feeling they knew more about the thinking of Australia's first people. Maybe these "first people" understood the world better than modern man.

They moved onto the next session that afternoon, which was a lesson of how to play the Didgeridoo. This was the same instrument Valentina had seen the shop owner play outside the store yesterday morning, whilst waiting for Mia to return from her time with Daniel.

It was a fun session, and both the girls had a turn trying to vibrate their lips, whilst using a circular breathing technique to create the droning noise that it made.

Both girls had minimal success, but they were both feeling immersed in the fun of participating.

After their lesson, they headed back to main part of the resort, ringing Steve to find out where he had gone.

"You will find me down at the bar. Just turn left towards the back, you will find me having a drink with some of my mates" Steve informed them.

The girls found Steve sitting with another three men of similar age to him, drinking beer and eating some snacks. The men were all chatting away and laughing when the girls walked in.

"Here they are," Steve announced. "How were the "cultural sessions?"

"Great" they both said in unison.

"It was interesting and informative, but now we need a drink" Mia said.

"I told ya, it was educational, but the best bits are still to come."

The men introduced themselves and offered to buy the girls a drink to quench their thirst.

"Tonight's a bit special" said Steve with a big cheesy grin on his face.

"How so?" said Valentina.

"I can't tell you everything before it happens or it won't be special anymore, but we are going to illuminate and electrify your night."

The men laughed as the girls just smiled.

"So, you will need to be at this part of the resort by 5.00pm for pick up by the tour bus, he told them pointing out on a resort map the meeting place. Wear pants and enclosed shoes. That way the snakes won't eat your toes when you're not looking."

The girls looked at each other and just laughed.

"Who wants another drink?" said Frank, the guy sitting nearest to Mia. They all shouted out the word 'me' at the same time. That afternoon, they laughed and laughed as Steve's friends were jokers who loved to spin a good "yarn".

The girls were ready and waiting near the designated area for the tour buses that were heading out that night. They still had no idea where they were going, but with tickets in hand all they knew from the pieces of paper was that it was called, *Uluru Experiences - Field of Light - Sounds of Silence.*

They waited to make their way on the bus and watched Uluru, the great rock in the distance. It was changing colour before their eyes. Everyone standing there watched in awe as they witnessed this phenomenon.

The girls boarded their bus and headed out for a short ride to a secluded place with a raised viewing platform, where they were served canapes and chilled sparkling wine, whilst they overlooked the Uluru-Kata Tjuta National Park.

Everyone took a seat, mingling with people from all over the world, who had tales of their travels and explorations around Australia and lands far away. All of them culminating here in this very place to witness one of the world's greatest wonders.

As the sunset and the darkness fell upon the land, they listened to the playing of the didgeridoo. It was all a little surreal, but so magical, as it appeared that every star in the sky was out for them that night.

For a moment it took Valentina away from the misery she had suffered months earlier. It brought for that one night some solace and distraction that she needed.

A bush tucker buffet was on display for dinner, and it did smell delicious. The girls were hungry as they realised, they hadn't really had a decent meal since brunch.

They picked at different types of foods, bringing them back to their table, whilst ordering more rich Australian wine. Wine in Australia is some of the world's best and they were given a treat of wines from all over the country.

People bubbled with conversation as they described what brought them here and where else they had been within the country. There were people from all over the world, including France, Germany, Malta and of course Australians exploring their own backyard.

Mia went over to grab some more "tucker" and came

back quickly without any food on her plate as she sat next to Valentina. She nudged her with her right elbow. Pointing her head in the direction of the next table.

"Isn't that the guy from Sydney and the plane?" she said.

Valentina looked in the direction Mia had been gesturing. The same guy they had seen at the Opera bar in Sydney was chatting away to people on the next table. Was this guy following them?

It's just a coincidence Valentina thought to herself. Then Daniel's words came flooding back to her.

"There is no such thing as coincidences, everything is by design." Surely this had to be the exception.

She shook her head and said to Mia, "I guess he is just being a typical tourist and exploring the outback. Just like us."

Then one of the tour guides stood at the front of the group of people assembled and announced that they would now be listening to the resident "star" expert, who will give a talk on the heavens above. Using a laser pointer, he pointed out the Southern Cross, the milky way and the zodiac signs.

The night was so clear, that it left a lasting impression on everyone. They all felt blessed and special that they were experiencing this under the brightest stars that many had ever seen in their lives.

After the presentation, Mia started up a conversation with a woman sitting next to her. Her name was Noemi Pascal and she told Valentina and Mia that she and her daughter had come all the way from her country of Romania to experience Australia. It had been her dream for many years and finally she had the opportunity.

Noemi was a very beautiful woman. She had auburn hair and was maybe no taller than 1.65cm or five foot five. Valentina guessed she must have been in her early forties. Slim build and her eyes sparkled when she smiled. She was a very engaging woman and Valentina enjoyed her company.

Noemi had a fascination with astrology and knew everything there was to be known on the subject. She carried an app on her phone and offered to tell Valentina a little bit about herself. Valentina was a little hesitant at first and didn't wish for Noemi to go to any trouble.

"It is no trouble" Noemi insisted. Explaining that Astrology was an ancient art from Babylonian times.

"As we are under the stars, what more appropriate time to look into your charts" she said.

She looked at her app, asking for Valentina and later Mia's birthdates and the times of their birth as she went on to explain more about their personalities. The girl's listened intently as Noemi gave an accurate picture of their current situations.

Noemi looked at Valentina and told her that her life was about to change. Something about Jupiter rising in one of her houses was taking place and that she was due for a major shift and that it had something to do with a foreigner or a foreign land, or potentially both.

Valentina listened and wondered what was coming for her soon. She thanked Noemi who now had others on the table wanting her attention and asking for her to do their charts as well.

After dinner, the girls and those that had paid for such an experience were taken out to the "Field of Light'. As explained to them, this exhibition was by artist Bruce Munro covering over 50,000 stems crowned with frosted glass spheres, that fill the whole landscape with colour and light. It was a spectacle.

The girls held each other's hands as they stepped out to the field to explore and wander through this artificial field of illumination.

They were like little children engrossed in amazement and wonder.

Mia was the more exuberant of the two and rushed ahead saying, "I will catch up with you when we get to the back of the display, I need to explore and your too slow Val." She said laughing as she skipped through the field.

Valentina treaded through the sands, enjoying the spectacle.

People were wandering everywhere, when out of nowhere she heard a voice speak to her in a strange accent.

"How are you enjoying your stay in Australia?"

Valentina turned and saw the man from Sydney standing next to her.

"Sorry to startle you," the man apologised. "My name is Christiaan Van de Berg and I remember you from the plane that departed from Los Angeles."

Valentina put her hand out to shake Christiaan's, as he had extended his own.

"Valentina Russo, nice to meet you."

Christiaan tried to make conversation as Valentina continued to walk, but Valentina excused herself saying that she had to catch up to her friend and walked away, apologising.

As she did so, Christiaan called after her, saying, "It was nice meeting you."

The girls reunited and before Valentina had an opportunity to tell Mia that she had spoken to this strange man, everyone was herded back into the bus to end the night.

It had been very special. Steve didn't lie that it would illuminate the girl's evening.

The girls hopped on the bus and found a seat together towards the back, waiting as everybody in the party found their seating, so they could depart back to the resort.

Then Valentina saw Christiaan walking down towards them, sitting himself down in the seat in front of them, that was yet to be occupied.

He turned around peering over the seat headrests and begun making conversation.

"Did you enjoy the night?" he asked.

Mia being none the wiser that he had approached Valentina earlier that evening, responded in the affirmative.

"It was downright magical. God, I love this country, I just wish it was little cooler" she said.

Valentina remained silent, trying to look out the window.

Christiaan made some small talk with Mia, explaining that he was originally from the Netherlands, which explained the accent.

When they arrived, Mia invited Christiaan to join them back at the bar for drinks. He gladly accepted and they all made their way down for a night cap or two.

It was Mia's turn to buy drinks and after taking everyone's order, she announced that she was going to buy

some fries for them to snack on. She took their orders and
headed off to the bar.

Now Valentina and Christiaan were alone. Awkward at
first, Christiaan spoke.

"I know that this will come as a shock to you, but I
have been following you for some time now."

Valentina stood up, frightened by Christiaan's
admission.

"Wait, Valentina." Christiaan protested. "What I am
trying to say is, I was there when your boyfriend Jacob
died. I have been trying to find the right time to tell you.
I guess there is really no good time is there?"

Valentina dropped back into her chair. Not sure if she
should just get up and leave or hear this guy out. She
chose the latter.

Christiaan continued. "I met Jacob in Thailand. We
were all recruited to do a job for him, but something went
wrong. Jacob didn't stick to the plan, and he pissed-off
some powerful people. I have been trying to tell you this
for a while."

"See there were three of us."

"A British man by the name of Robert Bastion, Jacob
who was the Australian connection and me."

"Neither of us knew the other until we met in
Bangkok. Jacob was the recruiter for a group of bikies."

"Both Robert and I met Jacob in a dingy bar. He was
an easy guy to talk to and it didn't take much convincing
that we could make good money transporting the "stuff.""

"Robert was unlike Jacob and me, he had a criminal
background and had spent time in UK jails on and off
since his teens."

Valentina instinctively knew it had to be drugs that
they were involved in. She had heard the stories of
Thailand before.

"Jacob had the Australian connections with these bikies
and our job was just to do what were told, but it all went
wrong."

"So, we were all recruited knowing we could make
some real money and maybe score something else, besides
the cash. It seemed failproof and then something
changed."

Mia returned in hand with the drinks and some hot

fries, which the Aussies like to call "chips".

"Sorry to take so long, I got chatting to this hot guy at the bar and lost time, but the drinks are cold, and the "hot chips" are hot."

Christiaan chose to stop telling his story as it was for Valentina's ears only.

Valentina grabbed her drink, looked at Christiaan and began to down the contents of the glass in a couple of gulps.

She then went to the bar and sat at the counter, ordering the barman to give her six more of the same and line them up on the counter in front of her. The guy at the bar did as was asked and lined up her six drinks side-by-side.

Mia watched from a distance, as she and Christiaan made some small talk. While nibbling away at her hot chips, she mumbled to herself, "It's going to start again."

Valentina continued to drink. First one, and then she gulped down the rest one after the other. She asked for another three to add to the six or seven she had already consumed. She began talking to anyone and everyone who was standing around the bar, trying to make conversation as her speech slurred, ever so slightly.

People started watching her as the alcohol began to take effect.

"Do you think we should intervene?" Christiaan insisted.

"You won't be able to control her," Mia replied, "she occasionally goes on these benders. She has ever since I have known her. She is harmless and sometimes downright funny, but we just need to watch her and make sure she is safe."

By the end of the night, Mia had convinced Valentina to go back to the room with the assistance of Christiaan.

They laid her on top of her sheets and Christiaan wished them a good night after offering to sit with them.

"It's ok Christiaan, thank you for your assistance. Enjoy the rest of your vacation" Mia insisted.

That night was made up of dark dreams of Jacob for Valentina, as she battled her demons.

The next morning Valentina refused to get out of bed. She was feeling a little seedy and somewhat embarrassed, but she couldn't get the story that Christiaan had told her out if her head.

Mia had gone out to get her a fresh coffee and was holding it under her nose.

"You can't keep doing this Valentina" she said in a gentle voice.

There was a knock at the door as Valentina sat up to take a sip of her freshly brewed coffee.

"Are you decent?" came the booming voice of Steve.

Mia opened the door slightly ajar.

"Val, kind of had a big night, I don't think she will be able to do too many things this morning."

Steve's big smile dropped.

"Well, I did have you booked into the Uluru tour this morning, but I guess we can make our trip back home."

"She" gesturing towards Valentina, "can sleep it off in the back of the truck" he said.

The girls showered, grabbed some coffees for the road and packed their luggage into the truck.

The next five hours for Valentina was made up of sleeping on the back seat and when she was awake, she would make some small talk with both Steve and Mia. The trip was boring, and she was still a little hung over, and so anything beyond getting some sleep was not of interest.

By the time they had pulled into their hotel once again back in Alice, Valentina was pretty much her old self. Chatting away, yet still quite embarrassed that she had allowed herself to get that drunk the night before. You would think she may have grown out of it by now.

Steve helped them unload their bags and then pulled Valentina aside for a brief chat.

"I hope you are feeling better Val, because I was speaking to Daniel this morning and he has requested to hold another session with you. Mia is aware that it is just you this afternoon. Do you think you are up to it?"

Valentina was quietly elated and a little unsure as to why she was getting another session with Daniel, when Mia wasn't.

Steve anticipated her concern as to why today Daniel

would want to catch up with her, when they were meant to be at Uluru instead.

Steve pulled his hat off his head, wiping his forehead from the sweat. He looked down at the dirt below his feet and then back at Valentina.

"Daniel is an unusual guy, Val. This ability that he somehow developed allows him to tune into energies of other people. I guess it's like a tuning fork. Don't ask me how it works, but you must have witnessed some of it when you spent time with him. It's up to you if go of course. No one forces you to do this, so if you are not up to it, then that's fine with me and with him. No one has told him about what happened last night, but he will know. He will also know if you need some adjustment to your energies."

Steve smiled. "God, now I'm sounding like him."

Valentina didn't argue, but instead decided she had caused Steve enough problems so far and that another informative session with Daniel would be a positive engagement.

"I've got a couple of things to do around town and I will pick you up in about half an hour. Be ready" Steve said as he got back into his vehicle.

Valentina nodded and headed into the hotel, gesturing for Mia to come outside.

"Let's grab a bite said Valentina, we have thirty minutes to kill before I go."

They headed towards Kangaroo Corner Cafū to grab something to eat.

As they walked in, the same waitress was there to greet them. They took a seat and the woman walked over.

"I thought maybe you had already left as I hadn't seen you for a couple of days" the woman said as she approached their table.

"No still here" Mia replied.

The waitress officially introduced herself.

"My name is Elizabeth, but everyone calls me Lizzy."

The girls also introduced themselves and gave their orders.

Two toasted cheese and ham sandwiches, which they called 'toasties' with some sparkling water.

As there were very few customers in the shop that day,

Lizzy had more time to make conversation with the girls and get to know them.

They both exchanged some basic details about each other.

The girls were both from Los Angeles, where Valentina worked in emergency at the Los Angeles Community Hospital and Mia was a high-end realtor in Beverley Hills.

"I guess you are born and bred here in the Northern Territory?" said Mia to Lizzy.

"Not at all, replied Lizzy. I was born in another part of Australia called Melbourne. In a suburb called Blackburn, but I have spent a good part of my life on the Gold Coast in Queensland."

"We are going to Melbourne next," Mia said. "Can't wait to get there. I have heard it is something special."

"Melbourne is a major city I believe, and if I am right, so is the Gold Coast?" said Valentina.

"Oh no, said Lizzy. The major cities are Sydney and Melbourne and I guess to a lesser degree Brisbane, but my ex-husband was born on the Gold Coast, and he loved to surf when he wasn't working, so it suited his interests. I moved there some time ago now. It's kind of a more relaxed, water activity kind of lifestyle. You know surfing, boating, and swimming. I just followed my husband when I was married, but I have lived here in Alice before too."

The girls finished their sandwiches, whilst they chatted to Lizzy about what they had been up to. They told her about Uluru and this guy Daniel that they had met who lived out of town.

Lizzy said she had heard about him and his 'abilities'.

The girls paid their bill and walked back around the corner to wait for Steve.

A couple of minutes later he pulled up and Valentina hopped in, riding shot gun, as they made small chit chat on the way to Daniel's. She was feeling more herself and ready for another informative session with the bush man Mr Switzer.

Intent

Daniel was waiting in his living room for Valentina when she walked through his front door.

At the front of the room was two white boards, on which Daniel had already written on them the words.

ENERGY and INTENT

"Take a seat Valentina, our time is precious, and you have not travelled all this way to not to gain benefit." Daniel was obviously not in the mood to waste time today.

Valentina complied, sitting down in a chair, and listening to his every word.

Daniel began with little fanfare.

"In our last meeting you learned about vibrational energy, but very few of us are able to maintain the harnessing of such energy."

Valentina's ears pricked up.

"If you remember from out last meeting, I talked about us being spiritual beings. Meaning, all of us are "spiritual beings." As a spiritual being, we have different properties to the dense properties of a human body. For a moment I want you to imagine that they are separated. A little like the movie Avatar. Have you seen it?" Daniel asked.

"Yes," Valentina replied. "James Cameron's movie Avatar the one with the blue looking people in it."

"That's the one" said Daniel with a smile. "In that movie, the Avatars are a little like our human bodies. Vehicles for the real us. They are not us, but they allow us to project the spiritual "us" into a physical world. Our will, emotions and feelings are expressed through our human avatar from our spiritual existence."

"Part of our journey on this earth is to rediscover these spiritual properties, whilst releasing ourselves from the thinking that holds back our own development."

"Many people that come to me ask for their lives to change. They don't always verbalise that is what they want, but essentially that is why they are here. For the most part they are consumed by fear, material wants and mental blockages of the past, that in most cases they are not consciously aware of."

"As we do live in the material world of humans, then

we will be exposed to all these things.

Our job is to move beyond this and become a more spiritual being with an improved perspective, instead of more human perspective."

"What comes with this change in consciousness are new abilities, new understandings, and new shifts in our physical world. We learn to focus on the present, rather than living in the future or the past."

Daniel stopped and pointed to the back of the room near the door, gesturing to the back of the room.

"Would you mind turning on the light for me please Valentina?"

Valentina stood up and did as she was asked. Strange request as the room was perfectly lit, but she was compliant with the request.

She flicked the switch and looked at Daniel waiting for her next instruction.

"Excellent," Daniel said, "and how did you achieve that task?"

Valentina was a little perplexed by the question but answered anyway.

"I stood up and flicked the switch and then there was light."

"What took place before you did all that, for it to happen?" asked Daniel smirking a little.

Valentina wasn't sure where this was going or how to answer him. Daniel continued, as it was obvious that Valentina needed more clarification.

"Before you stood up and turned on the light switch, to get the energy to produce light, you had to do one thing."

"You had to have a thought to do that. Now since you have been turning on the lights since you were a child. It must have been pretty much a subconscious thought that you are having, as most likely it is out of your awareness. Yet you still had to have it, to make something happen."

"This also happens in the physical world, to get a result in the spiritual world."

"Some years ago, there was a reaction across the world from a movie called 'The Secret'."

"Now there was an element of truth to its message and an element of naivety to it as well. It took me a while to understand this as I kind of bought into the whole premise like everyone else."

"The truth is that we do have the ability to create things on this earth via the power of thought. It is a unique gift spiritual beings have and are given as humans. When we became humans, we were given the physical ability to create. It is what makes us different from others in this universe. We don't just procreate, we have the ability, to create, both with our hands and our minds."

"Now the movie, The Secret gives us some of that message. It began to talk about intent. It's not really a secret, it is more that we misunderstand how to achieve it. It is not a matter of asking for something and suddenly it is there. I think a lot of people learned that the hard way, that there must be other element(s) to create what is beyond what can be seen."

"That is not to say that what you think does not manifest. It can and it does, depending on if it meets the greater design of your life's path."

"Prayer is a form of vibrational intent. Great spiritual leaders have taught us to pray to create a focused intent, so that we can tap into a higher self. To access the source of the greatest life energy, that many refer to as God."

"Are you saying that if what I pray for, or have a focused intent on, as you call it, will happen if it meets my path and I am meant to then follow that through?" Valentina questioned Daniel.

Daniel smiled, "You are on the right track."

"Just because you wish for a Ferrari, doesn't mean that it serves you on this journey. It also doesn't mean you won't have one."

"If you have been given the ability to create, then you can create. Every invention you have ever used in your life started with a thought, followed by an intense will to put into action. This is called intent."

"No inventor dreamed about something and left it as a dream. What happens when they begin this process is that they will engage struggle to enable creation. They put motion into play and then they 'tap' into the greater universe where everything that was ever invented or will be invented resides. Like a big book of ideas, just waiting to be plucked out."

"Have you ever heard of an invention coming to

fruition and then someone on the other side of the world, who has never ever met this inventor, or even heard of this invention comes to the same conclusion? Well, that is because they have both 'tapped' into the higher source, where all answers reside. Past, present, and future."

"Now the other part of this equation is belief. Intent doesn't really work without belief. How could you create without believing you have something worth creating? Belief is a tricky one Valentina, because many people will tell you they believe in something, but instead they have a 'want' to believe. They really do want to bring something to fruition, but the way their minds are programmed, they become their own worst enemy. We will work on this later."

"Finally, they need to engage what I call the creative "Fire Starter" or "spark" and that is visualisation. By visualising, you are putting all your mental focus on making something happen. Of course, this is not a one-time exercise. Speak to people who have created something. Be it big or small. All will say is that it started as a thought. Visualisation is now seeing in your mind's eye the target and make it more real. Deep visualisation changes the vibration of your focus and the creation process."

"Let me try to give you a more practical example to illustrate my point."

"I was single for many years as I put all my focus on my career and business, but it did not bother me, as it was my *intent* to put my focus where it was."

"As I moved into my early thirties, maybe for the first time, I felt that something was missing. My soul knew that I was not complete, and I began to think about a partner, but my work was always still at the forefront."

"I didn't consciously give it a lot of thought, except when I went out with other couples. It was during these times that I would begin to think that I was feeling a little incomplete, and that a partner would be nice to share my life with. I used to imagine it and visualise myself in those scenarios that other couples enjoyed."

"A year or two later I found myself living an expensive apartment on the Gold Coast in the Q1 building.

What was at the time the tallest residential building in the world."

"Of course, there must be struggle for you to grow and this happened six months after moving into my apartment."

"A downturn in world markets plummeted my company's profits and suddenly we were teetering. My hard work was falling apart and trying to keep the ship together was harder than I thought."

"I remember going home one Friday, choosing not to stay for drinks after work. I just wanted to get home and be alone."

"My staff were worried, and I was just trying to keep it together for them. I allowed fear in."

"As I drove home, I turned on the radio in my Mercedes SUV Coupe and went into a trance, not really knowing how I got home."

"I didn't cry, but I worried. The next day was Saturday and I spoke to one of my friends from Melbourne on Skype about what had happened. I felt tired and depressed."

"I wanted to kill myself. I think I even prayed to God to end it for me as there was not much for me to live for, as I potentially was going to lose everything that I had put all my energy into over the previous few years. Everything I had sacrificed to be successful, including love."

"I had been low before in my life, but now I was at rock bottom."

"I finished talking to my friend and took my iPad and phone laying on my bed, eventually falling asleep. Waking maybe two hours later, knowing that something wasn't quite right. I realised that I couldn't move properly."

"My back had seized up and my left leg couldn't be straightened. It had never happened to me before and I was a little fearful that I was experiencing this."

"My leg was in immense pain shooting through my back, with any little movement that I made."

"I was trapped on the 64th floor of the Q1 building. A prisoner of my own thoughts."

"I lived alone. I really didn't know anyone in the building, and I know my mother was having problems at home with her husband Jimmy."

"I tried to rest, but no improvement, so I thought maybe some pain killers to assist. I wasn't sure what was in my medicine cabinet in my bathroom, but I had to do something. I was certainly in no shape to go downstairs and walk to any pharmacy or to the convenience store, which was situated at the bottom of the building for any drugs that would relieve my anguish.

I couldn't lift my back up, so I rolled until I hit the floor with a thud, and then I crawled to my bathroom a few feet away. I opened the drawers of where I thought they would be. No luck, I guess I had never bought any drugs for pain. Too busy being successful."

"I crawled back to the bed, but there was one problem. I couldn't lift myself back up. I had the strength to lift my upper body, but the rest of me was in too much pain to follow up and over. I was in trouble. Who would have thought that I would find myself in this predicament?"

"I lay on the floor resting, until I found the courage to put myself through the pain threshold to somehow get myself back on the bed."

"I think that took about two hours."

"I lay there contemplating my future."

"Potential bankruptcy if I didn't change my circumstances. Losing everything I worked for.

Now I had a seized back in which I had no idea if it would improve, and finally no lifeline to help me eat, shower, or even move from the bed without excruciating pain."

"In other words, it seemed hopeless."

"No point ringing for an ambulance as no one could get into my apartment."

"I didn't leave that bed for the whole weekend. I was hungry and tired."

"My thoughts of killing myself had subsided and I wanted to just walk again. Funny how the universe finds way to change our focus. Funny how we are continually pushed back onto our path."

"I decided to bite the bullet and contact my mother. She looked worse for wear, but she was still a welcomed face and luckily, she did have my spare key to get in. She went downstairs and got me some Ibuprofen to assist with the pain. Eventually the spasm or whatever it was subsided, and I felt normal again."

"I was facing failure and life was losing its meaning for me."

"One Saturday morning, shortly after my back had gone out, I chose to have breakfast in the outside cafй at the bottom of my building. It was a nice day, and my daily ritual was to buy a Financial Review newspaper, whilst having breakfast."

"There on the next table was a beautiful woman with long blonde hair, reading of all things, a bible."

"At the time, it was not unusual for me to strike up a conversation with people in coffee shops. I guess when you are alone, sometimes you just want company. Work was my social life and since my injury I had avoided driving into the city. I guess I didn't want to face the staff."

"I made a comment about what she was reading, and the conversation went from there.

I wasn't looking for it to be any more than a conversation, but in a short period it started as a date and eventually became a relationship, and then my wife. Maybe not all that quickly, but you get the idea."

"So, what's the moral to my long-winded story?"

"Intent doesn't happen in your time frame. No matter how many gurus tell you so on YouTube. This only happened because my intent became aligned with frequency for someone to enter my life, which I set in motion some years earlier. It will come when the path is ready, and the timing is right. See within my path the downturn of my business was put there to help me, not hurt me. To re-evaluate what I wanted. Nothing was going to change whilst *all* my focus and energy was on making money and building my business. So, an interruption in my thought process was manifested. That is not to say that I let my business fall apart because I wanted a partner. It means that sometimes we lose focus of what should be important to us along the way, as we are striving hard to achieve a goal. Many of us have blinkers on that do not allow us to see beyond our small world that we have created."

"Remember Valentina, that it starts with intent. Then

it travels its journey until it meets fruition. Unlike 'The Secret' that portrays it like you have intent and then you open your door, and your car is waiting outside. Oh, if it was just that easy."

"I had always believed that I would find someone to care for and care for me, but in my case, career had got in the way. My intent was focused elsewhere, it was only when other forces made me take down my guard, that it took shape."

"In my case it was meant to be. My path was to unfold."

Valentina's mind wandered to her relationship with Jacob. Was his death meant to be? Was there something that she could have done differently? Does everything happen for a reason?

Bringing her mind back into the room, she sat contemplating and then spoke.

"Everything you just said. Well could it just be a coincidence that it happened, and your intent had nothing to do with it."

"As I have mentioned before, nothing is a co-incidence or happens by chance. The human world is by design, with one proviso. You are given the ability to make a choice as to where your intent is focused on, which can alter scenarios, but not necessarily Wisdom opportunities. You have opportunities to alter the frequency of your vibrations."

"Let us say you get into an altercation with someone one day and unfortunately that fight results in you killing that person. What that means is you will most likely end up in jail. That may alter the look of the journey, but if you look at your world through spiritual eyes, then it is what you are here to learn that is important, not the journey. The journey provides an opportunity, even if sometimes it just seems to be a road of heartache."

"If you are here to learn how to love. This may come from your time in that jail cell. Or it may come from someone who hurt you severely and it is your opportunity to discover a new way of handling what may be an ongoing issue for you across lifetimes. You do have a choice to learn, or you make the choice to repeat."

"Our Wisdoms come from several different sources,

repeatedly until we get the learning. If we do not, we are destined to living our own Groundhog Day."

"Let me tell you the story of the Two Burros Valentina."

The Two Burros

"**M**any years ago, an old farmer who was struggling financially, watched as his best draft horse was dying from colic. He was in a dilemma as he was not in a position to buy another one as times were tough. It was still the days that horses ploughed the land, well before machinery took over."

"The farmer scratched his head wondering what he was to do. It would be a massive task for one man to plough alone. He considered asking neighbours if he could borrow their horses, but they too needed their animals to plough their own land."

"As he looked out to his pastures, he saw his two donkeys or what the Spanish refer to as burros grazing in another paddock. He had bought them many years earlier to ward off any predators to his flocks of sheep that he had down the hill."

"Burros are natural protectors and will warn off other animals that wish to attack your stock. That had been faithful animals and so he had kept them for years."

"The farmer had heard that in a province not too far away there were a couple of farmers who were in a similar position as himself, putting their burros to work, to help plough the fields. He talked it over with his son and they agreed that this was his only option they had at their disposal."

"They made their way down to the field where the two animals were grazing and brought them back up with the intention of putting them to work."

"The son lined up the two donkeys' side-by-side, putting a harness on them as he held them in place as the father attached his plough behind the two beasts."

"The men were ready to start and tried to get them to move forward in a straight line, so they could begin making furrows in the ground, so he could plant his seeds for the next season."

"At first nothing happened as the men made loud noises, yelling at the animals. This wasn't a big task, they just had to walk from point A to point B in a straight line as the old farmer kept the plough straight and upright."

"Instead, these animals had a mind of their own. They were stubborn. One would walk straight as requested, but the other would walk off to the left, pulling the other off course."

"The two men were now frustrated. They knew that getting a burro to do what was asked may be difficult. but not impossible. Other farmers had done it before."

"Now while the men were scratching their heads, the two burros began to chat to each other."

"The older burro by the name of Sanchez definitely had a mind of his own and he was going to take his own path. Afterall, he had done that his whole life. He didn't know why, but if a human tried to get him to go one way, he would always do the opposite. It was his nature."

"As he told his counterpart, Santiago 'If anyone puts a harness on me, then I will move away as soon as I can. Or kick up my heels, so they know I don't like it. I don't know why I do it, but I have done that since I was little. I think someone tried to put a saddle on me when I was young."

"Santiago laughed and said, 'It isn't that hard to do Sanchez. You put one foot in front of the other until you get to the end and then you turn around. I have seen this before, when I was on another farm. It is back breaking work and sometimes you wonder if you will ever make it through the day, but you don't have to be a horse to be able to do it. We are better than horses anyway.'

"Sanchez was not having any of it. He was going his own way and he began to walk off further out to the left and away from the other donkey."

"The farmers had made the mistake of not buying a proper harness and were using a thin rope to hold the two burros together. It was also very long, yet they were still connected, but from a distance it was like they were not connected at all."

"No matter what the farmers did. They could not control the burros as they operated completely differently to each other."

"Eventually they brought in the famous burro whisperer, Isabella, to help them with their dilemma. A forty-year-old local who it was said that she could talk to all animals in their own language."

"The women first spoke to the father and son and then walked over to the two burros."

"At first the animals were mindful of any human that could talk their language, but eventually warmed to her. She explained to them that there was a path that they could follow that would make it much easier for them to get the job done."

"She informed the two burros that if they focused their minds on the task, then together they could achieve far more than if they worked separately. Even though they were obviously of different age and experience that if they moved their thinking in the same direction, then miracles could be performed. They just had to think it and make it happen."

"Although both Sanchez and Santiago thought the flimsy rope was a silly idea and was more of a hindrance. Isabella understood and explained that it was a good reminder that you are connected together, even if it was by a thin veil of a rope. In other words, they were never disconnected, even if one of them could occasionally go on a tangent."

"Yet if they both followed their path and focused their thoughts, they would get to the end of the job so much more quickly than if they chose to align themselves elsewhere."

"The two agreed, as they knew that the sooner, they did so, the sooner they would get their wish. Where they could once again graze in the paddock."

Daniel stopped as Valentina was listening to the story being told and sat down.

"I like the story Daniel, but what is the meaning behind it? Learning to work together?"

Daniel sat forward.

"There are many lessons for you here."

"The first one is that all of us follow an invisible pattern that for the most we don't know we are carrying out. Like the older burro, Sanchez, it had become part of his conditioning. When asked to do something, instead of finding a way to help get the job done, he kicked his hooves up and without any conscious awareness caused problems."

"Every human being has these patterns that seem to control us. Sometimes we are aware of them and other times, we cannot understand why we act them out."

"Let me give clarify."

"Now I know you have flown on a plane before. Are you also familiar with what happens in the cockpit out the front?"

"An interesting thing about pilots and flying planes is that for much of your flight, they are not actually flying the plane. They are at the controls when you take off, following checklists to make sure everything is working and that they have the right amount of fuel for that particular flight, but once they have you in the air, in most cases they revert to a mechanism known as the "Autopilot". I am sure you have heard about it."

"Essentially its function once turned on is to keep the plane flying at a certain altitude and speed. If there is a gust of air that may pick up the plane from its settings, it will bring it back to what that altitude was originally set at."

"Now we as humans have a similar setting."

"A lot of our autopilot was set when we were children. It dictates how we operate in different situations and brings us back to the original setting. Some of us kick up our heels, because we are running our autopilot."

"This autopilot is found in our subconscious. We are in many cases unaware of how we operate. We just do. It can be a positive or negative effect on our lives. Those that succeed in life don't do so because they were born into money or have an education and a top university. Both of those things give you a leg up, but I'm sure you know many "smart" people that really go nowhere in life. They work in dead end jobs, and they secretly envy the guy who started XYZ company that is worth billions."

"A lot has to do with their autopilot controlling subconscious actions that sometimes sabotage them."

"The positive is that all of this can be changed and when you do that, you are able to fly at much higher altitudes. You will find that you may also see people that you called friends differently, as you will identify that they are not necessarily good for you. They may not have you best interests, but rather their own at hand. They are playing out their own autopilots and flying at a different altitude to your own."

"These realisations come when you have removed past conditioning that has been imprinted on you from childhood. On the other hand you will also realise that you will gravitate towards those that are there for your benefit, and who do not wish to take away your energy, because they lack it themselves."

"All of this will make more sense as we discover the 3 Minds."

Daniel poured himself a glass of water and continued.

"Part of the secret to creation within the physical realm is to understand the connection between spiritual and physical. Like the connection between Sanchez and Santiago. They are connected. In this case by a thin rope. Just because you are connected does not mean that you are aligned with each other. Until you align your minds through this connection, then you will always be at the mercy of going astray. Pulling in different directions. To understand that all thought is a form of energy. A form of vibrational intent with true beliefs behind it. By putting it into words, it focuses the mind to bring about this intent."

"Two burros, connected by a veil called a thin rope, but yet they are still connected."

"Therefore, prayer is so important. The connection of many minds all with the same intent alters the physical world. It allows them to walk the straight line to plough their field."

"We as humans feel helpless sometimes, because when we are in our 'intent' mode, we put a time frame on when the result should take place. Some things are very quick, others must grow and mature. To germinate."

"Sometimes we put limitations and conditions on our intent. For example, if I don't get this within a certain period, then it is not ever going to work. Or God has abandoned me, because I really wanted to be with that person and now, they are with that guy. Or even worse he punishes me when I am such a good person."

"Trust me I have felt and said all of the above. When

you lose loved ones, it is a conversation you have with God sometimes."

"Sometimes we also feel that God or the universe has allowed bad things in the world to happen, when in reality, we as humans have created it."

"God does not allow wars. Man creates wars."

"God does not create evil sadistic humans. Men choose to take that path."

"God does not interfere with our decisions, as it is part of our journey. The good and the bad. Remember Earth is not Heaven."

"If your intent is in alignment with your path and the interacting paths of others around you, then your intent has power."

"For most people we put this intent out in the universe and then wait for the period we think is appropriate to us."

"It's a little like planting a seed and our expectation is that the seed we have planted, will appear as a fully grown tree a day or two later. That is *not* how it works, in the real world. Maybe in books or movies. Like a seed, it will germinate and wait until it becomes aligned to the path of what we are asking for. Sometimes it takes years as different paths are aligning. Remember you are not the only one have an earthly experience."

"If we pray for someone to get over an illness, but that person is not ready or it is not part of their path, then our intent will not override their journey. Of course, if they become aligned and in line with your prayers, then change can take place."

"No one can make Sanchez choose his path. It is his decision that he can focus his intent and get the job done. Along the way he may stumble, but these are part of his lessons."

"Remember everyone is here to learn from their journey. If you are to experience something, then only so much interference will be allowed to intervene. Someone who has decided to die after having been given the news of a death sentence by something such as cancer, is far more likely to pass within a short period, than someone who intends fighting it and focusing their intent on a positive result. Many people hear the words of a doctor that they have a couple of months to live and unfortunately commit their *will* to that thinking. This is very common."

"Valentina, the universe is all connected. Across every galaxy and being. No matter what they look like or act like. There is a binding mist of energy that connects. For the energy to burn brighter, we are given "opportunities" to turn up the brightness."

"So, when we despair at the pain and suffering in this world, we must remember we chose the path to learn how to turn up our brightness levels. Humanity is given a choice to turn up the brightness, unfortunately factors such as greed and power dominate this planet and so it is heading down the wrong path. It is given opportunities along the way to correct itself."

"By understanding intent, we can connect to the Source, but never expect the Source to be like Uber Eats and deliver just because you put an order in. It just doesn't work like that."

With that Daniel stopped and let everything he had given Valentina to sink in.

"I think we need a break," said Daniel. "Tonight's session is designed to open your understanding of concepts."

"What you will learn next may change your life, so it's time to have a mental refresh."

"Also, during the break, I am going to ask you to ring Mia, as this will be an all-night session. I will drive you home, as I can't expect Steve to come and collect you up so early in the morning."

"Are you ok and ready to be exposed to what is holding you back from your spiritual awakening?"

Valentina nodded and agreed.

"For what you learn about yourself here will show you how to open up your own possibilities. It will teach you the Wisdoms you need to know and the barriers you need to break, so that you can walk your path and sow your seeds of intent."

"Only once you have mastered what you are about to learn Valentina, only then will you find your WAY."

3-Minds

Valentina rang her friend Mia and explained that she was safe and was coming back to the hotel, early in the morning.

"Are you ok?" Mia said as the two spoke for a couple of minutes.

"Yes, perfectly fine," said Valentina, remembering Mia's concern from the night before.

"To be honest in some ways this is the most enlightening conversation I have ever had."

"Before you go," Mia butted in, "there were two guys here looking for you. "They bailed me up as I was about to go for a walk. Has something happened that I should be aware of?"

"No, I really can't think of who that might be," thinking that the police detective had returned.

"What did you tell them?"

"Nothing, I just said that I couldn't help them and left it at that."

"Ok good, I've got to go. Talk in the morning."

Valentina and Daniel returned to the loungeroom.

Daniel stood at the front of the room and cleared his voice, looking intently at Valentina.

He cleared his throat and asked.

"Do you think you are successful person, Valentina?" Daniel said in a low but confident voice.

"I guess many people would say that I am successful," she replied. "I am a doctor after all. I was pretty good at school, and I believe I am well respected in my profession."

Daniel paused while thinking.

"But the question is, do *you* think you are successful in your life?"

Valentina carefully answered, contemplating the question, and laying her cards on the table.

"No, I have never felt successful. I have always felt inferior if you must know the truth. Just because you are the top of your class, does not mean that life is a breeze. If anything, it just brings its own pressures."

"I never had a lot materially or financially growing up. My father died when I was eight years old, and my family made up of my mother and sister struggled through my teen years and early twenties. I was socially awkward, and never really fit into one group or another. As I got older it became easier as my friends for the most were my colleagues, going through the same pressures I was."

"To answer your question, I have always felt I was small and an outsider to this world."

"Thank you for such an honest answer, Valentina. Most people are good at hiding behind their masks that they create to get through this world, but you were quite transparent and maybe a little enlightened in your response."

"Oh, I still have a mask," Val replied. "I am generally pretty good at pretending that I am holding it all together, but I'm a mess."

"As our time is limited and we are going into the night, I want to start to give you the foundations to creating everlasting change, but before I can do that, you need to understand how you as a Spiritual Being operates within both the physical and spiritual spheres."

Valentina lay back in her seat, drinking a cup of hot green tea, listening intently.

Daniel walked to the whiteboard on the left and began to draw.

On the board he drew three circles. Evenly spaced one on top of the other.

On the first one he wrote the words, Soul 'Unconscious - The Answer (Spiritual Mind)'

On the second one below he wrote the words Mind 'Subconscious'- The Servant' and on the last one at the bottom he wrote the words, Body 'Conscious Mind - The Programmer'.

"Now I'm guessing you are familiar with the term Soul? As in someone has a Soul, not that they are a soul brother."

"Of course, Valentina replied. I do believe we all have a soul. I was brought up a Catholic, so I am familiar with the concept."

"And you would be right. The question is where is the

Soul? Is it within our bodies, and does it return after our death? Or is it elsewhere and do we reconnect with it at a later stage?

Daniel pointed to the top circle.

"The Soul is what I call the Unconscious Mind, sometimes called the Super Conscious. It is the divine God essence that everyone has. It is a continuum of our thinking, emotions, desires, and the Subconscious connects us to this mind. We sometimes call this Unconscious Mind, The Answer. The final step where all progression culminates." Daniel started.

"The Soul is the past, the present and the future and transcends time itself. The Soul does not have time. It just IS. A little like The Dreaming you learned about at Uluru."

"As the Soul is not of this earth, it can be here and there at any time. In other words, it does not reside on this earth. It resides only on heavenly plains, and it is projected into other realms. I know that can be a little hard to comprehend, but the Soul is reflected here and is part of you in spirit, that you find through the second mind, which we call the Subconscious."

"Now the Subconscious Mind sits between the spiritual and the physical worlds. It is the mirror of the Soul and holds the same characteristics, as well as the habits that we create here on earth."

"It is almost like part of the Soul resides here on earth through the Subconscious Mind. This mind is the conduit between the two worlds."

"Finally, you have the Conscious Mind," as Daniel points to the final circle. "This sits squarely in the physical world and uses the brain. The physical mechanism given to us for faculty thinking."

"What I have described here, are the 3-Minds that make up spiritual beings that we are."

"I call the Conscious Mind, The Programmer, as it has the ability consciously make decisions and a little like a computer programmer, input new data. If this data is correctly input, then the next mind will be influenced accordingly. Of course, if we don't remove some of the old programming, we have this "inner conflict" that needs to be addressed. Sometimes we talk about being in two minds when trying to make a decision."

"The Servant is the Subconscious, because it takes instructions and holds all our habits that are mirrored back and forth between the Soul and the Conscious Mind. Like I just mentioned, if we input bad data, then we produce bad outcomes, which are not aligned with our spiritual self."

"If we are truly spiritual, then why are we here?" asked Valentina. "I am sure you have told me before, but I don't get this pain and suffering part of it. I don't get this journey that we must endure" Valentina said.

Daniel took another sip of water from his glass.

"There are levels of Souls. Those that are closer to the physical world and those that are closer to the God essence."

"The goal is the God essence, but no one learns anything when it is handed to you on a platter."

"Do you remember learning to ride a bike when you were young?"

Valentina nodded

"My parents bought me one when one when I was 5 years old. It was a beautiful red one with its own training wheels and a bell on the handle. I think I got it for Christmas" Valentina said.

"Did you stay on your training wheels?" asked Daniel.

"Well no. If I remember correctly, I wanted to be able to ride like my cousin Paul, so I begged my father to teach me."

"One weekend, he removed the training wheels and held the back of my seat as I pedalled and tried to keep balance. I fell many times that day. Initially I cried, but my father encouraged me to get back on and try again. Eventually I gained my balance and stayed upright. I can still recall the moment he let go and I realised that it was all me."

"I yelled and screamed."

"It's funny I haven't thought about that for a long time."

"So, you are telling me, Daniel continued, that you fell, suffered maybe some scrapes or pain, but with the help of your father you learned to ride a bike that the day before seemed impossible. Now able to join other kids in riding your bike. It wasn't easy I'm sure, but you learned. You gained knowledge, and now you no longer give a second thought to riding a bike."

"The Soul makes choices to gain Wisdoms. Why? Because it wants to move closer to the God essence."

"Why earth of all places Daniel?" Valentina asked.

"Many Souls choose earth, as their university for knowledge. They come more than once to earth to gain their Wisdoms, until they improve."

"See the earth is difficult, if not the most difficult of the journeys. Souls choose it on a regular basis. It has the option of choosing other realms, and some do, but the progression for them takes longer."

"Earth gives you the ability to take your training wheels off earlier."

"That's a lot to take in," said Valentina. "So, are you agreeing with Eastern religions that we have many lives?"

"I am advising you that our Souls have the ability to choose the journey before we come back. Even if that journey means pain and suffering. In all honestly before you return to this physical world, you do choose what the journey will look like and then while you are here you then make choices as to how you play this life."

"If you don't learn the lessons that you came to learn, then you will find during your physical life, regular reminders, and opportunities to relearn. If you don't get it in this journey, then you may choose to come back to relearn it."

"This just sounds like I am in a game of some type" Valentina protested.

"No, you are sitting in the most powerful learning environment that is possible for a growing Soul. Do not dismiss its value Val."

"So, you have the physical mind, what we call the Conscious Mind, which we just described. It is able to make decisions here on earth about situations that you encounter, but you have to remember that what you bring to the table is what you bring to the table."

"What the hell does that mean Daniel?" Valentina asked.

"What it means that you can only operate to your fullest capacity with the tools that you have to date. Many things influence you here on earth. Parents, grandparents, colleagues, and circumstances put in front of you to assist or hinder."

"Each of those people have played an important part in your life as a child. They will impress on you their habits and mannerisms, which you will pick up without even being conscious of it."

"I call this "Generational Baggage"."

"Usually within a short period of knowing someone, I can pick these habits on an individual and when I ask the person, 'Which parent did you pick this up from?' They usually need to take a step back and think."

"Many times, they go to protest. In many cases the habit they hated in their parents the most, is the one that they are displaying themselves. Then usually they take a mental step back and say, 'That was my father or mother's habit'."

"Most of us are not aware that we have been influenced our whole lives, and we are running patterns that affect our progress. We need to make an adjustment for our own development."

"My father died when I was young, so is it possible that I picked up his traits?" Val interrupted."

"How old did you say he was when he died?'

"Eight."

"I have no doubt you have some of his traits. Maybe you can think of some if you focus on it."

Valentina drank some wine that Daniel had given her earlier. She held up the glass peering into it as she remembered her father.

In her eyes he was a beautiful loving man, but he had his faults.

"What did he die of Valentina?" asked Daniel.

"His liver failed?"

She paused

"He was an alcoholic." She continued.

Valentina never spoke much about her father to anyone. She loved him, but she feared she would become him. Alcohol at times would control her, especially when she was stressed out.

A small tear fell down Valentina left cheek. She hadn't ever thought that she could become her parents. That is why she strived to do well at school and become a doctor. She didn't want to struggle like them. Especially the struggle and poverty they experienced after her father's death.

"The beauty of gaining Wisdom, is that you can use the knowledge to alter your path. This is the reason why you are here."

"When you learn a Wisdom, you have an opportunity to remove the barriers to it. You will have the chance of integrating new thinking that becomes part of you. Once it becomes truly part of you, it then mirrored through the subconscious back to the Soul Consciousness.

Sometimes it takes several incarnations of one's life to perfect a Wisdom. Therefore, you find yourself thrown back into similar situations and wondering how in hell did you get into a similar mess as before."

"It's a learning opportunity."

"Your path will give you opportunities along the way."

"So now that you understand a little about the 3-Minds, you will be ready for us to work with them, to help you on your journey. In time as we work with you and if you choose to go down that path, we work on each layer, until we align your 3 Minds."

Daniel looked at his phone to check the time.

"I'm hungry," said Daniel, "time to eat. Hope you like Tacos?"

"Love them replied," Valentina.

Both were hungry, but one of them had so many more questions that she wanted answered before her time in Australia was over.

Daniel cooked and Valentina assisted with preparation. They sat down to eat and chill a little, as they enjoyed their food.

Just as Valentina was finishing her plate and was about to help herself to another Taco, her phone rang.

"Is this Valentina Russo?" a deep man's voice said on the other end of the line.

"Yes, Valentina replied."

The line then went quiet as Valentina tried to get a better reception moving around.

"Anything serious?" enquired Daniel.

"Wrong number, I think. I didn't recognise the voice."

After they had their fill of Tacos, Daniel jumped to his feet and announced that it was late, and he would rather get Valentina back late in the night, rather than really early in the morning.

Val picked up her handbag and phone and followed Daniel out to his Ford Ranger Wildtrak ute.

They hopped in and before Valentina could even put on her seatbelt, Daniel was off the like the wind down the driveway.

She managed to get on the seatbelt, and she held on for dear life.

"Trying to get rid of me?" Valentina squealed as Daniel flew out of his driveway.

"No, he replied" just want to make good time.

As they settled in for their ride back to town, Valentina got brave and felt comfortable enough to ask Daniel about himself.

"What's the Daniel Switzer story?" she asked with some confidence.

"Do you really want to know?" he said keeping his eyes on the road.

"Yep, I want to know as much as you will share."

Daniel's Story

"**I** was born in the State of Victoria, in the suburb of Chirnside Park. About an hour drive out of the city of Melbourne.

"It was a normal childhood, I think. My father was a commercial pilot, but not like the big airlines stuff. He flew much smaller planes for private owners. I think it was a good deal until he had a falling out with his boss and he then he struggled to find work.

"My mother had been a hairdresser, but her wage, although contributed to the household income, it was really dad that was the breadwinner.

"I had no brothers or sisters growing up. I guess the financial struggle put a stop to that.

"When I was still very young, my father found a job here in Alice Springs working for the Royal Flying Doctors Service as a pilot.

"They were good times, but I had to adjust. Big city kid, moving to outback town.

"We had a mix of white and indigenous kids. For the most we got along, but I really connected with the Indigenous kids the most. Maybe it's because I felt I was an outsider and at times they felt the same.

"I was ok at school, but I preferred my times outside the school environment. My indigenous friends were great, but I really loved the adults. Especially the grandparents and the elders of their people.

"After a while I became more like part of their family. So much so that the elders treated me like one of their own. They taught me some of the old ways. How to survive in the bush and they even took me to the men only ceremonies after I had completed my time going walkabout."

"Walkabout?" Valentina enquired. "I feel I have heard that term somewhere before."

"If I am correct walkabout was a term the white Australians used to give to the Indigenous workers," said Daniel, "who would suddenly stop work and disappear for periods of time. They would just go walkabout. So, it was considered a derogatory term given to what they perceived as lazy Indigenous people who just stopped working.

"That wasn't the reality. The workers were following traditional practices, sometimes attending ceremonies that they needed to attend."

"When you are around the age of ten to approximately the age of sixteen, travelling out in the bush for weeks on end is a rite of passage. A spiritual journey whereby you travel to ancestral sites of the land is important. It can last for as long as six months.

"In some way it's a little like a Bar Mitzvah for young Jewish boys, where they moved from adolescence into a manhood.

"When I was fifteen, my best friend Nullah or as he was known at school, Nick, was ready to go walkabout. We had both been taught for a few years on how to survive in the wild and both of us were ready to do our time.

"Of course, when you do go walkabout, you must do it alone. It is how you grow.

"My mother was hesitant and thought we were being irresponsible. My father felt differently. He had met many indigenous people in his time with his trips across the Northern Territory and had great respect for their rituals and the people.

"He felt it would toughen me up. That's not to say that he did not have his concerns. I was allowed to go walkabout for just over a week, which to my mother, is unfathomable and downright scary to think about.

"She knew I had been trained by indigenous elders and that I had the skills to survive in the bush. Probably better than any other white man out there.

"I won't bore you with all the details. None the less I did do my walkabout. I identified the plants I could eat and those that had healing properties. I built my own shelter and found my own food and water. Most importantly it allowed me to reflect and reconnect with the land. To connect with my spiritual guides.

"I grew from the experience, and it gave me a sense of spirituality, that I have taken into my life as I got older.

"Life was normal for the next couple of years.

"Then my normal changed one day.

"My mother got a call one evening from dad's work. He had a massive heart attack that killed him stone dead.

"One minute he was talking to a colleague in the office and the next meeting he is clutching his chest and fell to the ground. To think he worked with doctors, and no one could save him. I guess it was his time.

"Life got hard. Dad had no life insurance and suddenly we started to go without.

"Now my mother is a survivor and within a year she had met a truckie by the name of Jim. They married reasonably quickly, and we all moved to set up home in the state of Queensland on the Gold Coast, where Jim was from.

"I loved the beach lifestyle, but it was sad to leave my friends. Of course, I had a better chance of getting a university education if I lived close to one.

"I finished high school, got a degree in business, and moved into the corporate world to learn about finance. Working in it for a few years, eventually finding my way into a mutual fund manager, working with investments on an institutional level.

"I did my time there and learned the ropes, but I had yearned to be my own boss. I guess I was always entrepreneurial.

"In time after gaining sufficient knowledge and by some miracle I convinced some investors and colleagues to join me, setting up, Walkabout Funds Management.

"I guess in honour of my indigenous friends. Well kind of.

"The business took off almost immediately and I put together a great team of managers that helped us skyrocket.

"I now had my offices set up in Ann Street in Brisbane and life was good. Money was great.

I had it all. Cars, a beautiful apartment in the tallest residential building in the world at the time, The Q1, facing the beach.

"Life was busy, but empty.

"Anyhow you know the story about how I met my wife, and all seemed good as my business survived the global financial crisis. Now I was making more money than ever.

We even had a daughter who was the apple of her father's eye. Christina.

"We eventually bought a beautiful house on Sovereign

Island, and I was set. I now had the beautiful house, beautiful wife, beautiful daughter, and more money than I could spend.

"And then one day this guy walked into my office...

"A tall guy in his mid-thirties, beard and of slim build, wearing a three-piece suit.

He had made an appointment and was punctual. He had wanted to make a very large investment into one of our funds and said that if we were up to it, more would be coming on a regular basis.

"The name he gave me was Victor McEvoy and he said that he represented a group of investors that needed my services.

"I informed him that we would love to have his business. We set up the funds that day and I thought none of it until a few months later as Victor chose to make another visit. This time with a couple of men, not so well dressed as himself.

"This meeting was very different. He had informed me that the investors were impressed with our firm and wanted to invest hundreds of millions of dollars. Not once, but every month.

"The commission dollars rang in my head.

"Now I knew deep down that this had to be some type of mafia or drug money, and they were money laundering dirty activities, but hey I was into making it big at the time. I was not naïve, but greedy and who was I to stand in the way of my own good fortune?"

Valentina sat listening, surprised by what she was hearing.

Daniel continued as they drove along the dark highway towards town.

"Yes, I took the money, and I did it for maybe a year. I and the company made considerable profit from these transactions, but I wasn't brought up that way. I wasn't a bad guy, but greed had taken hold for a period, and I didn't look beyond the dollars. I didn't do what I would have once done and that is scrutinise a deal like this.

"For that whole year that I took the money, I suffered from headaches and stomach cramps. It just didn't sit right in my gut.

"Eventually we had a falling out, as I advised Victor

one day that we were no longer going to expose the company to this, as the government was cracking down and we needed to stop.

"Victor told me that his boss would not be so happy with this decision, but he would relay the message back.

"Some months later my wife, daughter Christina and I went to a friend's kids birthday party. It was a beautiful sunny day and we all had fun playing, drinking, and relaxing.

"I even went out with my friend on his boat in the waterways of the Gold Coast.

"We had a light dinner there and as the sun had now set, so we decided it was best to head home. It was only thirty-minute drive away.

"Not even five minutes after leaving the party, I was pulled over by a police car doing a random alcohol breath test. There must have been a blitz on at the time, cracking down on drivers.

"The officer said we were in an area too busy for pulling over cars and asked me to follow them to a quiet reserve to conduct the test. I obliged and followed the police vehicle to the wooded area. Both male officers got out of the car and asked us to wind down our windows, which we did.

"Then I got this feeling of pending doom. You may say I was crazy, but I used to refer to it as my Spidey sense. Something wasn't quite right.

"They asked for my driver's licence, which I gave them, and they headed back to their vehicle to check my details.

"They appeared to be making a phone call, as I watched them in my rear mirror. Not their police radio, but just a normal smart phone.

"My wife sat patiently in the front seat as they again jumped out of the car.

I looked at my side mirror and noticed the officer with his firearm drawn and what appeared to be a silencer on the tip of his pistol.

"Both men walked up to the car quickly pulling out their weapons, the man on the other side of the car put a gun to my wife's head and pulled the trigger. Instantly killing her. She fell back into her seat, splattering blood into her headrest.

"The other man shot me in the chest several times, whilst I could hear the back door opened and my daughter protesting as they pushed her down on the seat and shot her in the back repeatedly before you could no longer hear her whimpers.

"I could feel myself slipping away...

"Suddenly I somehow left my body and floated above it. It was a strange sensation if you could call it that. I could now see myself slumped on the front seat, covered in my own blood. I looked across the dashboard and could see my wife with her head back against the headrest with a clean bullet hole in the middle of her forehead. Her eyes were open wide.

"My heart sank as my gaze moved to the back seat. There I could see my daughter's blood splattered body slumped face down. No movement. I knew instinctively she had passed also.

"Before I could feel anything. I suddenly felt I was being pulled away and all I could feel was brightness and warmth. A little like when you go on holidays, and you wake up with a bounce in your step and the sun on your face.

"It's hard to describe Valentina. It was like one minute I am this body and then I move through the mirror of my mind and find myself in Soul. I had never felt anything like it before. I was so content. Not from what I had witnessed, but from the peace this journey was bringing me. Hard to explain. If I was on earth, I would be devastated, but I wasn't.

"Then as I travelled further, I could see figures before me. All my grandparents were there and their siblings, welcoming me. Giving me what I call their "light".

"The group parted ways and a man appeared. I had seen the shape of this being before, and as it got closer. The features became clearer and more pronounceable in appearance. As this being approached, I then recognised that it was my father.

"His beaming smile brought me absolute peace.

"We spoke for a while and he told me that I had passed, but I had yet to fulfill my purpose back on earth. We spoke about my family, and he assured me that it was their time and that they were well looked after. The "family" would look after them.

"He pointed behind me as if to gesture that I had to return to where I had come from.

"He told me that I had great work to do and that my mother still needed me back on earth.

I protested, but he just smiled and then as quickly as he came, he was gone, and I felt a tug from within my stomach and I was now back in my body with paramedics working on me in the back of an ambulance.

I was back."

"But you were dead?" said Valentina.

"Yes, and then I was alive. Human alive that is.

"Apparently, a man had been walking his dog that night and even though he did not see the events at our vehicle, he had heard the police vehicle take off. His dog dragged him to the scene. Animals are so in tune with spirit you know.

"Once he got to the car, he rang emergency services immediately.

"There was nothing that could save my wife and daughter, but somehow, I was still breathing after a concerted effort to bring me back to life. Obviously, they saved my life and the police investigated. Of course, no arrests were made, even though we suspected the cartel and bikies of the murders.

"The news had originally reported that all three occupants had died.

"That day Daniel Carboon died, and Daniel Switzer was born."

"So, you went into a witness protection program?" Valentina asked.

"No, I created my own, I moved to back to Alice Springs. It was where I felt safe.

Plus, I really didn't know if I could trust the police, so I just changed my name and disappeared. I knew how to move my money to my advantage, so I picked up what I thought was necessary and bought a house back here. The business I believe was bought out by some of my close colleagues and the money went to my mother, as she was my only living relative besides my younger half-brother."

"That is an incredible story Daniel, you have seen a lot

in your life. I am also sad for your loss. It must have been traumatic?"

"I hadn't seen anything until my death experience Val. What I experienced changed me. Not only did it take away any fear of death, but it was like a veil had been lifted and I could hear things and feel things I couldn't before. It was like this thin veil was now almost one and I was able to see things in others that I couldn't in the past. My losses were painful, but instinctively I knew that they were in a better place. They are only temporarily separated from me, and I will see them again for sure."

They were now about fifteen minutes out of town as Daniel looked up to the rear-view mirror for the first time, since starting his story.

He did a double take and announced "There is some idiot behind us with no lights on. Geez there are some buffoons out there."

Valentina turned her head to see what Daniel was talking about.

Maybe ten feet behind them was a black car. Neither of them could work out the type of car, except that it did not have it lights on, and it was keeping pace with their vehicle.

Daniel slowed down, so that they could pass them comfortably, but the car chose to remain at the same pace and distance.

He turned off the highway to head into town, closely followed by the vehicle. He put the foot down and the car kept pace.

"I think we are being followed; Daniel announced. Don't panic, it could be just young guys being idiots. There is enough of them in this town."

They made their way into town as the other car pulled up beside them, keeping the same speed, whilst the two cars covered both sides of the road. Valentina and Daniel couldn't see who the occupants were. Either it was too dark, or the windows were totally tinted out.

They could feel their eyes peering in, even if they couldn't see them.

The car sped up and drove off.

Daniel and Valentina finally hit town. It was late and the Alice is not always safe at night, but they agreed to go have a late-night drink at the local pub to relax.

Valentina paid for the drinks, and they sat in a corner booth talking.

"So, you have had an interesting life... and death I guess." Valentina said.

"Yes, like you, it has been made up of highs and lows and everything in between. I am following my path Val. No one said that it was easy. Our paths are meant to have some difficulty, or we wouldn't learn anything from the journey.

"Also, paths are meant to cross."

"You mean yours and mine?" Valentina replied.

"No, I mean all paths. If we are here by design, then we meet people in our lives who will have meaning. The good ones and the bad.

"Those that are of significance in our spiritual lives will travel with us across these reincarnations. You will have heard them referred to as Soul Mates or Soul Contracts.

As we come back for our lesson or re-lessons in some cases, each soul mate or soul pairing comes back with us, to help the other through the journey."

Valentina took a sip of her white wine and took a deep breath.

"Do you think that we only have one soul mate or many?" She asked sheepishly as if it were a silly question.

"Good question. I think we have many souls that come on our journey and we on theirs.

"The hardest thing about this human experience is suffering. Watching suffering from different angles is hard for most. It is hard to watch those that we care for, and it is hard to go through it.

"Watching my wife and child die horrifically is very hard. It's maybe harder when you know that they are in a better place, and you cannot be with them. You then look at humanity and say, 'How could a human being do this to another human?' It makes me cry for our Souls.

"What I do know is that we chose the journey."

Valentina was tired but was absorbing what Daniel was saying.

"We made a conscious decision to go through suffering before we come back to earth?" said Valentina. "So, you are saying you chose to see your wife and child being shot?"

"I chose for my journey to cross with hers and she did the same. Together, although horrific as it was, we needed to learn something from it."

"All I see is pain and the nonsense of this existence. What could you have possibly learned by the death of your wife and child?"

"I learned love. I mean real love. You only really appreciate something when you lose it. Until then at least for me, I took most things for granted. Even my wife and daughter.

"Their time had come, but I still had many Wisdoms to take from the whole experience. No matter how sick or perverted this may sound. We always struggle when death is brought upon a young life, because we think they weren't given a chance to live. When in reality they lived what was appropriate for this time around.

"When my father died, I was numb for a while, but I pushed it down.

"My spiritual experience gave me insight that most don't get. Firstly, I know it doesn't end here and secondly, I know that love transcends all barriers. You don't even understand love yet Valentina, but you will. You understand the chemical part of love, but the essence is so much deeper. It comes with the struggle of growth and experience together to become more."

They agreed on one last drink before calling it a night.

Daniel ordered another wine for Valentina and a bourbon and coke for himself. Valentina sat alone and waited as Daniel headed out for a toilet break.

Valentina pulled out her phone and pulled up a photo of Jacob. He was her soul mate as far as she was concerned.

As she scrolled through her photos, she noticed a pair of feet standing next to her.

She looked up and saw a young scruffy looking man who had a grin on his face.

"I don't want you to make a fuss, but I need you to come outside with me. Pulling up his jacket to reveal a pistol. We don't want to cause a commotion, do we?" he said as he grabbed Valentina's arm, physically dragging her outside.

She didn't dare resist and so no one noticed her distress.

Valentina walked out in front of her abductor to the carpark, where they were met by another man who got out of a car and approached them.

He opened the car door, gesturing for Valentina to get into the back seat. She looked at the other guy and tried to make a break for it, hoping that Daniel would find her. Or maybe she would make a clean break to get some help.

"Not so fast bitch" said the second man, as he grabbed her by the waist dragging her back to the car.

The first man grabbed her long hair and pulled it back. "Try it again and I'll finish you right here."

Valentina relented and began to get into the car. Just as she sat down, the door was slammed behind her, and she heard voices. She looked up and saw Detective Squires and two other men with guns in the hands, telling the two men to get on the ground.

The first accomplice put his hands behind his back and offered no resistance. The other tried to make a run for it as he was chased and taken down to the ground by one of the officers.

Both men were placed in the back of a waiting police vehicle.

Valentina slid her way to the other side of the back seat as all of this was taking place and opened the door jumping out of the car. She ran back into the pub to find Daniel who had returned to their seats and was now looking around for her.

They both walked out to see the two kidnappers driving off with the local police.

Detective Squires came over and said, "That was a close call, Valentina. We are going to need you to find a safe place until this blows over."

"Until what blows over, do you want to fill me in as to what is happening here?" she said with a concerned look on her face.

The three of them headed back into the pub finding a booth in the corner.

"Before I explain what is happening, please let me make a quick call, so I can involve someone who can fill in some of the blanks."

He came back 30 seconds later, informing them that his informant will be there within the next 20 minutes.

Detective Squires spoke.

"Guys, I sit on a special taskforce that looks into the activities of the bikie gangs in Queensland. We know that the Mongols gang have been heavily involved with Columbian cartel and the Asian import market into Australia.

"We have been working with international police forces tracking down these activities, getting ready to take them down with the Australian Federal Police. Now the reason why you fit into the picture is that the Mongols think you double-crossed them.

"Me?" Valentina protested. I have never had anything to do with bikie gangs, especially in Australia.

"No, but your boyfriend Jacob has."

The blood ran from Valentina's cheeks.

Valentina kind of slumped and looked up as Detective Squires as he was greeting his guest who had just arrived.

"Hi Christiaan, glad you could make it at this time of the night," said the detective.

It was Christiaan from Uluru. The Dutch tourist that Valentina and Mia had drinks with back at the bar.

"Hi Valentina, Christiaan said looking directly into her eyes. Maybe we can now finish that conversation we started."

Valentina grabbed her glass of wine and took a swig, drinking more than half the glass in one go.

"Take a seat Christiaan, I think it is time Valentina heard the whole story."

Jacob

Jacob Spriggs was born to two hard working parents who had met in a faraway outback town, when his father was passing through for work.

Jacob's upbringing wasn't easy, as his father was rarely home. When he was home, he was abusive and drunk.

His father Jim Spriggs was a man of little education. He was built like a 'brick shit-house' and knew more about hitting a woman than controlling his anger when he was full of beer.

Jacob grew up disillusioned and felt isolated from the world. Although he was charismatic, and people liked him for his carefree attitude. Jacob felt great pain through most of his life.

He enjoyed art and music and when he was old enough, he left home to live on one friend's couch to the other. He felt guilty about leaving his mother all alone, but life was becoming unbearable when the old man took to the grog.

His life changed one day when a friend of a friend saw his artwork and offered to show it to some high-profile people in the art world in Los Angeles California, who loved what they saw. They immediately made him an offer that he couldn't refuse to get him to the states and further his talent.

It was an all-expenses paid trip to LA. Including flights, accommodation, and tuition, as long as he could come up with the money for food.

Jacob had never been given an opportunity like this before and jumped at the chance of leaving the shores of Australia for the life in the big city of LA. Gold Coast had its beaches, but LA was different and kind of happening for a young guy like him.

He was able to pick up some "cash" work from contacts he had established shortly after arriving in the US. Picking up a job at a restaurant, who were happy to have a good-looking Australian waiting on their tables. The accent certainly did help with the patrons and Jacob earned good tips.

His main mode of transport was his skateboard that he

had brought from Australia with him, as well as buses and bumming lifts from friends and colleagues.

He also continued his recreational habit of smoking some weed. Nothing too serious, just enough to get mellow.

He never really got homesick, but at times he suffered from depression. The weed helped with that and over time he would take more and more.

One night he was out with friends, having a drink or two at a local bar, when they all agreed it was getting late and some of them had to work the next day. Joking and laughing, they strolled down the street. Jacob made his goodbyes as he lived only a few blocks away and chose to walk back.

He took a detour, deciding to take an alley way to save some time. He travelled down one alley way and then another, making good time with his shortcuts. Making a trip he had done maybe twenty or thirty times before.

Just as he turned the corner, three young guys past him in the opposite direction. Two in their early twenties and other was around seventeen years old.

The youngest one turned around and asked for a cigarette.

"Sorry, said Jacob, I'm all out." He had smoked the last one maybe two hours earlier.

Without word or warning, the same youth punched Jacob in the face, as he fell to the ground, holding his face from the pain that had been inflicted.

"That's ok, I really wanted your money" the teen said.

They searched his jacket and pockets, finding only a few dollars.

As Jacob protested, the tallest of the group pulled out a large knife, slashing Jacob across the leg, cutting into his jeans.

"This will stop you from getting any help, said the young man."

They ran off into the dark with very little prize to brag about.

Jacob was in extreme pain, but fortunately for him, the commotion from his protesting woke an elderly lady, who peered out to see what all the noise was about.

When she felt it was safe enough, she walked across

into the lane and checked on Jacob and then called 911 for an ambulance.

Jacob was rushed to the LA Community hospital. They put him on a gurney and pushed him through the corridors to emergency.

He was in pain and a little disorientated. One minute he is having a nice drink with friends, the next minute he was in agony and feeling violated. He had known about the streets of LA, but never thought it was anything more than good TV. Tough guys like him don't get jumped.

He was wheeled into emergency and left to wait. The bleeding had been controlled by paramedics, but he still needed something for the pain.

"Give me some bloody drugs" he yelled out.

Some nurses came to his aid after all his commotion, calming him down and telling him that the doctor in charge that night would be arriving shortly. She was attending to a motorcycle accident victim, and he was next on her rounds. He was safe and they were keeping an eye on him.

The doctor finally arrived picking a chart that they had prepared earlier by the nursing staff.

She was an attractive woman in her thirties with long dark hair and slender figure.

"Right Mr Spriggs, I believe you were in a fight, and you have been cut on the leg. My name is Dr Russo, and I will be assisting you today."

She asked the nurse to cut the bottom of his jeans off, so she could have full access to the wound.

"Hey, they are my best jeans. Can you at least save them?" Jacob protested loudly.

"Sorry Mr Spriggs, the doctor replied. Your jeans are the last of my worries here."

As his jeans were cut away, Jacob looked down at his leg. It wasn't pretty. The bleeding had been contained, but he was informed that he would need stitches.

"Do I really need stitches," he protested? "I'm a leg model," Jacob advised the doctor "and I'll never work again". He laughed through the pain as the doctor touched the area around the wound, inspecting it.

Dr Russo smiled, knowing she had a prankster on her hands.

"Now let me attend to this as we prepare you for amputation."

Jacob looked at her in disbelief, sitting up as she smiled at him and winked.

"You know doctor, you are pretty hot. I guess this is where the best-looking women must hang out in LA. Had I known earlier, I would have cut my own leg."

Dr Russo asked him to remain still, ignoring his comment.

"Where is your accent come from Mr Spriggs?" Asked Dr Russo.

"Ever heard of a country called Australia?" he said in the most Aussie accent he could put on for her.

"Yes Mr Spriggs, I think I have heard of that country. Land down under, right?"

Dr Russo finished her stitching and advised Jacob that he should just rest for a few minutes, but he should be right to go.

"Best first date I've had in a while" Jacob chuckled.

"I've had better" the doctor replied with a smirk.

"You don't know what better looks like until you have had an Aussie." Jacob replied.

Dr Russo laughed out loud. "Ok Mr Aussie, off my table, there are a few more Americans that need my assistance tonight."

Jacob was wheeled out to the taxicab by one of the staff. He gingerly hopped into the back of a cab making his way home.

A few weeks later, Jacob was invited to a boutique art exhibition held by one of his friends in Beverley Hills. He dressed appropriately and arrived to be welcomed by champagne and canapes. His friend, who was putting on the show greeted him and said let's catch up next week for coffee and we can discuss how successful the night has gone.

Jacob began to wander around, critiquing in his mind, what he liked or disliked. Or would have done differently. Overall, it was a great exhibition, and many well-dressed people were invited for the opening. His friend had done well.

Taking another red wine that was now on offer from the waiter, he turned to look at a painting that resembled a large male appendage. He took another sip as he analysed what it may *be*. Possibly it was just an ink blot, like those psychiatrists use.

"Who would have thought that they would let Australians into art galleries?" came a voice from behind him.

He turned and to his delight saw the nice doctor that had stitched him up some weeks earlier.

He held out his hand to shake, saying, "Ah Dr Ruskin I presume."

"Russo actually, but you can call me Valentina for tonight."

"Pretty name," he replied. "My name is Jacob, and you can call me Jacob," he grinned. "May I get you a drink? Your glass looks like it is running a little low."

The two spent most of the night chatting and interpreting the art on the walls.

Valentina and Jacob were inseparable after that night. When Valentina was not working at the hospital, they would go to the Comedy Store on Sunset Boulevard in Hollywood or catch up with either of their friends for drinks or dinner.

Valentina's friends and family were enamoured with Jacob. He had them eating out of the palm of his hand, with his mixture of charm and harmless bullshit.

They all loved the accent. The boy from Oz was settling in.

Even though Valentina and Jacob seemed to come from different sides of the track.

They were really from the same side.

They experienced a relationship neither one of them had experienced in the past. One of true honesty.

For Valentina, Jacob was her soul mate. He understood her. He was so passionate in bed, unlike any other man she had been with, that it "rocked her world".

He understood her at another level. Deep down, they both had scars from childhood, both relating to their father's treatment and alcoholic addictions.

His father was an abusive alcoholic, and hers was just an alcoholic who drank himself to death.

And of course, that was their common denominator.

The drink.

When Valentina wasn't working, she could often drink to excess. She thought nothing of it. For Jacob, it was a way of life for him. He knew no other path.

They were both so in love, that neither saw the destructive behaviour they both had.

Life continued as per normal, until one day Jacob received a call from his mother back home in Australia, asking that he come to visit as she intended leaving his father. She couldn't take it anymore and was going to move closer to family elsewhere.

Jacob kissed Valentina goodbye at the airport, and they cried at the temporary separation.

They knew it was only for a few weeks, as he would help his mother pack and he would also catch up with old friends. It had been some time since he had been back to the Gold Coast in Queensland.

Jacob's arrival was not met with any fanfare. No one picked him up at the airport, he grabbed an Uber and headed home.

His father was as abusive if not more so than ever, now that his mother was getting ready to pack up and leave him. He never knew how much control his father held over him until now and he fell back into needing to drink even more, whilst also being high from weed.

Jacob saw his mother off at the airport and headed back home in the old rust bucket of a car he used when he was younger. She was now going to start a new life without her abusive husband.

He kissed her goodbye and she assured him that she would be fine. She told him that once she had settled in, she would advise him of her new address, and he could then visit one day.

Jacob decided to ring one of his friends, who went by the name of Wongy. His name was Kevin Wong. Half Australian and half Chinese on his father's side. Jacob and Kevin had been friends since high school. The friendship started when Jacob tried to copy Kevin's answers during a test one day at end of term exams.

They both liked to get high, even in their school days. It was not unusual for the two of them to do detention after school for getting caught, but they were best buddies and best buddies do everything together. Even detention. Jacob's dad didn't care. Kevin's would go ballistic. They were mates for life as far as they were concerned.

Wongy was always the entrepreneurial type, and it was nothing for him to try something new to make money. For the most part, he failed at all his endeavours, but one.

Sometime after Jacob had left home. Wongy fell into selling small amounts of drugs on the street. He was smart guy, but gullible and saw it as easy money. It started with him being the consumer and then moving to the bigger stuff, selling to his friends.

Wongy was making good money and now drove around in a flashy white E-Class Sedan Mercedes Benz. He was the envy of all that he went to school with. Of course, none of them really knew what he did for a living, except for those that were his customers.

When Jacob called him a few days after arriving, they agreed to meet at his supplier's place of residence.

Wongy gave him the address and Jacob drove up to what looked like a warehouse. They met at the gates of the clubhouse of the Mongols bikie club and were greeted and let in accordingly, as they recognised Wongy.

It looked like a normal warehouse to Jacob and reasonably non-threatening as the two stepped inside. Wongy introduced Jacob to the members who were there, including the Sergeant at Arms, Seamus Preece.

Seamus was a short but stocky man. His arms covered in tattoos with a tooth missing at the side of his mouth when he smiled. A souvenir from a fight with another member, many years earlier. He wore the patched leather jacket of the Mongols proudly as the men shook hands.

Jacob's eyes panned the clubhouse. It had a pool table and bar. Off to the side was a garage where the members parked their bikes and cars.

Out the back were other rooms, that Jacob assumed were some forms of accommodation and kitchen area.

The men sat down at a table and Jacob was offered a beer.

"What type of beer do you like, Seamus called out peering into the fridge. We have Vic Bitter, XXXX and Boags."

Jacob settled on the Boags.

The men sat and chatted as Seamus and Wongy each puffed on a cigarette, offering Jacob one, who accepted gladly.

"Wongy tells me you are a good guy, Jacob. Went to school together, I hear?" Seamus started.

Jacob nodded. "Yeah, we have known each other since high school."

"He also tells me that you live in the states, in Los Angeles. You know the Mongols, started in Southern California."

"I did not know that" Jacob replied.

"He also informs that me you are a trustworthy guy and thinks you may be interested in potentially doing some work with us. What do you say to that?"

"What did you have in mind? Jacob enquired, not really wanting to mess with the Mongols.

Seamus looked at Wongy and then back to Jacob.

"We need someone to go for an all-expense holiday to Bangkok Thailand and move some goods for us. Easy work. We do it all the time."

Jacob looked at Wongy and shrugged his shoulders.

"Not really my thing" Jacob advised.

Seamus put his chin in his right hand, looking down at the floor.

"You see Jacob, Wongy owes us some favours and he was hoping that you could help him repay them."

Wongy looked at Jacob and then turned away.

"See Jacob," he continued, "Wongy kind of stuffed up, and well we need to put it right. There is a job we need done in Thailand and with Wongy's, let's say criminal record, he can't get over there without bringing attention to himself."

Seamus took another puff from his cigarette.

"Well, we all thought that you would be a good bloke and help one of your mates out."

"Wongy may be a dickhead at times, but he has never brought to us anyone we can't trust and plus we checked you out before we allowed you in the front door." Seamus said placing his hand on Wongy's shoulder.

Jacob looked at Wongy. Obviously, his good friend and mate had planned this, knowing that Jacob was back in town and would contact him before his departure.

"So, what if I don't choose to do anything? After all I am only back for family reasons."

"Please, begged Wongy. I really need this favour. I was always there for you when we were kids."

It was true Wongy was always there for him. The nights he would cop a hiding from the old man and sneak out, climbing out his window and up Wongy's drainpipe to his bedroom. They would chat until sunrise smoking dope and drinking some alcohol that one of them had stolen from their parents. They never got caught.

Well not often.

Wongy was a good friend but working for bikies never seemed like a good idea in any one's book.

Of course, Jacob relented against his better judgement. He knew that Wongy's life may be in jeopardy and the Mongols were not a group of people worth messing with. It could have also been the fact that that his mind was a little clouded by the dope he had smoked an hour earlier.

Jacob sat back and for a fleeting moment got a picture of Valentina in his mind. What would she say? Should he even mention it?

The deal was agreed to. Jacob would go to Bangkok, pick up some parcels that he would bring back to Australia. Plane tickets and accommodation was organised and paid for. It was settled and Jacob's fate was written.

Jacob made his usual call to Valentina that night with some trepidation.

"Hey babe" were Jacob's first words, as Valentina took their regular Zoom call.

Valentina smiled as she looked forward to these meetings where she could not only hear him, but also see his face.

"I'm well honey, busy as usual," she replied, "I am looking forward to you coming home, so I can kiss you and the rest."

"Well... about that," Jacob replied. "Some business has come up and I need to head out to Thailand."

"Thailand?" Valentina querying his statement.

"Yep, one of my old friends needs a favour and I need to go on his behalf. Maybe you could come with me? Make it a work/vacation?"

"You know that is hard with my job honey. I would love to go, but just not a feasible proposition at this moment" Valentina replied.

Jacob's head dropped a little as he lost eye contact with Val.

"Babe" he protested.

"Ok" he replied, "well I am leaving in the next 24 hours, so I'll talk to you when I get there. Send me an email of your work hours and I'll send you a text to chat."

They kissed each other goodbye, teasing the other as they did. Valentina never thought that this was the last time she would see Jacob alive.

Christiaan now took a seat near Daniel as he scooted over into the booth, looking at Valentina, who was not sure where to place her eyes.

Detective Squires spoke first.

"So, before we begin, I want you to give Christiaan a chance to tell his story. I know he tried in the past and that didn't go down too well, but what he has to say will shed some light on a few things."

"She will be fine detective" Daniel said as he grabbed Valentina's hand.

Christiaan, cleared his throat, pouring himself some water from a jug on the table.

He began.

"As I was saying back at Uluru, I was there when Jacob died.

"As I had mentioned previously, he was our recruiter. He hired us to transport drugs over the border out of Thailand. It was what we thought was easy money and Jacob said we would be looked after.

"Jacob hired us on the Thursday, and we were told to be ready by the following Monday to pick up our parcels for our departure from Thailand.

"We had a couple of meetings. Drinking sessions as you may call them, to discuss how things were to work. How we would get through airports undetected and what we were to say to authorities if we happen to be pulled up.

"One afternoon Robert Bastion, the English guy was out buying some cigarettes and supplies, and Jacob asked me to meet him in his hotel room.

"He was kind of serious at the time and I wondered what was wrong. He explained to me that he was only doing this "mule business" because he had owed a favour to a friend, but he was regretting his decision. He wasn't sure why he agreed to do this in the first place.

"I asked him why he was telling me all of this.

"He said that he had a girlfriend back in the States, and he knew that by doing this he would be letting her down. As I was the youngest of the three "Mules", I think Jacob took pity on me. Maybe he saw a bit of himself in me. I don't know why, but I am eternally grateful."

Valentina grabbed Daniel's hand a little tighter now.

Christiaan continued.

"He told me that he was against this importation of drugs, which were headed back to Australia. It would create drugs like ICE that would kill kids. He said and he had seen enough pain in his life.

"He really did have a good heart. I didn't see that when I first met him. I just thought he was another heartless drug dealer.

"We spoke for a while and he then he confided in me that he couldn't go ahead with it and help these people. Even if it meant his friend who was back in Australia would get into trouble. His friend had dug this hole and it was really his own mess to clean up.

"He was concerned that he was letting Valentina down. He told me he had a plan to dispose of the merchandise. It had been delivered a couple of days earlier and he had hidden it, so that no one would find it.

"His plan was that he would substitute it with something of a similar substance and give it to Robert, the English guy that he also had hired. He was telling me all of this, because he knew it was risky and that I had a lot of life to go. He wanted me to get out before it was too late. He should never have hired me in the first place, he said.

"The bikies or cartel, whoever he was working with only knew of Jacob and the English guy. According to Jacob, the English guy Robert was a prized asshole, and a drug addict and if he died from him betraying them, then it was probably a fitting end, as he was going to kill himself of a drug overdose anyway.

"He told me that he really loved his girlfriend in the states. He also said he knew he didn't deserve her. She was smart and beautiful, and he truly loved her more than his own life.

"He said he was such a damaged individual, that he had no idea why she would love him back."

Valentina tried to hold back the tears.

If only he had known that she had felt damaged as well.

"All he told me was that you had the key and that I was to find you and tell you just that.

He said to me tell her "No one, but you are the key."

The three men looked at Valentina, hoping she would

shed some light on the message.

Christiaan continued.

"Jacob tells me all of this and then asks me to promise him, if anything happens to him, that I would find Valentina. He gives me your details and then says, "do me a favour mate and go get me a dozen Singha" which is the local beer in Thailand.

"I leave him and walk down the road. It took me around 40 minutes before I got back, buying something to eat whilst I was there. Carrying the beer on my shoulder.

"The accommodation Jacob was staying at had two entrances to his kitchenette room. One was at the back and there was also the one that leads to the hotel front entrance. The back was kind of a hidden entrance. I doubt if most people even knew it was there. I usually came through the back as Jacob always felt it was best that both Robert and I were never to be seen and to use the rear entrance for our own protection.

"As I was approaching, I heard two voices, it was Jacob and Robert arguing about something. I'm not sure exactly about what, but I guessed that Jacob had told Robert that the job wasn't going ahead or something like that.

"Anyway, I was about to open the sliding door to come inside when there was a knock at the front door. I waited outside listening and watching.

"Robert opened the door and was pushed aside by a large burley man with tattoos on both his arms. There was a second man who walked in after him and told Jacob and Robert to sit on the beds.

"I chose to keep out of sight, whilst I heard Jacob do most of the talking.

"It was obvious Jacob knew exactly who they were. I gather it was his bikie contacts from Australia. The accents sounded Australian.

"They seemed quite agitated and were yelling at Jacob and Robert, saying they didn't like to be double-crossed. Both men sitting on the bed denied ever trying to double cross them. Jacob tried to get up off the bed to speak, but they just pushed him back in his place."

"The second bikie spoke.

"You don't think we trust piss-ants like you with our goods without keeping an eye on what you are up to.

"You fuck. I ought to put a bullet in your head right now. But first, tell me where my merchandise is?" he yelled.

"Robert protested loudly, offended by the statement.

"He got up to berate the second man and quicker than the eye could see, a knife was produced and slit across Robert's neck. It was a pure reflex from the intruder. Robert began to gurgle as the blood filled his throat and he fell back on the bed grasping his neck, covered in his own blood as it dripped down. Choking on the liquid seeping back into his passageway.

"Jacob remained quiet as Robert was dying. Maybe he was a little stunned or scared.

"Now, we have had this place bugged since you have been here and we know you intend hiding our goods, you piece of shit" said the first man to Jacob.

"I never heard the guy's name," said Christiaan, "but you would never miss him. He was bald with a beard. He had a tattoo of a tear under his eye and when he turned around, I saw that he had a tattoo on the back of his neck, saying "Respect Few, Fear None'.

"At the time I didn't know what that meant, but later on I found out it was the motto of the Mongols bikie gang.

"This guy walks right up to Jacob, pulls him up off the bed with two hands and pushes his face against his, screaming at him. 'What have you done with our goods?'

"Jacob leant back pulling away from the man, stating that his goods were safe and what was his problem."

"My problem is." He barked back at Jacob. "Is that your room is being fucking bugged, and we know that you have no intention of transporting our property. You have stolen it and sent the key to your girlfriend."

"Save us all the time now and tell us where it is before I shit down your neck."

"Jacob pulled back from the bikie's face. 'I don't know what you are talking about, I could hear Jacob saying. Give me a day and I'll get it to you if you are worried,' he said 'I have it, just not here of course. I wouldn't keep it on me, would I? I don't need to be caught in a police raid.'

"The British guy Robert had stopped gurgling and breathing some time ago.

"Jacob tried to make a run for it, heading towards the back entrance where I was hiding. Before he took two steps, a bullet was put through the back of his skull. He dropped to the floor, and I just knew he was dead. I couldn't bear to look at him in case they caught me, but I knew he was dead.

"The two men made a phone call to the local police, which I thought was strange. Until a couple of uniformed men arrived and took the bodies away.

"The room was searched for any signs of the drugs, but without success. The men made another phone call in which I heard them say 'get me the girl's information.'

"All parties left, and I then lay there paralysed. I cried for Jacob," Christiaan said to Valentina, looking directly at her. "I cried for both of them."

"I was saved by twelve bottles of beer that I had gone out to get for Jacob. My friend Jacob.

"I guess that is all I can really tell you Valentina" Christiaan said now relieved he had finally got most of his story out.

"I was told that he died from an overdose" Valentina said through her tears.

"They said it was heroin, but I knew it couldn't be. Jacob would never touch that stuff, no matter how depressed he may have been."

"At first, I was extremely frightened and concerned that I would be next, said Christiaan. I hid out for a week, worried that they would find me, but they never looked. Or maybe they just didn't know I existed, which was more likely the case.

"I gathered the courage to do something about it. I knew that they would go after you Valentina. Even though I didn't know you." He said looking at Val. "I knew that I owed Jacob. If it weren't for him, I would also be dead."

"I contacted the Australian consulate, who at first weren't sure what to do with the information. They wanted to report it to the local authorities, which I begged them not to do or they would put my life in jeopardy. Luckily, I found someone there who listened and said that she would get in touch with authorities back in Australia. She said it sounded like something that they were enquiring about in the last month and my information may be of interest.

"I eventually got to speak to the Australian Federal Police, and they wanted more information. Not so much about Jacob's death, but more about the drug transportation and the relative connections.

"As I wasn't the main contact with the gang, they weren't so sure that anything I had to say was of interest, until I told them that it was a good chance that they would go after Valentina and that you had been sent the key to the drugs.

"At that point they brought in the US Drug Enforcement agency and the two groups decided that they would begin surveillance, but they wanted me to also be involved, as they couldn't afford the manpower at that stage.

"Highly unusual I know, but I'm not sure they saw it as being a high priority. They said that they would fly me to the states for an interview first to discuss if there was something worth pursuing.

"I met officers in the states and then we agreed that I could keep an eye on Valentina. I already knew your whereabouts, as Jacob had given me your details and the officers confirmed that was the case once they checked out my story.

"From that point I stayed in Los Angeles, and I guess kept an eye on you. I rented an apartment in the same building. I'm surprised you never noticed me as I was never far away.

"I remember when I first saw you," Christiaan continued. "I thought Jacob certainly has great taste in women, why in the world would he need to be a drug mule."

"It didn't take long before the gang found you and began to follow your every move. At first, they were discreet, but then over time it became more apparent that they had stepped up their surveillance around the clock.

"Then one evening, they knocked on your door and pretended that they were looking for a friend in the building. I couldn't hear them, but they had tried your neighbour's door first. Maybe in case anyone ever looked at the video footage, it would look like they were lost."

"How did they get into the building?" Valentina asked.

"That is a security building."

"Security or not, nothing stops someone following someone else into the building once they have opened the front doors.

"I hid behind a pillar watching them as they spoke to you and then pushed their way into the apartment. You made no commotion, so I suspect they pulled a weapon on you.

"They must have been there maybe an hour or so. I saw them leave and I rushed over to your apartment to see if I could hear anything. I was a little afraid to come in immediately as I wasn't sure if they were drug cartel or someone that you knew. So, I waited for around 10 minutes. I saw that the door was slightly ajar, and I peered inside and saw you on the ground. You were lying on there with tablets surrounding you. It was obvious you had overdosed.

"Whatever they had said to you, must have been so upsetting that you decided to end your life off the back of that conversation. The place was a mess, so I guess they searched the apartment. Obviously, they didn't find what they were looking for.

"I rang 911 and called for a paramedic, who took no time to arrive. I opened the door for them, and they began working on you straight away after asking me a couple of questions. I said I just happened to see the door wide open and noticed someone passed out on the floor. I then walked away as I didn't want to have to answer too many questions."

"I don't recall what they said or why I took so many pills? I don't even remember their faces. I guess they must have pushed me over the edge, and I saw no alternative." Valentina blurted out.

"I remember seeing you at my side when the paramedics were working on me," she said to Christiaan. "I just couldn't quite work out what you looked like. I guess I was too drugged out at the time."

"That isn't possible," said Christiaan, "I met them at the door, answered some questions and left. After initially finding you, I was never at your side again. I wanted to make myself scarce.

"You must have imagined it."

"Maybe you are right," said Valentina.

Detective Squires brought the conversation back to the topic of the key that seemed imperative to this case and the hiding place of the drugs.

"So maybe you can fill us in as to where the drugs may have been hidden. I gather you also have some type of key that can open a box or a vault? Our counterparts in Thailand would be very interested, as are the Australian Federal Police and the Drug Enforcement agency in the US" said Detective Squires.

Valentina looked at the three men. "None of this makes any sense to me. I am not holding a key of any type. Jacob even begged me to come to Thailand. Why would he do that if he knew there was danger?"

"Maybe he was scared and didn't want to do this alone or possibly he just didn't think it was too big a deal. Thinking he could combine it with a nice fully paid holiday." Detective Squires suggested.

"Again, can you tell us where the key is Valentina, it is important to this case?" the detective continued.

Valentina had no idea and told him that if she did, he would be the first to know.

"Well tonight you are safe, but they will send more in their place, once they don't hear from these two that were sent to track you down. We will need to find you a hiding place for your own safety."

"Yes, we were followed by them all the way up the highway, I'm surprised they didn't run us off the road." Daniel said.

"That was us," replied the detective. "We have had Valentina under observation since she has been in the country and Christiaan has been our eyes from LA to Australia. Unfortunately, he gave you a bit of a scare, dropping part of Jacob's story on you without notice."

"I need another drink," said Valentina.

"Detective," Daniel said. "I think I can protect her better than you. They know that you will have her under protection, so they will be watching you and your men. Maybe it's better that Valentina and I disappear."

"What are you thinking?" Said Detective Squires.

Daniel looked at Valentina.

"I think it's time we went Walkabout.

"Let's grab you a few things from your hotel. Maybe pick up your backpack, some fresh clothes, suntan lotion and any snacks you can find. You can say goodbye to Mia without telling her anything more than we were off on a retreat for a while."

Valentina agreed.

Walkabout

Steve picked up both Daniel and Valentina at 9am from Daniel's house and drove them to a designated spot a few hours out of Alice Springs. They hid Daniel's truck at a friend's place, which was to be dropped back off after a certain date. Everything was now in place for them to disappear into the outback.

"Meet us in 40 days from now," Daniel told Steve. "That should be around this date," as he looked up his diary in his phone to find the exact day that they would return. "We will meet you at 2pm sharp. I have a watch, so we will know exactly the time and date. Does that work for you?"

"Yes mate," Steve replied, "I'll keep in touch with the detective and bring you up to scratch when I see you next. Good luck buddy, look after her" he yelled out at as he hopped back into his truck. He stuck his head out of the window and spoke to Valentina.

"This guy knows this land like the back of his hand. Hate to say, he knows it better than I do. You will be safer out here for now, until things settle down."

Valentina waved him goodbye with some trepidation, wondering what had she got herself into?

The two began to trek out into what just seemed like barren land. Daniel seemed to know where he was going and clearly showed no concern as they began their journey.

Daniel's prowess in the bush was evident as he knew how to find water and food. He explained that the spirits created the lagoons and water holes for the Indigenous people to use. The land and the people were one.

He warned Valentina about the snakes and not to bother them. Some were venomous, but none of them want to interact with humans.

"So don't poke the bear. Or snake in this case" he advised with a smirk.

"If you remember this is their home, Daniel informed her, then you will remember that it is about respect. Just keep your eyes open to not to accidently step on one. Snakes don't usually attack humans unless, they feel cornered or threatened. Otherwise, you will be safe.

"Australia may be a beautiful place, but there were certainly parts that were dangerous. Unless of course you are in sync with the land and show the respect that the Indigenous people had for thousands of years."

The first day was tiring as they tracked, hunted, and prepared for nightfall.

Daniel was always in control. He knew the land. Of course, he was trained by the Indigenous people, even though he was not one himself.

They ate nuts, fruits and roots that they had collected. For dinner Daniel had killed a kangaroo, which he stunned with a boomerang, that he had packed with him. Valentina struggled at first to eat this beautiful animal, but after a day of walking and searching for food, she was happy to eat just about anything. Surprisingly it was delicious, Valentina thought to herself, it is just like regular meat, but according to Daniel much healthier.

"Maybe tomorrow we might eat some snake" Daniel laughed.

Valentina wasn't sure if he was being serious or just pulling her leg.

"You will learn, Val, that everything is sacred and so when you kill an animal for food, you don't waste it. In the western world, we have a meal and throw out the bones and everything that we haven't eaten. Indigenous people would make tools etc from these bones. If our world acted this same way, then we would not be a planet of waste. We would respect what we have killed and understood that it is there for our use as long as we honour it."

Val sat and contemplated his comments. As they both sat and watched the very bright stars. As if they were just above their heads. Valentina had seen stars before, but these were exceptionally bright. Like they were putting a show on for them.

Whilst looking at the stars, Daniel began to speak.

"Now is the time to do the real work that you will require in your life. To find out the real reason why Australia became part of your path. I have given you some of basics, but now is the time to begin the transformation. Tonight, let's give you the foundation for this to take place.

"It is time to return to the DREAM TIME, and this is done by following a process to achieve that.

"If every being is here to learn their true spiritual nature, then they need to learn and unlearn what has been presented and imprinted on them over time. Over potentially many generations. Remember that the Dreaming has no beginning, past, present, or future. It all one continuum.

The process funnily enough, that I use, is called DREAM.

It stands for:

(D) Delve
(R) Recognise
(E) Extract
(A) Amplify
(M) Motivate

"I'll explain some of those as we work through it, but no earlier.

"The first few steps are important in moving forward with anything in your life. The first few are why people's intent fail. Why they feel that all they do is try but are hampered by something which appears out of their control.

"It's not out of their control. It is out of their awareness and so they keep maintaining patterns, that does not serve them well. Sometimes destructive patterns. Patterns that interfere with their ability to arise above the noise."

Valentina lay back on her backpack, which she was using as a pillow. She was really wanted to know how to move on from what she felt was holding her back.

"You will find, Val, that I will repeat some of my messages that I have gone over before. This will reinforce the messaging, as it becomes important that what you learn helps rewrite the subconscious."

Valentina was curious, "So this a technique of the indigenous people of Australia?"

"No" Daniel replied, "this is a technique used by someone who has seen the beyond.

"Shall we start?" he asked

"Fire away" Valentina replied. I am open to anything."
Daniel continued.

"I may have mentioned before that, we are a product
of many things, but we are a product of our childhood
and the influences of that period. Be it a parent or
whoever was our greatest influence at the time during our
formative years.

"Let me ask you a question Val to get us started.

"Is there anything about your mother that you really
dislike or maybe even hate? It maybe something she does,
or even something she says?"

Valentina thought for a moment.

"Yes, I really hate that she works herself into the
ground. Ever since I was a kid, she was a workaholic.
Never knew when to stop. I guess she experienced struggle
and hardship, which is why she pushed me."

"And how are you any different?" Daniel enquired.

Valentina thought hard. No one had ever asked her
that question before.

"I guess I'm not, if I am being honest. I do the same,
which is why I am successful at work."

Daniel delved a little deeper.

"Who is your mother emulating? Where did she get
this habit from?"

Without thinking, Valentina blurted out, "My
grandfather. He was the same. Apparently, he worked so
hard back in his village, back in Italy, that he died at the
age of 42 from a heart attack. His nick name was "testa di
maiale". It means I believe, "pig-headed".

"He would get told to slow down, but no, he would do
just keep working and working, until it killed him.
Neglecting his family along the way."

"You have been trained to run yourself into the ground
and remove balance from your life, haven't you Val?"
Daniel asked.

"Well, no," Valentina protested. "I had a balanced life
when I was with Jacob. It was loving and we did a lot of
things together without me having to work as long hours."

"What about your drinking to excess? Where did you
learn that?" Daniel fired back.

"See balance is an important part of development and
transformation, but if you have learned excess in your

life, then you need to determine the source of why you act this out repeatedly. It really is a mask for an in-balance and pain from your past.

"Excess in your work to the point that you lose the greater sense of things in life, becomes a form of drug. In your case, you not only overworked, but you chose another mask. One we call alcohol. You used those excesses to hide from pain in your life."

Valentina looked at the stars once more.

"You know, Daniel, I never thought that I was doing anything to excess, but you are right. I drink because my father drank, and his father drank. Maybe I am like him, it allows me to forget."

"You may be right, but this pattern you are exhibiting, has been impressed upon you over time.

"See as children for the most, we want to be just like our parents. Imitating what they do. As we mature, we think we are running our own ship and thinking for ourselves, but we are running programs that have been imprinted on us from childhood. Some good. Some bad. This then becomes our "Autopilot."

"Now these habits didn't start with our parents. It started way back as we discussed before. Generations ago. Your ancestors had some of these habits, which have been passed down and blended when a member of your family married.

"The passing of these habits, I call "Generational Baggage".

"It's almost like an unseen force, travelling through many lifetimes, until you correct them. Unfortunately, they usually are unchecked for most of our lives, and they continue to control us from the subconscious level to our Soul Level.

"This is partly why we return each time to learn from them and then help future generations to move on until we have changed the vibrational energy.

"Now identifying your habits. Your patterns as it may be, is an important part of your transformation. Once you have corrected them, then you are able to become flow.

Flow meaning, that you have brought your conscious mind, subconscious mind, and unconscious mind into alignment. A state of Focus.

"Once you have alignment, many things will change for you.

"Let me try to give you an example.

"Have you ever had to decide on something, but you are at a crossroads and not sure which option to go with? Sometimes you may even refer to it as being in two minds.

"The conscious mind is trying to decide, but the subconscious, that hold the habits that you have learned over several lifetimes, has different ideas.

"This is a dilemma as we find ourselves lacking this state of true focus. That is why we first need to delve into what those habits are. Where they may have been formed and then break that nexus, by bringing it to the forefront for us to face maybe for the first time in our lives. When and if you break that, then, and only then, will you begin your transformation.

"See Valentina humans bury emotion. Very deeply sometimes. So much so, that it becomes part of our being. Now some emotions are healthy and others, well, downright dangerous."

Valentina lay there absorbing everything Daniel was saying and thinking about how her life had formed. The habits that she may be displaying without really noticing that were potentially hampering her own progression.

"Some of us never let it go." Daniel continued. "We are traumatised, by events, even though we bury it deep in our subconscious. We think we are fine, but the Soul knows better. You have actions that replicate those of the ostrich. Putting your head in the sand and ignoring it. Burying it until it is no longer is within your consciousness. Instead, it has been buried deeper into our subconscious.

"Some events we don't think as traumatic. We think they are just events in our lives, and you move on. It becomes engrained in your cells. How you react to an event, determines if that event owns you or not.

"Since you are a medical professional, why don't we discuss how this affects your health."

"You mean the mind body connection?" Valentina said.

"Yes exactly. We generally do not pay much attention to how much we are connected through our minds.

"To move that little finger on your hand starts with a thought, right?"

Valentina agreed

"Everything we do starts with a thought, even when we are not conscious of that thought.

"Following that train of thinking, what if the thought is negative? A memory of pain, which affects our thinking.

"These negative thoughts, just like positive ones, can move in a couple of directions. They are either expressed in the creation or movement of something, or they are retained within our subconscious to fester. In the very cells of our being.

"As a doctor in a medical emergency ward, you see the outcome of body trauma and so you can stitch it up, operate on it or remove it. How about trauma that is buried within the mind? How do you operate on that?"

"That is what psychologists and psychiatrists are for" Valentina added.

"Yes true, but many of our traumas are never tackled by an external person. The reason being is, we don't know that we have a trauma. We can't see it or touch it or have the tools to identify and tackle it. In many cases it happened so long ago that we were too young to identify it. It just became part of us. Getting greater as time goes on, eventually affecting our human bodies. Becoming larger as we pile on other traumas.

"For many people, it will eventually manifest in the body somehow, or we just cover these traumas with other things. Such as drugs, alcohol, and self-harm to take away or mask the memories and the feelings. Pain has many faces.

"As we established earlier, a thought can move part of your body. And that was a positive thought.

"Imagine a negative thought that doesn't leave you after you have had it. It becomes part of you and stays there for literally years.

"This Valentina is unhealthy.

"If I am correct, the Indigenous Hawaiians talked about this effect on the body. They said if a person buried these negative emotions deep down, it was like putting all of it into a little black bag. Then one day it would have to release itself, as the bag would be too full to contain. With its own devasting effects.

"We call this Dis-Ease.

"The mind is not at ease and as we established that every thought somehow affects the body.

"Therefore, we have issues such as cancer."

Valentina interjected, "Do you really think that is what causes cancer? Not even the scientists know the answer to that one."

"You know Valentina I am fascinated that literally *billions* of dollars have been donated towards cancer research and I'm not convinced we are really any closer after all these years of really curing it.

"Not until the medical profession identify its source, which seems to elude them, that we will cure it once and for all."

"They are closer" Valentina insisted.

"Well maybe it is my sceptical side, but if we can send people to the moon, then after all the money and years we have spent on cancer research, we should have solved this riddle by now. Don't you think?

"Of course, there is no money in curing cancer."

Valentina stood up. "What do you mean by that?"

"Think about it Valentina, more money and jobs come about from not curing cancer than curing it.

"For anyone to start their journey towards bringing their 3-Minds into alignment, they need to understand the power it carries."

Valentina wasn't sure to be offended or to maybe be open to the fact that she may have been blind. Afterall what tends to happen in society is that one falsehood can be told and sold to another, until it becomes truth.

She was told that Jacob had died from an overdose of heroin and initially she believed it. Why wouldn't she? She was told by authorities, who were told by other authorities their truth that they wanted us to believe. Yet all of it was perpetuated on a lie.

Maybe the whole world worked this way.

Science vs God

"Whilst we are on the topic of science, and it influences over our development," said Daniel. "Let us talk about Science and God and how they do or don't intertwine."

Daniel turned on his side to now face Valentina. He could just make out her features in the light from the campfire.

"Many people on earth think that we somehow evolved from an organism and by some miracle we somehow have grown from an ape species to now be a human species.

"Unfortunately, many people think this is called science. By providing very little evidence other than apes look similar to us and suddenly we teach that in schools. It is already a failed science, but we persist with it, because believing that there may be something greater than us that could possibly have created all of this, is too far-fetched. In addition to that, science can't prove it.

"The truth is that a greater power created what we see on this earth. Can I prove it like science? No, but science is not necessarily great at proving their theory either. I don't pretend to be a scientist. I am about belief and faith, which for many is not enough, I understand. In time science will just prove what we have been saying for centuries. Of course, by the time they catch up, I think there will be a great reveal from behind the curtain."

"How is it a failed science?" asked Valentina, interrupting Daniel's train of thought.

"Okay, well it is known as the Theory of Evolution. We have a few of these unproved theories around the world that we give a lot of credence to.

"The Theory of Evolution was a theory by Charles Darwin. He thought that what he was witnessing what was one species becoming a completely different species. That is the theory that he proposed.

"What he witnessed were birds that were evolving into another type of bird. He was not witnessing a bird now becoming a dog. His theory is that one species becomes something else. A completely different species. Like an ape now becoming a human. Ever since his theory was written, there has not been one species of animal become a completely different species of animal. There are birds that have evolved into a different type of bird, but they do not jump to a completely different type of animal or even a man. Yet we do see so called discoveries, which do not prove this theory. His theory has never been proven and never will.

As I said it is a failed science. One that is perpetuated through some school systems as being fact.

"Did you know that the "science community" were conned back in 1912 and believed wholeheartedly for some time that evolution was a real concept?"

"Really?" Valentina said, now turning on her side to face Daniel.

"In 1912 there was a guy by the name Charles Dawson. Many scientific articles were written about Mr Dawson's find, that was called the "Piltdown Man'. It was claimed proof of the connection of the evolution from apes.

"He even produced a skull that was part man and part ape. Amazing right?

"Amazing if you don't check the lies put before you. What Dawson was doing quite skilfully was putting together a human skull with an ape's jaw and it looked very convincing. Unfortunately, not very scientific. He had them fooled for a very long time. Decades I believe.

"Eventually he died at a young age, and they found him in his basement with the tools he used to fool the scientific community. It is believed he died from potentially the fumes that must have built up in his basement that he used to glue these fake structures. His wife died of the same fate shortly afterwards. Apparently, it was quite a convincing hoax. Perpetuated by the scientific community.

"Now the reason I make this point is that humans need to move away from the notion that science has all the answers, when in many cases there is no science to the science.

"This is not to say we do not see some great gains for humanity through science. The lesson here is to understand motive before you accept that this is a solution. You need to realise that the "scientist" may have a lot to gain and will do anything to obtain that gain.

They are human after all.

"I'm sure the average scientist is like the average worker. Just trying to earn a living and do a good job. It is those above, who may have ulterior motives.

"I believe that everything science says about spirituality will one day blow up in their faces as they prove God's existence and those that believe will think quietly to themselves:

'I already knew that.'

"The problem Val. Is that according to many scientists the world is still flat. Or the brain cannot be changed after birth. Or a lobotomy will cure mental illness. All these thing's science told us were truths. The sad thing with the lobotomy is that the guy who invented that procedure was awarded a Nobel Prize for physiology. All fallacies that science expected us to adhere to.

"...And so, they will in time, come to the realisation that there is one pure energy vibrating at such a high frequency that can create anything if it so chooses. When science spends more time understanding frequency and how to bring frequency into alignment, then real medical breakthroughs will take place.

"The problem with mankind is once upon a time God and science were synonymous with each other in some ways. Science accepted God as the truth. Then somewhere in our history, science decided that it was larger than God. Science looked to measurement of facts, when religions asked us to believe in what we had been taught. So, the two separated.

"Understandably when you feel you cannot measure something or test in in a lab, then maybe it is not true, but there is enough evidence of people's experiences that support the existence of this pure vibrational energy. Unfortunately, when they are having these experiences, there is no scientists sitting there measuring it. Yet there are literally millions of people that have had an experience. Just like when I passed on. No scientist has the opportunity or the knowledge that I would have moved to the other side of the veil and then return. Only I know the truth.

"My advice to anyone, Valentina is don't make science your god, as it shows time and time again to be a floored god at that.

"One day the two may converge again, but I think you will find that God will reveal his face well before science ever catches up."

"I understand where you come from," said Valentina. "As a scientist myself, I have struggled with my beliefs versus what we are told are truths."

"People get caught up in mythology and think that because ancient man described their experiences in what we now call primitive, then their beliefs must be primitive. Daniel said, now lying back on his back. "When they are so advanced on the thinking of the "professionals", that the "professionals" are playing catch up with what is already known.

"Please don't take this conversation that I dislike or hate the science profession. What you must understand is that science constantly proves itself wrong over time. What is fact today is a proven fallacy tomorrow. This is science.

"God is naturally a harder concept for humans, as we do not see this form, but we do get exposed to it the same way we do in the lab. It happens in many subtle ways.

"In our coincidences that lead us down a path that we would have never taken. Or the near-death experiences that some of us are exposed to.

"In these near-death experiences like mine, we are given a glimpse into the unknown.

"One Day Valentina, God will reveal, and science will melt away.

"Now get some rest, tomorrow we will do some heavy lifting and we will delve deeper into how to create change, using your 3-minds.

"Every lesson builds on the other. Knowledge becomes power, becomes understanding. Your role is to gain your understandings or Wisdoms as I call them, so you can make your trip back to the ultimate source."

Daniel, then went quiet, placing his hat across his face and he began to sleep.

Valentina looked up at the stars and wondered about Jacob. She wondered if he was in the Dream Time, and if things would have been different if he had chosen to not to go to Thailand or maybe she had just joined him.

126

She also thought about what Daniel had taught her to date and maybe he was right that the health of the world was being influenced and, in some way, corrupted without anyone realising.

Transformation

Each day was similar for Valentina and Daniel. He would teach her how to hunt and forage for food. During the night they would have in-depth conversations to assist in moving her mind.

Valentina was missing the home comforts, but she was also proud of herself and the newfound skills she was attaining. The outback could be harsh, but fortunately she had packed her sunscreen and hat to protect her from the rays of the sun. She really didn't need anything else, except for Daniel's guidance.

They never went without, but the luxuries she took for granted were now a thing of the past. It was just the two of them and the elements.

There were two reasons for this journey. One was to expedite her own spiritual path and the other was for her own safety. The latter was always sitting in the back of her mind. Would it be safe for her to return to a normal life? What is a normal life after you have revisited your current one and then make the choice to change the way you perceive it?

That evening they ate dinner and the two sat facing each other crossed-legged, just like children.

After they had eaten, Daniel chose to begin this evening's work.

"For tonight, I need you to be very relaxed," said Daniel. Placing his hat on the ground next to him. "In order, for you to do that, I will ask you to find a comfortable place to lay down. Place any clothing underneath you, if that helps."

Valentina did as she was asked and rolled up some clothing to use as a pillow.

She looked up at the clear sky. She had grown accustomed to the peacefulness of her surroundings.

"Ok I will get you to close your eyes and just now listen to my voice." Daniel began.

Valentina closed her eyes and laid there.

"I want you to imagine you are back at home in your comfortable bed, just about to fall asleep. You notice that just before you sleep, your legs become very relaxed starting at the toes, working their way up. Becoming more relaxed as you move through your body. As you do this, you imagine sleep falling over your body. Making its way up until it reaches your head.

"Now picture yourself standing at the top of staircase. As you look down, you notice that it winds down like a spiral as you begin your decent. Taking the first step and then the next, as you begin to fall deeper into sleep."

Daniel's voice dropped slightly and slowed down in pace.

"You notice that all you can now hear is my voice as the thoughts in your head now focus on the land around you and the significance of this land.

"You become sleepier as you feel your eyes becoming so heavy that you have gone all the way down.

"As you lay on your bed, you imagine yourself opening your eyes and you find yourself back in Australia, but in another time. A time way back when the indigenous ancestors roamed the earth. They were one with the land and they were one with the Dreaming.

"As you take each step, you fall a little deeper within your mind. Noticing that you are feeling relaxed and safe.

"I now want you to jump to your childhood and tell me what you see. Tell me what life was like for small Valentina?"

Valentina recalled vividly seeing her father. He was not a tall man. He wore a moustache and overalls. It was obvious that he did not have much to his name. His fingernails were dirty, and she could see that he was feeling alone and sad. It was almost like she could read his thoughts.

She described what she was seeing to Daniel.

"Very good Val, now move inside *his* mind and tell me what you are feeling?"

"He is angry and sad all at the same time. He feels cheated by his life and his sadness comes from his childhood."

"Very good, continue." Daniel urged her.

"I feel there was some type of abuse in his life, and he doesn't know how to process it.

He is reaching down and looking for a bottle. His

favourite poison was whiskey, and he drank that most of the time.

"The emotions are so mixed and painful." Valentina said out loud.

Valentina was now feeling her father's discomfort with his own life.

"Ok Valentina, but this is not your pain. Come back to your own body now. Whilst still asleep, I want you to feel yourself rising above it and look down.

"I want you to analyse your own life and your own pain. Where did it begin?

"Imagine that there is a thin line called Valentina's life. This line goes all the way back, not one life, but all your lifetimes. You can see it clearly from the height you are hovering at.

"Notice that along this line, are events that have contributed to who you have become."

Valentina looked down and saw many lives. Each event had both joyous and painful feelings attached to them. She noticed that she had played different parts in different lives.

Sometimes she was a man and other times she was a woman. Gender didn't seem to make a difference in each of her lives. Each life was there to give each incarnation, an experience.

She couldn't see who she was in these periods, other than being a man or a woman. She did know from her feelings that she was in different human vessels, but all of them were still her.

"Now remembering that struggle is an important part of journey, I want you to move back along your line, as far back as you feel is necessary. Giving yourself permission to forgive the decisions made during these times and take learnings that you need. Checking in and understanding that there are emotions attached to each event and that they have travelled with you and imprinted on your Soul. As you check-in to each emotion, I want you to check below the surface of that emotion.

"Even though you may feel anger, you may find below that emotion are other emotions that are the real reason you have been held back. The story is never the story. There is always the truth below.

"All journeys have been chosen by you. How you have chosen to react to them has been of your own doing. If they are repeating themselves, then you have still to learn the lessons. That is why they are still being put in front of you in each incarnation.

"It is time to release them one by one and ask your higher self for the knowledge to move on."

Valentina floated all the way back along her line, tapping into each event and its accompanying emotion, and then releasing it until she came back to now. At one point during her journey, she came to Jacob's death. She could feel the emotion of pain and anger that was attached to that part of her life, but she could not conjure up an image of Jacob dying. She later put it down to the fact that she had never seen his actual death or his body. He was on the other side of the world when it happened.

She expelled air from her lungs, like it was the first time in her life and breathed in what she would describe later as spiritual air.

She felt like she was now moving through a dark tunnel, which then became a blast of bright light. She couldn't see anything, but just feel the light, as if it was a beautiful spring morning.

Although she could see nothing, she spoke to the light, asking that she be given the opportunity to take learnings from her lives and be given the knowledge to move on.

Then as quickly as it all happened, she felt herself being pulled back along the same line she was looking down on before, until she was back to now.

Daniel had been monitoring her and spoke.

"I want you to just soak up the feeling Valentina. To take in the knowledge you are given. To understand that you have been relieved of past sufferings and that all sufferings are part of your learning process.

"To understand that everyone that influenced you, from friends and family, colleagues etc, were also on their own paths with you. Not necessarily at your level, yet still on a similar trajectory.

"Now I want you to take in a deep breath and let this now integrate within yourself and to have the knowledge that you will be ready to begin your transformation.

"When you have done that, come back to me in your

own time, remembering that you have now adjusted your own line. That past events hold no control over the present but were part of the continuum. The obstacles you experienced in those lifetimes were just that, obstacles, that have now been released and pushed aside to clear a path for your renewal."

Valentina lay there for a while. She knew she had to wake up, but she felt so good laying there. It was like she had just had a thousand sleeps all rolled into one. The tension from her shoulders subsided and she began to return.

Eventually she opened her eyes and waited for them to adjust to the darkness.

She sat up and looked at Daniel.

"How do you feel?" he said.

"Different, but a good different" she replied.

Daniel reached into his backpack and pulled out a pen and notebook. He handed it to her and told her that she was now to make notes when she felt the need to get her thoughts down. Any type of thoughts. It was like downloading from the internet, but this was from her mind. It would transfer some of her issues or thoughts during the day to paper. Almost relieving the burden of over thinking.

"Do you remember Val, when I explained the 3-Minds to you?" Daniel said.

"Yes" Valentina replied.

"Then you will remember me talking about the Programmer, whose job is to input new habits and programs into the Subconscious, that then feeds up to the Unconscious. This sits on the human side of the three minds. It can sometimes get in the way of you developing your Soul.

"The reason for this is it plays a dual role. The Programmer is also one of the gatekeeper. It is your critical mind, analysing things and at times is sceptical as to what it hears. So, when you wish to change the subconscious, it is this conscious mind that blocks any new messages.

"There is way to bypass this gatekeeper and create everlasting change in your life and that is by talking directly to the subconscious. This is best done via stories and metaphors.

"When a person is exposed to a story that is of interest, then the Programmer or conscious mind is distracted and listens intently to the story being told. The gatekeeper is now occupied.

"What is happening behind the scenes is that the subconscious is now free to make the connections that relate to the meaning behind the story. When the subconscious does this, it is now open to suggestion. Open to change.

"If you have ever listened to great teachers, prophets and world leaders, they have a great ability to take you within yourself. So much so that you can see in your mind's eye exactly what they are talking about. This combination of story and meaning behind the story helps people transform themselves. By listening to great teachers or reading books that help your subconscious begin an evaluation process, you begin a communication with the mind that works directly with the Unconscious or Soul State.

"The message here is that if you wish to really change your life then you need to learn methods to open this subconscious, so that you are creating real change."

They both sat and chatted for a while and then Valentina's mind moved to Jacob. She had been thinking about him a lot lately since that day, when they sat down with Christiaan and Detective Squires.

She looked down at her watch and saw that it was 9pm.

Death & Dreams

The next morning, she felt lighter. As if many burdens were now removed, but she wanted to know more about the beyond.

Daniel has explained that last night was just the beginning of the transformation stage and that it was an ongoing process.

Valentina was curious about what happens when people pass on. She wondered if those we love, somehow go through their own transformation when they leave this earth.

"Can you tell me more about death please Daniel, I think it will help me process Jacob's passing?"

"What would you like to know?" He asked.

"Well, more of what is it like. What happens when we die? Do we feel pain when we go?

Are we judged by God? What if we didn't live a good life on earth."

"Ok, I think I have got it," he acknowledged.

"I guess I was lucky to experience some of the afterlife and for some reason I have this insight into the rest, so you will have to trust me on what I am telling you."

Valentina nodded.

"When I died, it was a state of peacefulness. I saw a light as I was heading down the tunnel. As I got towards the end of this tunnel, I saw my loved ones. They looked the same as I remembered them, but I now know that they are just taking on a form, so that I would recognise them, and it would assist me to crossover without fear.

"In all honesty, they, and you, are just conscious energy. Able to take on any form in this environment. You just think it, and you are it. I know it sounds weird, but you must remember that you are no longer a physical body in that environment. Everybody identifies each other via their vibrational signature, so they know who you are.

"Not long after you arrive, you will meet the Masters. They are advanced beings and vibrate at a much higher frequency. In this meeting the life you have just lived, is "Reviewed". It is a quick process, but you will feel the pain you have inflicted on others during this period, so that you understand the implications of your actions here on earth. It is a fleeting experience, but it is important that you understand that your choices and actions do impact on others. It helps you decide the next journey.

"For some time, you will remain in this realm. It will be fun, and you will enjoy it. You can meet everyone you loved as their souls reside there.

"Then at some stage, to further your development, you will be given the opportunity to decide as to where you may go next. It may be back on this earth or somewhere else to help you get your knowledge and experience.

"There are many places to choose from, by the way. Earth is known as the hardest place to get this learning, but many of us choose to keep coming back repeatedly for that very reason."

"Why would anyone do that?" Valentina asked. "It is such a painful way to exist."

"True, Daniel replied, and it is the best learning ground. Vibrating at such a low energy means we feel everything. We get to see our actions in motion, and we get the chance to create and become better spiritual beings, not better human beings.

"It is here that many choose to go to, because it is here that we suffer and struggle.

"It is here we get the opportunity to grow.

"No one learns anything when it is given to us on a platter. As spiritual beings we chose not just where we will learn, but also what we are to experience in that incarnation."

"So, if I get cancer for example, is that part of my journey that I choose?" Valentina enquired.

"Yes" replied Daniel, "but if you make certain choices and gain the necessary learnings, then it can be avoided or reversed.

"You now already know that the mind influences everything, and part of our learnings are to understand, overcome and grow. So, if you choose cancer as part of your journey before you arrive here, then you can learn how to overcome it through your choices on how you react to your traumas in this life.

"As our choices influence our existence, then choices to smoke and damage our lungs is something we could have avoided, right? The way to look at this, is that the story line was written before, but like a video game, there is an outline and then depending on what you do determines what is the next scene. Like what weapons you will use or tokens you will pick up to move to the next level or gain more lifelines."

"Yes Daniel, but what if they didn't live a good life or someone commits suicide for example?"

"Good question. We are now talking about Heaven and Hell.

"Okay, so I believe that we have a misunderstanding of these concepts. Even if you listen to teachings of Jesus, he really is talking about choices and consequences of choices. He tells us that one choice leads us to God and the other means we no longer exist.

"It is not about fire and torment, it is about returning to the ultimate source or rejecting that source and eventually we are extinguished. No pits of fire, burning for eternity. You choose to enhance your soul, which can be a difficult path. Or you choose to darken it, which will in time have finite existence after several lifetime opportunities.

"When someone who has not lived a good life or has even committed suicide, they will travel the same way as I have described before. Of course, in their "Review" they will experience all the pain they have inflicted by their acts on others.

"One day there will be some type of judgement in which a decision is made on each Soul and if they should live forever or be extinguished.

"Every thought, emotion and deed are recorded as we live each life. This will then become part of a final "Review" when the ultimate energy decides it is time.

"So those that commit suicide are not judged. They do not go to a hell. They, like all of us, return to the light and will then be given a "Review". This is to show them how they lived that human experience, and they then will feel what others felt because of what they did to themselves. In this case take their life. Then they get the opportunity to have another experience of their own design to try again or maybe choose another reality elsewhere to assist in their development."

"You refer to elsewhere," said Valentina, but what do you mean by elsewhere?"

"Humans are a funny species. We think that God only created us. Like we are the only beings placed on one planet, when he created numerous planets and galaxies. Is it not arrogant to think we are the only ones and earth is the only place? I tell you that spiritual beings have choice too. Some choose earth and it speeds up their development and others want a different experience. Maybe one not so challenging.

"All I will say at this stage is that the Creator created many environments for us to reside and to learn.

"Let us continue the heaven and hell theme for a moment.

"The use of heaven and hell has been used by organised religions to keep people within their parameters of their teachings for thousands of years. As a new division or breakaway group takes place from those organisations, then the concept of hell is perpetuated. It becomes truth if enough people speak with authority about its truth.

"Earth of course is the ultimate learning ground due to the density of the vibration and how there are more struggles when you have a body.

"Regarding suicide, no one wants someone to take their human life.

"Those on earth struggle with the loss of this individual and those Souls in the light also know that it means the learnings have not been met and will need to be found elsewhere in another incarnation. Cutting short your learning means you are destined to repeat it until you understand it.

"I hope that this gives you some insight, Val."

"I guess it does. I just wondered what happens if you were to end your own life and now, I have a better idea. Thank you."

The two agreed that was enough for one night and both retired for the evening.

Valentina lay on her back and thought about a lot of things. Her own attempted suicide. Jacob's death and everything that she was learning whilst in hiding.

She began to doze off, and suddenly she felt a tap on

her shoulder. Naturally she assumed it was Daniel and slowly opened her eyes.

As her eyes adjusted, she saw a figure near her head. It was a man, but it wasn't Daniel, she could tell by the shape of this individual. Although it was dark, the stars always gave its natural light, and she could tell the man was of a dark complexion.

It startled her and she sat up abruptly.

Before she could say a word, the person put their finger to their mouth and then whispered to be quiet. He pointed to Daniel, indicating that he was fast asleep and not to awaken him.

She felt paralysed at first, but for some reason she wasn't afraid.

The person held out their hand, gesturing for her to stand up and go with him.

She did as she was asked, taking his hand and following him to a nearby watering hole.

Once she got a better look at him, she realised that he was an indigenous man. He held a spear in his right hand and was wearing what to her looked like war paint, as he had white lines across his face.

Although they never actually spoke, Valentina was able to communicate perfectly with him.

The man told her that the Rainbow Serpent was nearby and to ready herself.

Valentina didn't really know what he meant but listened anyway.

He pointed to something in the distance. Then as it got closer, she saw it. A large snake moving quickly, slithering in their direction.

It was very large and in some way menacing. It moved near her feet as she stood perfectly still as it passed her. As she watched it, it began to shed its skin, leaving what looked like a carpet behind. A beautiful snakeskin carpet of many colours.

The man gestured for her to walk across the skin, and she obliged. She had no shoes on and she felt the sensations of this serpent's coat that it had left behind. It was a strange feeling.

She walked back and forth and felt a sense of contentment as she did so.

The Serpent looked back and then moved on.

Suddenly Valentina felt as if she was being lifted into the air and like a tumbleweed was blown back to her position on the ground next to Daniel.

The Serpent was now gone, as so was the man.

She lifted her head up and noticed that Daniel was fast asleep. She looked at her watch and noticed the time.

She put her head back down on her make ship pillow and went back into a deep slumber.

The next morning, they woke up nice and early. The morning sun always had that effect on them.

Valentina looked up to the sky and remembered the Serpent and the man in the loin cloth. The indigenous man who spoke no words but communicated with her anyway.

She decided to tell Daniel what had happened, but she wasn't sure if was real or not. Maybe spending all this time in the bush was sending her crazy, but she was sure that the previous night's meeting was very real.

Daniel sat on a rock and contemplated.

"Have we ever discussed dreams? I don't mean the process of your transformation or the Dream Time. I mean actual dreams that we have."

"I don't think so" Valentina replied.

"Dreams have their purpose on earth as does everything else you experience. Generally, they have two purposes. As an outlet for what is happening in our waking life. It helps us release some of the pressures of our existence and it is designed to replenish us. Dreams also have a deeper reason for their existence.

"They are also designed to give you either prophetic meaning or messages for you to tap into. Whilst you sleep, the soul is awake. It can pass on messages that may be beneficial to you. The soul witnesses everything and at times will send its own messages to guide you.

"You will see in history or even the bible that there were people that could decipher their own dreams or the dreams of others.

"I think your dream is more about spiritual meaning.

"You talked about a big snake? A Serpent? It sounds like the great Rainbow Serpent, which all relates back to the Dreaming.

"You say he slithered past you and then shed his skin and you walked upon it?"

Valentina nodded.

"OK, here is my interpretation of this dream.

"Firstly. Let us talk about the Rainbow Serpent, which relates to the Dreaming. Now this term 'Rainbow Serpent' was coined by white man. The indigenous people use different names for it.

"This "snake" represents the giver of life. Although each of the indigenous tribes have this theme, it can vary slightly depending again on which part of the country you are in. It is considered a giver of life and has an association with water.

"When you see a rainbow in the sky, it is said that the Rainbow Serpent is moving from one waterhole to another.

"Your dream is about "new life'. The Snake represents you entering a new phase in *your* life. It is your message to you that it is time to shed the old skin of Valentina Russo. The girl that was held and imprisoned in her own mind by the past, and for a long time, it was shaping her future. It was making her unhappy.

"It was shaping the people she was meeting, and she was joining her energy with those that had limited ability to help her find purpose.

"Although the past is very important for us to maintain memories, so that we do not forget our learnings. Living in the past, especially when it does not benefit our growth can be detrimental. To both our growth and our health, physically and mentally.

"The message you have been given is that it is time to move on. Don't forget the past, but don't let the past own you.

"Shed your skin, Valentina. Shed the habits that have defined you. Shed the thinking that has confined you.

"It is time for new life."

Mashda's Energy

Daniel then took both his hands and held them maybe a foot part, palms facing each other as he asked Valentina to do the same.

"When you are ready Valentina, you will begin to feel the energy between these palms, as you move them closer together.

"Here, copy my actions and slowly bring them both closer together, feeling for the energy. They should not need to come completely together, because you will begin to feel that energy between the separated hands at some point."

Valentina obliged, watching Daniel slowly bringing his hands closer together. She emulated the actions, until her hands were now clasped.

"I don't feel anything Daniel, sorry. What am I meant to feel?"

"Energy emits from all humans and when you do this exercise, you will feel a slight resistance. It is not from the mechanics and angles of your hands. It has to do with the energy that is being always emitted from you. This vibrational "pushing" allows you to experience energy.

"As humans, we are so far removed from our energy source, that we struggle to feel energetic vibrations of others. Yet, 'on the other side' where we are spirit, that is all you feel. There is no physical body to interfere with this source. There is no pain. There is no struggle. There is just conscious energy.

Valentina tried a few more times, but to no avail. She couldn't feel what Daniel was experiencing.

"It will come, Daniel assured her. You are emitting vibrational energy. You just are not yet attuning to it. You are very much still in the physical right now.

"Tonight, we will work on that, but today we will find some more food. Don't forget to put on some of that suntan lotion to protect your skin as the Australian sun is like no other in the world."

"Did you know we have now been out here over two weeks?" Daniel told Valentina.

"Wow, it went quickly. Not like the first few days, they

seemed to go on forever. To be honest it was hard. But you know they breed us LA chicks pretty tough in the US."

They both laughed.

"Today I don't just want you to see your surroundings, I want you feel them. I want you realise that in some way you are part of them. The rocks, the lagoons.

"Maybe touch them and feel for their energy. No matter how strange a request that may sound. Everything is giving off its own energy force. We associate this type of exercise with the "tree huggers" and so there must be something wrong. If you want to be scientific for a moment, then realise that everything that is living has its own energetic vibration. Which is why looking after it, is so important, because it assists us to balance our own energies.

"When you touch, try to feel a connection. No one is watching, so you won't be judged. Just become one with it."

Valentina agreed to do that today. Yes, the request was strange, but Daniel had never led her astray and there was always a purpose to his requests. She did as she was asked and would touch a tree or a rock as she was requested.

She would reach out and with great reverence, gently touching a rock nearby or some type of flora to connect to it.

The ancestral spirits lived in these places and so she treated it with the respect that it deserved.

She wasn't sure if she was doing it right, but she liked that Daniel had this respect and considering that there was no one else around, but the two of them, she didn't feel so self-conscious about this act. Instead, she felt like she was being let in on something special. Something beyond this earthly realm. A secret that has been forgotten, except for older generations who preserve it.

The day continued and once again night fell upon the land.

As usual they ate together.

Once they had their fill, Daniel said, "let us go for a walk."

They came to a clearing and Daniel picked up a stick. He drew a large circle in the middle of the clearing and asked Val to sit within it.

Val obliged and moved to the middle, sitting down crossed legged.

She watched Daniel as he walked around the circle a couple of times and then stopped to face her.

He asked her to place her hand on her knees and relax.

"If you truly want to transform Valentina, then you need to learn to connect back to source. Back to the light. This is done by bringing what sits in your soul consciousness through to this physical world.

"We do this through meditation. By opening the pathway between the conscious mind, all the way down to the unconscious mind.

"If you can think about it as a highway.

"For most people their highways are cluttered with debris and old cars blocking the path. For many people they rarely take this road. Mainly because they are unaware that it exists and because keeping the road clear is not always so easy.

"Yet there is still a road, which leads you back to a higher self.

"We have worked with you for the last few weeks in understanding what is in the road. We have also helped you work on some of those blockages and how they may have got there. Now you have come to the crossroads in this superhighway. You need to bring this a point of realisations.

"If the road has been cleared, then the drive is smoother. Of course, that does not mean you know which highway to take.

"Therefore, we went through several exercises to clear it. Now we need to do is bring it up to consciousness, so you own it. To tap into the higher source, so that you are connected and ready for growth.

"Although part of our process is to guide you through this. What I need you to do is learn how to also do this for yourself."

Daniel asked Valentina to close her eyes and take a deep breath.

"Nice and deep.

"That's it.

"Now exhale noticing your breath.

"I want you to visual each breath as you go deeper.

"Keep your focus on your breath and notice that your thoughts are disappearing. If a thought comes into mind, take your focus back to your breath unto you have full focus on it.

"Now when you have that, I want you to imagine moving from the tunnel of your mind down the shaft, through your subconscious (whatever that manifest itself to be and look like.) All along the breath. As you inhale and then exhale. It will push your mind along."

As Valentina went deeper into this state, she could hear Daniel begin to tell her a story. It was like she was listening to him from a faraway place, but she still could perfectly hear everything that was being said.

Daniel continued.

"Way back in ancient Sumer many lifetimes ago, there was a ruler by the name of Mashda. He was a tough ruler on his people, and he lived in fear that one day there would be an uprising that would topple his kingdom.

"There had been many revolts by groups of people over time within his kingdom over the way they were treated. Mashda believed that ruling with an iron fist was the only way to keep order and power.

"Every day he would tell his wife that the people were becoming more unruly and that to be honest he hated them with every fibre of his being. He would think up ways of punishing them to maintain his control and rage. He felt that in some way he was paying them back for their insolence.

"Mashda was a simple man, who thought that there were many gods that ruled the world. There was a god for the sun and a god for the moon. A god for love and a god for war.

"He was no different to the people of his times in that these gods resided with them and protected their cities.

"One day Mashda fell ill. He felt very weak and was not sure what to do. His physicians were helpless to assist him in changing his circumstances. His condition was now grave.

"He summoned his wise elders to his chambers to advise him. He was deteriorating very quickly and was concerned that maybe he had in some way offended the gods.

"Once upon a one time, Mashda was known for his bravery and strength. He fought in wars and was feared by even his enemies for his brutality both towards them and his own people.

"He demanded answers from the elders as did his wife, Queen Sidhuri.

"Sidhuri was a wise woman and decided to call upon one of the gods who resided not far from their land. His name was Enki, and he was known as the "healer" god. If anyone could cure Mashda from his ailments, it was Enki.

"Enki was summoned to the court and a dispatch with a message from the ruler was sent with an urgent request to come as soon as possible.

"It took three days and nights before Enki finally arrived. He went to the ruler's bed side as Mashda lay helpless and in pain. Queen Sidhuri never left her husband's side, holding his hand as Enki walked into the chambers.

"The ruler raised his head in hope that the great healer would perform magic on him and out of respect Mashda bowed his head as best he could.

"Enki raised his hands and then ran them across Mashda's body about an inch above it. Hovering over areas and stopping at times as Mashda felt a tingle at different points. The healer was totally focused on the task, and it appeared that he had gone into some type of trance.

"Both Mashda and Sidhuri wondered what the great healer was doing, but they didn't dare question it. It would have been an insult to do so. You never question one of the gods.

"Then the great Enki stopped his ritual and looked at Mashda and spoke.

"The reason you are sick, my great ruler is that you have many ailments, which has to do with your energy lines within your body. Like sand from the desert, it can block the doorway to a temple and make it almost impossible to pass. Unless they are cleared and restored and aligned, you will continue to deteriorate.

"These lines are important as they connect to your higher self. Until you bring your energy back into alignment, then your fate does not look promising.

"Mashda," Enki said.

"Your energy is failing you."

"Mashda and Sidhuri looked at each other and pleaded for Enki to provide a healing.

"Enki pulled his long flowing robe back off his shoulders and sat down.

"For too many years Mashda you have ruled your people with an iron fist, not with love. Love flows two ways. To both to others and to yourself. This does not sit well with your spirit. Instead, you have chosen not to be aligned with your higher self. You have held back emotions, that have become your sand to your doorway, blocking it. If you do not correct your ways and unblock these lines, then your body will continue to become weak, until it is time to take your spirit away.

"Mashda," Enki said. "Every thought you have ever had towards your people is transmitted out to them. Then this energy becomes stronger as you put it into words, such as a how you say you "hate" your people or give a command to hurt them."

"Mashda was taken aback by the god's words that he was hearing.

"Finally,' Enki told the ruler, you then put your energy into action. The strongest of the energetic proposals. Not with love, but with hatred. These thoughts are now in motion, affecting those that are in your care.'

"Enki stepped closer and whispered to Mashda.

'Unfortunately for you Mashda, every thought you have, does not just affect others. It affects yourself. These thoughts attach themselves to you and even though you think you are directing this energy outwards to those that you despise. The one you are really hurting is YOU. Each thought amplifies on those that you despise and makes them want to repel your thinking through their uprisings.'

'Until you understand to forgive others and yourself, then nothing will change in your kingdom. NOTHING, including your health. All if this has been created by you.' He now said in a loud booming voice.

"Mashda was now panicking. He was usually always in complete control, but now for the first time in his life, he had to re-evaluate the way he thought about the way he lived it. The way he treated others. The way he thought about others.

"It was affecting his energy and according to Enki, this would be the end of his earthly existence.

"Enki turned around as the courtiers moved aside for the great healer as he walked away, glancing at Queen Sidhuri.

"As he got to the end of the chambers, he turned around to face Mashda and Sidhuri to give them one last final warning.

'Learn to free your energy Mashda, by changing your thinking and allowing it to flow back to a higher source. Your forgiveness, not your threats will save you.'

"With that warning, Enki left and Mashda and Sidhuri were left to contemplate their fate.

"In time Mashda changed his thinking and released from his body what was holding him back. In time he returned to balance and in time he truly made his kingdom great."

Daniel's voice faded away, as the story ended and Valentina, still focused on her breathing, absorbed the learning.

Once again after a period he spoke again.

"When you are ready, still focusing on your breath, you will begin to come back through the tunnel, until you are ready to come back to now.

"The learnings will come with you and will give you a sense of knowing and peace. Everything that once defined you, has now altered. You are now with source.

"When you are ready, I want you to come back, with the knowledge that you can do this for yourself at any time when you so wish to."

Valentina eventually opened her eyes. She described the experience as uplifting and peaceful. There were no thoughts, but somehow, she felt clarity.

She didn't know why, but she was ok with Jacob's death. It was like everything she had been learning for over a month now, was integrating within her.

She couldn't really put it into words, but she knew that she was developing new understandings about not just herself, but also the greater world she lived in, and that of beyond the physical.

Daniel then informed her to repeat the exercise, which they had tried before by getting Valentina to hold her hands apart and slowly bringing them towards each other. Feeling for the energy.

Valentina held her hands about a foot apart and slowly brought them together.

On this occasion it was different from her past attempts. She felt some type of resistance between her palms. It was subtle and she could feel that there was something there. It was strange. Valentina had never experienced energy before. She had no explanation as to why she should feel anything between her hands as she slowly brought them together.

She giggled with glee. "It's working," she shouted. "I can feel it between my palms. It has never done that before."

Daniel smiled. "Maybe you have learned the sensitivity that comes with being attuned to energy. We all obtain it at different levels. Mine came after my near-death experience. I not only feel energy, but I see it. When it is in balance, your earthly and heavenly bodies align.

"Everyone gives off energy. I can see it around them, and it has different types of colours which I have learned over time, tells me what state of mind and health the person is in.

"You have now obtained a basic stage that most humans should be able to attain. That is the ability to feel energy. Sometimes you feel this energy is drained from you when you are around people who lack their own balance or who lack congruency between their 3-minds. These people seek out others to make them feel better, because of this lacking.

"Of course, they do not necessarily have your best interest at heart, and you will feel this draining in your body and mind. I am sure you have felt them before. Every time you are with them, you know something is not quite right. Sometimes you feel physically or mentally drained in their presence."

"Yes, I can relate to this, Valentina replied. I have had even people I call friends, who do this to me."

"We have all experienced them Val. Sometimes it takes us years for us to remove them from our lives. Rather than add to our energy they usually deplete it. Only when we begin to reflect on our relationship with them do we begin to see life differently. Our path puts opportunities for us to see circumstances and relationships clearer. Our alignment also creates new relationships, potentially with people who meet our spiritual needs.

"Once we do that, we allow ourselves to move on."

Valentina and Daniel now lay on their backs, looking up to the heavens.

Over a month had now passed, and it was time to get back to civilisation.

A lot had been learned, but they did need to return and face the real world. Daniel explained that learning does not stop with just delving into the mind and clearing it of the past, but it was an ongoing lifetime process.

"You will come across guides in your life, who may come for a short time or maybe a long time." Daniel said.

"These guides can be acquaintances, colleagues, lovers, or those sent by spirit to move you on."

Valentina sat up. "Explain those sent to move me on."

"Well, we did write the script of this life some time ago, before you stepped back on this earth. For that script to be fulfilled, you will be given what I will call a nudge to kind of get you back on track.

"Of course, if you are being influenced by past baggage, then your choices are reflected by these influences, until you go through a clearing stage like this DREAM process, that you are going through.

"The nudges I refer to are from those that have been charged to look out for you. Other Souls can be called upon, but they are not around you all the time. At least not the Souls that travel with you from one incarnation to the other.

"They come when they are called upon, otherwise they are not around.

"There are also other humans who will nudge you in a direction that sometimes seems like an innocent action on their part. But spirit moves them to act and push you back towards your path.

"Sometimes you act upon these nudges and other times they seem like a nuisance, but they are all part of your journey. Both good and bad.

"You are never alone Valentina; we do travel in packs."

The next morning the two of them tracked back to the spot they had been dropped off over a month ago. It wasn't long before Steve appeared from around the corner. Beaming with a big Cheshire grin. He stopped his truck on the side of the road and leaped out, hugging both at the same time.

He couldn't hold back his exuberance for the two of them. He knew that they would be safe with Daniel's background, but there were always that niggling feeling in the back of his mind.

Both Valentina and Daniel were tanned, and both looked healthy and well fed.

After their hug fest, Daniel enquired about the situation surrounding Valentina.

They got back in the truck and Steve informed them that the Australian Federal Police had been watching this gang for some time and several arrests had been made within the country, but it wasn't the bikies that we needed to fear, but their connections overseas in Asia and Canada.

'Canada', both Daniel and Valentina said in unison.

"Well, Detective Squires can fill you in, but apparently there is some type of big drug dealer that was originally working in Australia at some stage and ended up in Canada. He wouldn't tell me much more than that, but it sounds like they are closing in on this guy.

"For now, my friends you are free to get back to the land of the living."

The drive back was a long one and Valentina had wanted to see Mia and explain everything she had experienced.

Steve informed her that Australian Police had felt it was best that Mia calls off her Australian holiday for now, until it was safe again. He believed that Mia did make a trip to Sydney on her way back to the states, but never got to Melbourne.

"Here," he said, pulling out an envelope from his top pocket. "She wrote you a letter."

He handed it to Valentina who was sitting just behind

him in the back of the vehicle.

She thanked him and sat back to read the letter from Mia, that had been written on the stationery from the hotel they had stayed at.

'Hey Bestie,

I don't really know what to say. What started out as an amazing adventure, turned out to be so much more. All I wanted for you, was to gain some insight from this guy Daniel and of course to come and see some hunky Australian men.

Who would have thought that there was trouble lurking around the corner, but from what I understand, it all has to do with that ex of yours, Jacob.

It sounds like trouble followed him wherever he went. Unfortunately, you got involved and it sounds like the saga continues.

The cops won't tell me a lot, except that you had to hide out for now, until the heat subsides. I did suggest to them that we just go back to the states, but they told me that it was too risky, and the bikies had chapters back home too.

I do miss you and I am a little worried for you too.

Steve assures me that you are safe.

I have been told to head back to the states for now as the Australian police don't need to be watching me as well.

Hoping to see you soon. Stay safe and I'm sure we will be drinking again at a bar back at home.

Love you my friend
Mia

Valentina shed a tear. Drying it away with her finger.

"Thanks Steve. I'm glad she is safe, I was a little worried that they may go after her next, but it sounds like she is back home. I hope I can see her again soon. She has been a good friend to me."

Steve turned down the radio, which was playing AC/DC's 'Highway to Hell'.

He spoke.

"Trust me Val, she'll be right. Thing's kind of sort themselves out, even when everything seems to have gone pear shaped.

"Now I bet you are parched. I know I am and would like something else to drink instead of bloody water. Can I interest you in a traveller?"

Valentina laughed and asked what the hell a "traveller" was.

"A drink you have while on the road. Next to you is an Esky, open it up and you will find some Vodka Cruisers."

Valentina looked down and saw a portable cooler on the seat, she guessed this is what they call an Esky out here.

She opened the lid and grabbed herself a drink, whilst passing the boys some beers.

Steve then turned up the volume and you could hear AC/DC blaring away in the distance as they headed down the road.

The three of them arrived back at Daniel's house a few hours later.

Besides the obligatory toilet stop, Valentina dropped everything and headed to the bathroom to go have a long hot bath, where she was able to reflect on the last couple of months and feel clean for the first time in a long time.

She dipped her toe in before totally immersing herself in the nice warm bath. It was a feeling she had missed. Having nice hot water covering her whole body was bliss, but she didn't regret the experience she had with Daniel. It just wasn't one that she would like to sustain for a lifetime.

Valentina was still on vacation and so she wasn't worried about work yet, but she knew at some stage this whole episode of her life was to end and it would be time to enter reality again. Although she was beginning to question what reality was.

All three slept at Daniel's that night. Steve parted ways early that next morning as he had tourists from Germany to look after that day. They were making a trip to the Olgas, a famous tourist destination in the area and he didn't want to miss their flight that was arriving later that morning.

Daniel felt that it would be good for both Valentina and he to not be so isolated and so they headed into town for some breakfast. A change of scenery was in order he said.

They sped out the driveway and headed back into the town that neither of them had seen for over a month. Nothing had changed of course in their absence. It was still the same big country town.

There were some indigenous kids playing on the side of the road as they pulled into a familiar carpark, directly opposite from the Kangaroo Corner Cafй.

"This is where Mia and I used to have breakfast each day. Our hotel is literally around the corner" Valentina announced as they pulled into the carpark.

Daniel opened the door for Valentina as she walked into the cafe. They took a seat and looked at the menu. They were both hungry and were keen to have a nice hot breakfast. It would be nice to eat something different.

Both their heads were deep in their menus as their waitress arrived to take their order.

They looked up and saw it was Lizzy. The women that Valentina had met before on previous outings. Lizzy was dressed in her usual outfit with an apron on the front and note pad in hand with pen behind her ear.

Lizzy looked at Valentina and then at Daniel.

"Where the hell have you been honey?" Lizzy said.

Valentina went to answer her as the two had spoken in the past on her previous visits.

Instead, Daniel stood up and gave her a big hug.

"How are you mum? It's been a little hectic lately, but

all is good. I'm here now."

Lizzy hugged him as the two embraced.

Daniel introduced Valentina, but Lizzy acknowledged that they had already met. Lizzy looked Valentina up and down as if there was something wrong with her clothing.

Valentina assumed the look related to her having breakfast with her son.

They both gobbled down their meal, enjoying the selection of foods that was at their disposal. A prized treat from the lack of variety over the last month.

It was a Saturday and Lizzy advised them that she was about to knock off work and would love to sit down with them at the local ice cream parlour and find out all the gossip of the last forty days.

The three headed out when Lizzy finished work, walking to their destination a couple of streets way. Lizzy hugging her little boy as they strolled along the streets of Alice Springs.

Valentina was now acclimatised to the heat and felt she was now one of the locals. In the past she would have been constantly fanning herself with a piece of paper to keep herself cool.

They sat down and Daniel bought Lizzy and Valentina an ice cream each, returning with the flavours they had chosen. Valentina wanted choc chip cookies and Lizzy had salted caramel.

They filled Lizzy in as much as they could about their adventures, telling her about almost being taken by the bikies here in town and their escape to the outback, living like Crocodile Dundee. Just without the crocodiles.

Then Lizzy turned to Valentina. Putting her hand on hers.

"You know honey, I thought I knew you from somewhere and I was right" pulling out her handbag and opening it up. She reached inside, fiddling around in a side pocket.

She pulled out a couple of pictures, placing them on the table in front of her, side-by-side.

"See she said" pointing to the photos that she had just laid down.

Valentina looked down at what had been presented on the table and saw two photos of her and Jacob together.

She had to do a double take as it wasn't what she was expecting.

One of the pictures had been taken when they had first started dating and had gone to Disneyland for the day. Jacob was making a silly face and they were both pointing to Mickey. Mia had taken the photo from recollection.

The other was in front of the hospital where she worked, taken by a colleague. It was obviously at night-time just before she was going to start her shift. Jacob had insisted, so he could have one for his wallet.

"Where did you get these?" Valentina asked quietly.

"I told you, I knew you from somewhere, Lizzy replied. Jacob is my son and he sent these to me a couple of years back when you started dating.

"He said he had this wonderful, smart, beautiful girlfriend that one day he would like to bring back to Australia."

Valentina stood up and hugged Lizzy.

"How did you get here? I mean don't you live in another part of Australia?" Valentina asked.

Lizzy looked at Daniel, who was now taken aback by the whole episode. She pointed to him, saying.

"Daniel brought me out after a difficult marriage to his stepfather. There was nothing for me there, especially with Jacob living in the states and Daniel in Alice. This is where I spent some wonderful times here with my first husband. Daniel's father.

"I was living in Queensland and times were hard, so Daniel brought me out to live back in Alice Springs. Setting me up in my own place. Jacob was already living in the US and in many ways I was alone.

"Actually, Jacob was in Australia at the time and saw me off at the airport. It was the last time I saw him."

Then Valentina remembered the conversation in the truck with Daniel about his family. She couldn't believe that Daniel and Jacob were related. Half-brothers.

She was about to say what a coincidence but stopped herself short looking at Daniel.

"So, you knew about me and Jacob?" now directing her question to Daniel.

He shook his head. "This is news to me as well. I

wasn't close to Jacob. He was a bit younger than me, and I had already moved on by the time he had grown up."

The three chatted for a while before Daniel's phone rang.

He excused himself walking out of the door to take the call.

Upon his return, he told Valentina that it was Detective Squires on the phone. He had arranged a meeting back at the pub to discuss what was happening.

They gave each other a hug and a kiss when it was time to leave, and both Daniel and Valentina headed over to the pub. Waving Lizzy goodbye after seeing her to her car.

As they walked in, Detective Squires was waiting and held out his hand to shake theirs.

They ordered some drinks and settled in to chat in more detail.

"Hoping you have some good news," said Valentina.

Detective Squires looked at them both.

"Yes and no.

"We have raided the Mongols club and have arrested those in Australia that were chasing you. We are confident they will do some time and won't bother you again."

He then looked down at the drink coaster in front of him and played with it.

"Spit it out" Daniel demanded.

"Well, the job isn't quite finished. The Australian Federal Police have asked me to speak to you about helping to flush them out."

"Who are we flushing out?" asked Valentina.

"There is this guy is Canada who runs his cartel called Sam Gor. Its means in Cantonese, I believe "Brother Number Three."

"The guy who runs it is of Chinese origin and his guards are made up of men trained in Thai boxing. Well trained killers.

"Not a lot is known of him, as he is unlike some of his counterparts in the world. He is very secretive. He is obviously very smart, very protected, and very wealthy, allowing him to buy off some police forces around the world. That has been one of our challenges.

"We have some trusted counterparts in Thailand that

we know will do the job, but we need to flush this group out and break the back of such a powerful empire.

"If we can get one of his "managers" to come out of the shadows, then we may be able to link this guy back to Canada. That may be our chance to bring the empire down.

They are literally killing kids around the world guys.

"There is a lot more to this than I can reveal, but you would be helping us and the memory of Jacob if we could get your cooperation."

Remembering that these guys had killed Jacob was motivation for Valentina. She was scared, but knew she had to help.

"There are risks, but we will be watching at all times." Detective Squires advised.

"What do I need to do?" said Valentina?

"Our plan is that we organise a meeting between you and the local manager. They still believe that you know where Jacob held his consignment of drugs. It was considered to have been quite large as it was destined to come to Australian shores.

"Unfortunately, Australia is quite a lucrative market for these guys.

"By getting them to come out into the open, this then allows us to either capture or connect them back to the leader of Sam Gor. Our goal is that we can then begin arrests around the world."

Daniel said nothing. He knew that Valentina was compelled to do this. Instead, he offered to go with her. If she was to be in danger, then he would put himself in the fire with her.

They agreed to meet at the airport in two days, in which they would fly to Sydney and then onto Bangkok airport.

The Double-Edged Sword

All three met at the airport and flew together to Thailand, taking a cab to their hotel in the centre of the city of Bangkok when they arrived.

They were careful not to be seen together and each were given rooms, side-by-side. Valentina was in the middle room with Daniel on one side and Detective Squires room on the other.

As they arrived at their rooms, Detective Squires took out a little black piece of equipment, that looked like a flashlight with a flickering red light on the top. Putting his fingers to his lips, indicating that no sound was to be made. Daniel and Valentina did as instructed and kept quiet as the detective walked around the room, checking for bugs.

The meeting had been arranged via an intermediatory in the police force that was known to be corrupt but was pretending to use his influence to curry favour with his superiors. He was their best shot at making inroads with the gang.

The room was clean of bugs and Valentina felt slightly more comfortable knowing her conversations were not being listened to. This exercise of 'sweeping' the room was done daily, twice a day.

Daniel and Valentina went out for lunch as Detective Squires stayed at a distance in the background, watching for those that may be watching them.

It was a Thursday and the meeting had been arranged to be held in their hotel room on the Saturday morning. Just Valentina and the cartel's contact. Daniel and Detective Squires would be in the next room listening.

At lunch Daniel checked in on Valentina to see her state of mind.

"I am calm, she said. I am completely at peace. The meditation is helping for sure."

Daniel explained that as she becomes more proficient at finding congruency of her

3-Minds, she will then find that everything will become aligned, and her vibrational energy will have changed considerably.

"So much so, that when you reach this state, he said, things that caused you anxiety or were considered difficult, will now be commonplace and you will wonder why they were such a big deal in the past.

"By changing it, he said. You will be in a better position to handle almost any situation. Even people that have known you for years will not know you. This is because your vibrational signature is playing at a higher note and some of your friends will no longer be friends because it is you that has changed, not them."

Valentina understood and was comfortable with his explanation.

They had been told that the meeting was to be held at the hotel as agreed. All the gang wanted was information about the merchandise location and the relevant key which they wished to interview Valentina about. There was to be no harm to the girl, in exchange for this data and keys. If this was provided, then there would be no trouble. The one problem is that Valentina knew nothing of a key or where the merchandise was held.

"This is fraught with danger Val, but we are assured that they have this covered with the federal authorities and will arrest them when the time is right." Detective Squires said.

They all agreed that this was something that had to be done and that Valentina would be in no danger, as long as they had eyes and ears on her.

Daniel and Valentina wanted to make the most of their overseas trip and decided to do some sight-seeing, knowing that they were most likely being followed. At least they had Australian authorities also watching them.

The next day was similar with them visiting a temple and doing some shopping. Daniel haggled at the local market for a designer handbag for Valentina. He felt she needed her mind taken off the case at hand and getting involved with the local culture of haggling was a bit of fun. They settled on a nice red Burberry knockoff handbag that matched one of Valentina's outfits.

Night had now fallen and the two of them met in a restaurant, walking distance from their hotel. It was a lovely warm night and if the situation had been different, it would have been a splendid evening.

They arrived at a small Thai restaurant, which the locals were eating at. This is always a good sign when the locals choose a place to eat. They sat down and were greeted by a man who welcomed them and gave them some menus.

Shortly afterwards Detective Squires also arrived and sat with them.

After some initial chit chat about their last couple of days sight-seeing, Detective Squires began to speak in a low voice, but loud of enough for Daniel and Valentina to hear.

"What I am going to tell you, may disturb you" he told them both.

He reached for his red wine that was sitting in front of him and took a sip.

Turning to Valentina, he spoke.

"Earlier in the year there was an attempt on your life. Two of the Sam Gor men were sent from Canada to extract information from you about the key and the location of Jacob's stash. They were a little too exuberant and obviously misinterpreted their instructions and instead gave you enough pills and alcohol for it to look like a suicide attempt. I assume they forced you to take it.

"Luckily for you, you were found in time by Christiaan and survived."

"I thought I was told that I overdosed at my own hands, not someone tried to kill me?" Valentina responded.

"The cartel honestly thought you were dead and from all accounts, so did the two bubbling idiots who were sent to get information from you. They misunderstood their instructions or were too exuberant and instead piled you with pills.

"We only know this because, we have operatives inside the operation in both the US and Thailand.

"I'm not sure as to all the details, other than they tried to kill you. They were meant to extract information from you first, but I guess you didn't know anything. So instead, they tried to ensure it looked like a suicide attempt. I'm guessing you weren't given many choices. Take the drugs or get a bullet in the head, which would not work well for the group. Too much of a mess to clean up or explain."

Detective Squires took a breath as Valentina gathered her thoughts. Thinking back to the time she had committed suicide. Or thought she committed suicide.

Instead, she didn't try to commit suicide, someone tried to kill her. She must have blocked it from her memory.

Daniel then spoke.

"If they think she is dead, then why have they been following her and now want to meet?"

"Good question," the Detective replied.

"As I mentioned, we have people on the inside, and they were able to get word back to the "executive" of Sam Gor, that you survived, which is why there are two dead fools that were sent to get you. This operative is not someone we trust, but we too use him for information.

"Therefore, you have been under our watchful eye for quite some time now. We knew, and when I say we, I mean international police operations across four countries, that they would want to pursue you.

"For a long time, nothing happened, and we assumed that you wouldn't be a target, but then our intel told us that they were now focusing on recovery of what Jacob had been given. A directive from the top had been made."

Valentina gave out a small grin. The type you give when you are not impressed with something that is said.

"So basically, I have been in danger all this time?"

"No, you have had more protection than any citizen in this country or the United States for that matter. You just didn't know that you had it."

Valentina was quietly composed. Even though this would have seen her in the past drink to oblivion, for some reason it didn't faze her. She knew that she was in danger, and she now knew that she didn't try to end her own life. In some small way, she felt relieved

Part of her knew deep down that this was her path and that she had made choices in her life, that led her to this point, and so she could make further choices that either altered this path or accepted that it was part of it. Daniel had told her once that all things happen for a reason. Both the good and the bad.

She remembered a conversation that they had once had

about children and their paths.

She had asked him at the time, why do children get terminal illnesses, when they did not have time to build up a "dis-ease", that would have come over time? Her questioning was to disprove Daniel's theory. Instead, Daniel explained that a life on earth is for the most part about us gaining knowledge. Some Souls return as part of their final journey to help others gain their learnings.

At the time, she couldn't fathom that God would allow a child to suffer in the process potentially destroying a family.

Daniel flipped that notion around and said, 'if you remember that we are spiritual beings and that you should be looking at this through your spiritual lenses.

"The individual that is a child in our world, may very well be a very old Soul that has come to the end of its spiritual development, and so comes here more for those souls it travels with for each incarnation, to help them with their learnings.

"If you recall Souls tend to travel together through incarnations. Today they may be your mother. In the next incarnation, they may be your brother. Together you help each other on your journey.

"So, when a child comes and goes through what they experience in a physical sense, it can be devasting, because we love this child. We honour this child, and it breaks our hearts to lose them. From a spiritual sense, those around them are given opportunities to see life and life around them differently.

"Some people fall apart when this happens, and this is more than understandable. Some never recover from this segment of their lives and others will learn resilience. There will be others that choose to stop living in the physical and material world and begin to focus on love. As it is love that helps them grow. A love for others and an understanding of loving, rather than loathing oneself. Making the most of your time on earth, as it is short. The child never dies, they have served their purpose on earth, for not only themselves, but those that love them.

"Their life continues, we are just not there to witness it, right now."

Valentina kind of came back into the room after going

165

into this daydream about this part of conversation.

The detective and Daniel had been chatting amongst themselves, so it made no difference to the conversation.

They then turned their attention back to her.

"Are you ok with all of this?" Daniel said to Valentina.

"I know that this is meant to happen, and I know I also have a choice, but if I can stop these guys, then yes I am willing to do this" Valentina replied.

The plan was that they would meet the Sam Gor guys in their hotel room at 1pm. That had already been arranged. Detective Squires and a team made up of two Australian Federal Police and Thai drug enforcement would be in the next room.

Once they had heard enough, they would make arrests.

They finished up their meals and final drinks and agreed that a good night's sleep would be an excellent idea. The problem was finding a way to get some sleep.

Daniel and Valentina decided that they would meet at 10.30am for a brunch the next morning. Over brunch, they could discuss how they would tackle the meeting with the members of Sam Gor. They knew they would be safe due to the number of bugs in the room placed by the enforcement agencies and the fact that the police would be ready to pounce when the time was right.

Daniel and Valentina walked well ahead of the Detective who now had to do something at the reception desk as they made their way back to their rooms.

Daniel wished Valentina a good night's sleep as she placed her room card against the lock for it to open automatically.

She pushed opened the room door, looking forward to getting a good night's rest as she was drained. She would meditate for a while to recharge and then hopefully sleep.

As she walked in the door, her eyes focused on two people in the room. The first was a big burley Asian man with tattoos and a singlet and shorts, who was sitting in a chair near the desk.

The other was a slim woman, dressed in black silk pants and a loose-fitting black top. Long black hair and plenty of makeup. Valentina's guess was that she was of Chinese origin.

Upon seeing them, she knew straight away who they

were and began to turn to make her escape. Instead, another man was standing behind her, blocking her exit. Closing the door as Valentina turned back to face the woman.

"I'm guessing you know why we are here" said the woman in an American accent.

Valentina nodded her head and said that she did, wondering how did they had gotten into her room?

Anticipating what Valentina's had been thinking, the woman informed her how they were able to get access to the room, so easily.

"Hotel workers are easily bribed in Thailand. The money we offer is like a month's wages," said the woman. "Naturally it is very persuasive tool to open a door and let people into a room."

The woman motioned her hand for Valentina to take a seat, offering her some water from the mini fridge.

Valentina acknowledged the offer, but politely refused. She was hoping that if the opportunity arose, that she would make a break for it and wanted to be on her feet.

The women's demeanour changed, and it became more aggressive.

"I want to know where our goods are, and we ask that you hand over the key for us to open wherever it has been hidden" she said.

Valentina hesitated, not sure what she was to say. This wasn't the plan. All of this was to take place tomorrow and the police by now would have taken these people down.

She tried to think quickly, but she was outnumbered. If it was just the woman alone, she may have tried to make a run for it.

Knowing Daniel was in the next room, she took the only course of action she thought was available to her. She screamed at the top of her voice and tried to move to the door to make an exit.

Before she knew what had happened, something struck her from behind and she fell smashing against the lampstand, knocking it to the ground.

One of the men put a bag over her head as they tied her hands. Valentina attempted to scream once again.

The woman looked out the room door and motioned

the men to take Valentina out.

Just as she was being carried out, Daniel exited his room. He had heard the commotion and wanted to check on what was happening. One of the men put Valentina's feet on the ground and rushed at Daniel, throwing a punch. Daniel side stepped the blow, turning to face the man once again.

The man mountain came for a second time, this time lunging at Daniel hips with the intention of picking him up and throwing him against a wall.

He bent down grabbing Daniels hips as Daniel braced himself, but no matter how much he tried, he was unable to lift him. Although Daniel was in good shape, he was by no way so heavy that a man of this strength would not be able to pick him up.

The man stood back as the woman told him to get him out of the way as they were wasting time.

The second man lay Valentina on the floor and chose to throw a kick at Daniel's face. Daniel lifted his hand and blocked the man's leg. Another kick was thrown, and Daniel repeated his blocking of his leg.

Then without any notice, Daniel felt a sharp pain from behind as the woman jabbed a needle in his neck. Daniel began to feel woozy and lost consciousness.

Valentina was once again picked up and transported down the fire escape stairs within the building. She was put into a car and all she remembered after that was waking up with the bag now removed from her head and sitting in an empty room with Daniel sitting not far away from her.

The back of her head was now aching from the blow, she had received earlier.

Daniel came to, maybe ten minutes later. It took some time before he spoke, as he adjusted his eyes to the room.

"What the hell happened?" he said, as he realised Valentina was sitting near him.

"I think we have been kidnapped" Valentina said.

Before either of them could say another word, the door burst open. The woman from earlier with the silk pants was with one of the men, stepping into the room, locking the door behind them.

Valentina was picked up from the floor and placed on

a chair as Daniel continued to sit in his position. His eyes had now adjusted to the light and was mentally trying to work out how they were to get out of their predicament.

The woman grabbed another chair and sat directly opposite Valentina, crossing her legs and lighting up a cigarette, blowing the smoke in Valentina's general direction.

She looked Valentina up and down and then leaned forward now blowing the smoke directly into Valentina's face.

"You have something we need, and I need you to give this to me now. Location and key," she screamed. "Time for games is over."

Valentina wasn't sure what to say. She had neither.

She went to open her mouth, but nothing came out.

The woman slapped her across the face.

"We really have no tolerance for idiot westerners who think they can fool us and take what is ours. Do you know who we are?"

Valentina nodded in the affirmative.

"Good, then let us stop playing and give me some answers" she demanded.

Daniel came to her defence trying to explain that she did not know where the "goods" were being held.

The man gave him a backhand as Valentina corroborated Daniel's answer.

"Jacob was my boyfriend, but I didn't even know he was doing work for you, and he never shared any locations or gave me keys" Valentina answered raising her voice.

Just as she finished her sentence, the woman's phone rang, and she began to speak in Chinese stepping out of the room.

Moments later she returned, informing them that they needed to leave, but would return later that evening. The woman summoned the man that had accompanied her, and they left without hesitation.

Valentina looked down at Daniel, who had a welt across his face from the heavy handiness of the bodyguard.

Both were in some sort of discomfort. Valentina was suffering neck problems, that must have come about from the blow she received earlier at the hotel, as well as a slap to the face.

She stood up, walked awkwardly towards Daniel, and fell to the floor next to him, placing her head on his shoulder.

Daniel encouraged her to begin breathing. To take control of her own system via her breath. Together they did this for around five minutes, until the pain from their faces had subsided. Until they had brought themselves back to a state of focus.

Valentina's legs were tied, enough for her to walk with difficulty, but her hands had been freed when they picked her up and put her on the chair. She had marks on her wrists as the ropes had been held tightly around them and they had been restricting the blood supply, which may explain why they let her hands free.

Daniel was the opposite. They had tied his hands with rope very tightly, but his legs were free. Not that he felt like he could run too far, considering the door has been shut and locked after the pair's departure.

He lay back against the wall with Valentina's face now dropping on his stomach.

Suddenly Daniel sat up, jolting Valentina up as well.

"As your hands are free, he said. I need you to feel around in my pocket for an item I have in there."

"What am I searching for?" Valentina enquired.

"Just put your hand in my left pocket and you will find a metal object, I don't think they would have searched me that thoroughly as they would have been looking for firearms."

Valentina reached in, rummaging around until she felt a small metal object.

"Okay I think you have it, pull it out." Daniel said.

Valentina pulled out this small metal object and held it up in front of her. It was metallic in look. No larger than an oversized matchbox with buttons on the top and side levers. It looked like a kid's toy.

"What is it?" she said.

"Our way out, hopefully." He replied.

He pointed his forehead towards the gadget.

"See the knob on the top there?"

"This one?" Valentina asked.

Daniel nodded.

"Place the base of the gadget against the hinges, I think that will be the weakest spot in the door."

"What the hell is this James Bond gadget Daniel?" asked Valentina.

Daniel ignored the comment and kept instructing her.

"Ok, yes place it right there. Now hold it flat again the hinge and turn the knob gently to the right."

Valentina did as she was instructed. She heard a little noise emitting from the box and waited.

Nothing happened.

"What exactly is it meant to do?" she asked.

Again, ignoring her questioning, he gave further instructions.

"Keep holding it flat and turn the knob to the right just slightly."

Valentina obeyed and waited.

A minute had passed, and she noticed the hinge was trembling. Another minute passed and the hinge snapped.

Valentina turned to Daniel in disbelief. Mouthing the words, 'Oh My God'.

"Quickly move down to the lower one". Daniel firmly asked.

Valentina was straining slightly as her legs were still tied, but loose enough for her to move.

Placing the gadget on the next hinge and waited for a similar reaction as to before. The same thing happened as a couple of minutes earlier. The metal began to vibrate and then crumble.

Daniel stood up.

"Ok now near the keyhole."

Again, the gadget was placed near its target. The keyhole of the lock.

"Turn it up slightly" Daniel demanded.

Valentina did as she was told, knowing that the pair could return at any moment.

A minute passed and nothing happened. Valentina still held the gadget against the door as she had been instructed. They then heard a buzzing noise as the door was being compromised by this little machine in her hand. Suddenly the door cracked and the lock broke.

Without any more effort from this contraption the door creaked open, half of it almost falling completely off its hinges. Only the rust kept it from not falling down to the ground.

Whilst Valentina had been working on the door, Daniel had been working on his ropes. He had been able to manipulate his hands, so that he could wriggle out of them.

He dropped to the floor once free, and untied Valentina's legs.

They grabbed each other's hands and quietly moved down the passageway, being careful not to make any noise. Daniel put a finger to his lips indicting no sounds were to be made.

It was eerily quiet, and they moved with stealth. It appeared that they were at the backroom of some type of call centre. As they could see through glass windows there were people with headsets talking. All sitting in cubicles.

They unlocked the door which led into the call centre and casually walked through as if they worked there, trying not to make eye contact with anyone as they passed through.

They did stand out as being the only non-Asian people in the place, but in places like this, it was not unusual to have non-Asian workers walk through and be given a tour of the facilities. They received funny looks, but most people just focused on their phone calls. And kept their heads down.

Daniel and Valentina found the front door and walked out onto the street as if it was something they did every day of the week, like any other employee. They looked around for their captors, who were nowhere to be seen and scurried down the street hoping not to be noticed.

They ran down a couple of streets, until they ran out of breath, looking for a telephone booth so they could ring Detective Squires and inform him as to their whereabouts.

To no avail, they never found one box and assumed that they must have been removed some time ago.

Daniel had taken notice when they first arrived in the country of where the American and Australian Consulates were situated, just in case they were going to need assistance. Something had told him that with the seriousness of the situation, that there was always a chance that they may need these agencies one day.

As they were unable to go back to the hotel in fear that their captors may return and seek them out there, they decided that a consulate would be the safest option.

They hailed a Tuk Tuk, recognising that it was a form of transport and hopped in, giving the driver directions to get there as soon as possible, as they were in a hurry.

That was a mistake the moment they took a seat as they found no seatbelts and had to hold on for dear life as they whizzed through the streets of Bangkok.

Finally, they arrived, and Daniel paid the driver.

They entered the US Embassy and were taken to meet a consulate official for an interview.

After explaining their ordeal. They were issued with temporary mobile phones to help them in case of emergency, as well being given food and some money. As well as a haven to sleep within the embassy.

Even though Daniel was not a US citizen, it had all been arranged with the Australian authorities, that it was best to keep the two of them together for the time being, until an alternative arrangement could be made.

Detective Squires was called and advised that they were safe and to come to the Embassy for a meeting.

It was not long afterwards that the detective arrived with two officers from the Australian Federal Police (AFP) who were working on the case in Bangkok.

It was evident that the AFP were in charge and Detective Squires was not giving the orders, but instead had been brought in as a conduit between the parties.

The person in charge was a tall man with a chiselled face, by the name of Tom Watkins. Good looks with short dark hair and in good shape. He could have very well been a movie star.

The three men entered the room taking a seat and the five of them sat down to discuss what had happened in the last 24 hours.

"Obviously they suspected that you were being watched or someone tipped them off," said Officer Watkins. "Either way we may have to handle this a little differently. We will place guards on your rooms 24/7 until we can make contact with them once again and work out a new plan. We suspect that someone from within the Thai police, may be an insider, tipping off the gangs.

"What we do need from you is the location of where you were being held, so we can stake that place out.

"We know who the main 'handler' or manager in the country is. He has been under surveillance for some time now. We need to draw him out, so that we can effectively link it all back to their main operations and hopefully take them down globally.

"This problem isn't just one for the Thai people, but especially for Australia. These gangs are working with the bikies there and importing death on a large scale.

"The help you are providing may save many lives. I hear you are a Doctor Ms Russo in an emergency ward, so I guess you see some of the outcomes of the work of these gangs on people that are brought in from drug overdose etc?"

Valentina nodded in the affirmative.

"Yes, I know the damage of drugs," Valentina said. "I have seen it firsthand and the damage that is causes to individuals and their families. Of course, I will assist."

"Thank you, Valentina, we know there is danger, and it is not our usual approach, but we think we are close, and you are of interest to them. They obviously think you know more than you are letting on. This is an opportunity to blow wide open this syndicate.

"We will have our Thai contacts get in touch with them and set up a potential meeting. This time, we will be there with a larger contingent of officers. We won't let you out of our sight."

Daniel and Valentina looked at each other and smiled.

"If you wish for Valentina to do this for you, which is of course of her own free will, then I will need a few things before that" Daniel said.

"And what is that?" asked Officer Watkins.

"If you can give me a piece of paper, I will give you a list of things that I need."

The second AFP officer handed him a notepad and Daniel began to write.

Valentina peered over his shoulder. Trying to get a look at what was so important that it was required to assist.

From what she could see, Daniel was asking for:

- ☐ Screwdrivers
- ☐ Large funnels
- ☐ Wood
- ☐ Metal dials

The list was not long, but long enough.
He handed it to Officer Watkins.
The officer looked down at it and said that he thought that all on the list was possible.
"Oh, and by the way," Daniel added. "I need a workshop that I can work uninterrupted."
The officer tore off the list from the notebook, handing the remainder back to the other AFP officer and spoke.
"Leave it with me. I'll get back to you shortly with our next steps. They will not be happy that they have lost you, but they won't try anything in here at least."
The men left with Detective Squires shaking hands with both of them and telling them that they had a plan and to just be patient.
Both Daniel and Valentina looked at each other, thinking the last plan didn't work, but they agreed to cooperate.
"Don't worry," said Daniel. "I have a plan too."
"What is it?" Valentina asked.
"Can't tell you at this point, but it will blow you away literally."
A consulate member entered and asked them to follow her to their rooms. Following the young lady down a rabbit warren, they were directed to two rooms side-by-side, where they found their belongings, which Australian police had collected and brought to the embassy.
The young women explained that further down the hall led to the toilets and a luncheon room with tea and coffee facilities. They were welcome to use all facilities, but not to enter beyond a door that she pointed out with a sign saying, 'Personnel Only'.
Valentina and Daniel entered their rooms to find that their belongings had been brought from the hotel and were neatly placed on their beds. They rifled through

their belongings to make sure that they still had everything, which to their relief appeared to be intact.

They met in the hallway and walked down to the luncheon room. Valentina made a coffee and Daniel a green tea.

They made some baloney sandwiches and sat to chat.

"I gather that you don't fear death?" Valentina asked.

Daniel just looked at her and calmly spoke.

"With everything you know of me, do you think that I fear moving to a better place? Of course, that doesn't mean I wish to die suffering. I am still in this human shell that is prone to pain."

"I know we have talked about death before," Valentina continued, "but when I was an intern, we used to get told stories of people who would hallucinate prior to their deaths that they were seeing loved ones or old friends and they were talking to them. It was put down to it being the drugs that they were receiving. But now after everything I now know, I would like your take on it. I'm not sure what made me think of that. I guess when you face your own mortality, you question a lot of things."

Daniel sat back in his chair.

"Well, I have told you a little bit about what happens to a person after their death, but prior, well that is an even more interesting conversation.

"You are right that the medical profession thinks that it is just drugs playing havoc with someone's mind. Sometimes they are right. Most times they are wrong. If you do some research, you will find studies that show that in many cases, these people are not on drugs that create any type of hallucination."

"Well, if it isn't the drugs, then what is this phenomenon?" Valentina enquired.

"People always think a human has passed over when the body has died. That is just an indication of human finality for this journey. The end of the avatar, called the body. Essentially when someone is ready to pass, the physical and spiritual worlds begin to merge.

"I liken it a little to having a foot in both camps.

"Sometimes the individual gets confused. They think to themselves, what is happening to me? Other times you may even verbalise that out loud. It can be confusing. They are here and they are partly there. They can't understand what is happening to them as they are beginning to get glimpses of the other side.

"Our loved ones, be it siblings, colleagues, friends that have passed now become visible. As plain as day as you see me now. You will sometimes hear them talking to them as if someone was in the room.

"It gives them solace, but to the outsider, not experiencing this transition, it looks like they are losing their mind, and the only explanation for the uneducated is that it must be the drugs or maybe a lack of oxygen to the brain.

"Instead, the mirror of the soul we call the subconscious is now withdrawing from this earth and the veil is being pulled back and it begins to move to a point that they may even see themselves lying in the bed, wondering who that person is. They may say something like "there is a person in the next room, and they look just like me."

"As the transition is nearing completion and assuming the physical body is in a state that allows them to talk, you will notice usually in the last hours that they are at peace. That the person in the next room, assuming that is what they are seeing, is actually themselves.

"Spirit now begins to talk, as the physical is about to subside."

"You know, that is really beautiful Daniel. I was too young to understand my father's death or observe his passing. It gives me peace of mind to know that.

"I have no fear of what is now coming, even if something were to happen to me in the next few days. I know that life does not end. It just transitions."

Daniel sat forward, placing his hands on Valentina's.

"Your passing is not due yet, Val. There is more work for you to do here. Remember that your life is about your spiritual growth, but it isn't just about your own. Everything you do influences and impacts on other physical beings who are trying to transform their own spiritual journey.

"I believe that you still have personal growth to come. Not just for you, but for others that will need to interact with you for their journeys to progress.

"I have a plan, so let's just take this journey, one human day at a time."

"What plan?" Valentina squealed, and then lowering her voice, remembering where she was.

"All in good time" Daniel replied as he looked directly into her eyes.

The afternoon was uneventful, and Valentina and Daniel chose to meditate together, like they did in the outback to re-energise themselves.

There was a knock on the door and Tom Watkins with Detective Squires stepped inside excusing themselves.

"Sorry to bother you, so late in the afternoon, but we wanted to inform you that we have a plan that we wanted to run by you first, so we are all on the same page.

"We have a Thai officer who is also on the take with the gangs and is our inside source. He tells us that the gang has set a place to meet, and they want him to be your escort to their hideout.

"Our thoughts are to let that happen.

"You would be picked up by this contact, in which we will have their car tracked and we will be close behind at a safe distance. We would then follow them back and capture the whole gang with the senior manager.

"It is our understanding that they will create a diversion and block the vehicle you are travelling in. That way they will be able to take you.

"I know that sounds dangerous, but we will follow you back to their location. Our man will stay with you and will tip us off when the main manager is in the house. When it is safe for us to enter the building and extract you, we will make our arrests."

Daniel protested. "That is way too dangerous a plan and you are using Valentina as bait."

The officer turned to Daniel. "If we arrest them at the initial car blockade, then we will not be able to get to the main man. That's the goal, he insisted. Without the main contact in this country, we have no chain of command back to Canada where we wish to make further arrests and potential take down the whole empire."

Valentina was now sitting on one of the single beds in the room.

"Does anyone want to know what I think?" she said.

"Of course, we do," they all said in unison.

"I think we sometimes forget that these people have never batted an eyelid when it comes to life and death in this world.

"They never sit back and think that what they are doing destroys families. Destroys kids. The same kids I try to save in an emergency ward.

"Do I really want to be put in the firing line? No.

"Do I really want to be just another statistic of this killing? No

"What I do want is to make them pay. If I can't stop it, at least I can reduce it.

"Jacob deserves that. If anything, his life was worth something and this is how I will honour it.

"I have decided, we will do this."

"Ok" said Officer Watkins. "It will happen in around four days. I'll be in touch."

As he was about to leave, he turned back to face Daniel.

"Oh, by the way, we have your workshop and supplies ready to go. You will be picked up in the morning by a driver and it will be ready at your disposal."

The men said their goodbyes and promised to return in the next few days.

Daniel and Valentina looked at each other.

"You know Val, you have an unwavering courage that I admire. Most of us would never agree to this. Why are you?

"Why put yourself in such danger?"

"We both know, she said, that we are not physical beings. We are spiritual. Yes, I may suffer for agreeing to this, but my soul will suffer more for not acting on something that could have benefited mankind. I do this out of love, not recognition."

"Now that was profound," Daniel said. "I wish I had said that."

Daniel sat down on the bed opposite Valentina and crossed his legs.

Valentina went quiet for a while as it was obvious, she had something on her mind.

"You know Daniel, for some reason, I have no fear of dying. I'm not sure why. Something in me has changed and I can't put my finger on it."

"Maybe you have begun a transformation. When you see things from a different perspective, what was important, now loses its shine. What was masked by your own insecurities is no longer based in a lower frequency of fear."

"Can I ask you a question?" Valentina asked.

Valentina put her hands in her lap.

"Just to change the subject a little?"

"Of course, replied Daniel. Nothing has stopped you to date."

"That is true" she continued.

"Ok here it is. I seem to get on a regular basis, dreams, that I'm not sure if sometimes they are real or not. A little like the one in the bush, but in most cases, they are about Jacob coming to visit me.

"Now I know you have explained dreams to me and that is fine, but each time I have them they seem to take place at the same time. I know because I look at my watch or a clock.

"I know this is not a co-incidence, so why is this happening?

"I hope this doesn't sound too weird?" she said.

"Not at all, Daniel replied. If anything, you are receiving signs. A repetition of a number is something from spirit trying to communicate."

"So, Jacob is trying to tell me something?" Valentina asked.

"Potentially this is the case, or one of your guardians that have been assigned to you are giving you hints. It is your job to follow the trail and find out more.

"You get these for various reasons, but one is to sometimes signify something that needs to be heeded or changed. Most of it is found within numerology.

"Now I know a lot of people have mixed views on all of this. Some think it is bullshit and from past superstitions, past down from generation to generation. Maybe they are right or maybe man was more advanced thousands of years ago.

"It is like Astrology. Most people think it is good fun, but nothing more to it. Yet if you read the New Testament in the bible, the three wise men or kings that they refer to follow the stars to find baby Jesus.

"Don't you find it strange that just by looking up at the stars they decided to pack up and leave their kingdoms with expensive and precious gifts, because a star was shining brightly? People who study the stars are astrologists and astronomers. In those times, they are more likely to be astrologists.

"Anyway, I am diverting from your question.

"So what time are these dreams being held?"

"Every time I look at the clock it is 9pm." Valentina answered him.

"Well let's look at numerology and see what it tells us about the path number 9.

"What is your date of birth and see if there is a correlation with this time?"

"The first of July nineteen ninety."

"Ok so 01/07/1990." Daniel said out loud.

"Let's pull this apart starting with the date

"So, you have 01, which equates to 0 +1 = 1.

"Then we have the month, which is 0+7, which equals 7 and finally the year, which is

1+ 9+9+0= 19, which you then add to the other numbers 1+7 +19 = 27. Which when you add the final two numbers of two and seven, you arrive at nine.

Daniel writes it down on a piece of paper for Valentina to see how he got to the nine.

Date =1
Month =7
Year equals= 19

Equals 27 (2+7 = (9 path)

"And funnily enough we come back to a life path of nine as I thought. So, you are a nine path.

"Let me read this from the numerology site, numerology.com. This might give you a little bit more information about this life path, I think it is accurate.

'The 9 Life Path is sensitive to humanity and puts its heart and effort into supporting the greatest good. These people are tolerant, loving, and deeply connected to

their inner wisdom. In this life they'll need to release past pains by learning to address their own needs and values.'

See those in the nine path have massive hearts, but sometimes they forget to help themselves as they are going through their own struggles.

That has been you. Your past resembles many people, in which it holds you back, but you have been transforming and learning the lessons for this path."

"What if my number was something else?" Valentina asked.

"When we talk about the recurrence of numbers, yes, they can have other meanings, and are most likely are signs. In your case I think it is your life path, but of course it could mean something else. Maybe it will reveal itself if that is the case. Each person as I have said many times before is following a path in order to gain Wisdoms. Numerology and numbers can give insights as to what is lacking."

Daniel stretched out his arms. I don't know about you, but I think I need to go for a walk, even if it is in the hallway."

Valentina agreed and they walked around for hours, trying not to disturb the people that worked there as they wandered around within their restricted area.

They retired early to bed that night as Daniel had a lot to do on his 'secret' project'. Even Valentina wasn't privy as to why he needed supplies and a workshop, but she trusted Daniel and knew whatever it was, it would be interesting or helpful.

The next morning Daniel was up bright and early. He grabbed some breakfast and popped his head into Valentina's room to tell her he was leaving as the assigned car would arrive shortly. Valentina begged to join him, but they both knew, she was too important to be leaving the compound until their date in a few days.

Daniel said his farewells and headed out to the lift that took him down to the carpark under the building, in which there was a waiting car, ready for him to be escorted to his workshop location, a short distance away.

He arrived twenty minutes later and was led by his minder/driver into a dimly lit old garage that was assigned to him. In the corner were old car parts and along the wall were different types of tools. There were some new ones in there, which Daniel had requested, as well as soldering irons etc.

It reminded him of his grandfather's old tool shed when he was a kid. Lots of tools lying around. Some on benches and others in their correct place. Mostly dirty and functional. His grandfather was a bit of a handy man and he passed on that trait to his grandson.

Daniel wasted no time, checking that he had received everything he had asked for. Working his way down the list he had in his inner pocket, within his jacket. When he was satisfied that he had everything, he told the soldier that he could leave if he chose to, or he could stand outside to guard.

The soldier chose the latter as he had been assigned to Daniel to ensure his safety.

Daniel set to work, pulling out a blueprint of a contraption from his inner pocket. It was a rough sketch, but Daniel had built something like this before and so it was more a guideline for him.

To the layman, the sketch looked no more than a box with dials and levers. To Daniel, it was going to potentially be Valentina's salvation over the next few days.

He worked solidly for two and a half days on his masterpiece, placing his creation into a vault each night that he had requested to have been placed within the garage. It was a large vault, with a combination, that had been revealed to Daniel before leaving the consulate on his first day there.

Each day he would return to the compound as usual, never discussing his project with Valentina or anyone else. Even though Val would enquire about his day, probing him as to what he was doing whilst away from the compound. All that Daniel would say was that he was 'tinkering away on something.'

An arrangement between the "inside man" who was working with both the police and the drug dealers had been made. The "inside man" had been working directly with the Thai police, but it had been questioned internally as to where his allegiances may lay. His job today was to drive Valentina to her designated destination, which was chosen by the gang, somewhere in a city building a few towns away. The agencies had asked themselves if he was a wise choice, but also knew that it must look like the "inside" informant was independent of them.

Unbeknown to the gangs, the police would be following the vehicle and intended to capture the main 'handler', who they anticipated would eventually lead them right back to their head operations in Canada.

They now had not just the Thai and Australian agencies, but the Drug Enforcement Agency (DEA) from the US and their equivalent from Canada were also involved.

Officer Watkins and Detective Squires were Valentina's contacts and were giving her daily updates as to the timing of the operation.

One afternoon a contingency from the various police agencies arrived as scheduled at the US compound to discuss how they were to tackle the day in question. Daniel was also there, having finished at the workshop for the day.

"Ok, tomorrow is the day," Officer Watkins started. "Operation "Takedown" is now in play."

"You will be driven in a black van with windows fully tinted. Bullet proof of course. We are told they will provide a roadblock around here."

The officer pulls out a map, spreading it across the tables. Pointing to where the roadblock will take place.

"We will place within Valentina's clothing a tracking chip, which will be sewn into the lining. This will be undetectable, even with a pat down. Of course, we will have you followed by a single vehicle, which will keep a visual. Once we are convinced that the big wig has arrived, then we will move in with the teams from the various agencies, supported by Thai police.

"We expect that this will be a straightforward operation, as we will have eyes on you at all times. All we ask of you Valentina, is that you stall them with the information that they require and keep your head down if you hear any shooting.

"Hopefully it won't come to that, as we think they will be outnumbered and choose to try to flee or lay down their arms.

"Any questions?"

"What if they don't lay down their arms?" Daniel asked.

"Well, our man will be on the inside with Valentina. He will tip us off as to numbers of captors with her and their location. We can send in a crack team to extract her when the time is right."

Daniel sat there thinking, this plan is fraught with danger. They have not taken all contingencies into consideration before hatching this plan. In reality this was designed to get them their outcome, without looking at what may happen in the process. We are now too far down the rabbit hole, he thought to himself. Valentina was committed to this cause and had pledged to go ahead with it.

Moreover, didn't they say they didn't really trust their "inside man"?

All, but Daniel was in agreeance that this was the right approach. The men shook hands and said that they would meet the next morning.

Daniel and Valentina bid them a good night and then returned to their rooms.

Valentina dropped onto the bed, laying down and contemplating what was to take place tomorrow. A lot was running through her head. It was now happening all too fast.

Daniel knocked on her door and asked if he could come in.

"Of course, grab a seat" Valentina offered.

"What do you think about tomorrow? Am I doing the right thing? Am I honouring Jacob by doing this?"

"I think you have been honouring Jacob, since the day you met him. Your heart knows if this is what you need to do" Daniel answered her.

"Well, it's too late now, Dan. I said I was in, and I am in" she replied.

"That's fine," said Daniel, pulling out a white box from his pocket.

"Before you go into this, both of us need to have a plan. Our own contingency plan."

Valentina sat up on the bed.

"What did you have in mind?"

Daniel opened the box and inside were what looked like mobile phone ear pods. Like the Apple Air pods.

"What are these for?" asked Valentina. "To communicate with?'

"Before you leave tomorrow, I need you to put these in your ears and hide them behind your long hair, Daniel informed her. No one will notice them if you keep them covered.

"Got it?

"All I will tell you is that, when we give you the sign, you must drop to the floor and lay as flat to the surface as you can."

"But why?" She asked.

"Best not explain. Best you just agree" Daniel replied.

Valentina agreed and asked what the sign would be.

"Think air raid siren. If you hear one, then you are to immediately drop to the ground. Do not even think about it" Daniel insisted.

Val agreed and placed the ear pods on her bedside table, so that she would not forget them the next morning.

Daniel then asked Valentina to test for energy, by placing the palms of her hands apart and slowly bringing them together.

She did as she was asked and instantly felt the energy pulsating between them, as she drew them closer to each other.

"You are ready for this, Daniel insisted. Remember whatever happens, you will need to follow the instructions I have just given you."

Valentina agreed that she would do this.

"Best we now get some sleep. Tomorrow is a big day," Daniel told her as he closed the door to her room.

The next morning, all parties arrived for the pickup. The driver who was the "inside" contact opened the door for Valentina. She was to be escorted alone. Her jacket with the chip inside was delivered to her room the night before and she wore a bullet proof vest underneath it for protection. The informant/driver was not made aware that a "sting" was to take place that day and their whole Asian operation was to be dismantled.

Valentina stepped into the vehicle, which was black on both the outside and in. The windows were a dark tint and there was no way anyone could see inside if you were trying to look in from the outside.

The doors were closed behind her and she buckled up, ready to go. A single vehicle was to follow the van at a safe distance and relay movements back to the team, who would pursue once their destination was established.

Daniel was to ride with his private escort. The soldier that had been with him for the last few days.

His name was Private Peter Whittaker. Daniel felt reasonably safe with Private Whittaker. A tall, well-built African American, who had a wicked sense of humour, which Daniel liked. They both liked to joke around and give each other stick about the other's country and its peculiarities. Australians speak funny and all live in the outback with the crocodiles and Americans spend all day eating hamburgers and fries.

Valentina's vehicle pulled out of the underground carpark. Just her and her Thai driver.

He asked her if she was comfortable and told her not to worry as everything had been planned to an exact time frame. She was in safe hands, he informed her.

He drove at the speed limit, watching the clock on the front panel.

As they drove closer to their target, Valentina calmed herself down, Watching her breathing. Lifting her energy levels. She knew she had to be on her game.

She could hear on the radio between the van and the following vehicle that they were ten minutes out from target and to be on the alert.

Suddenly the driver without warning took a detour and sped up, jostling Valentina around on the back seat. He rushed through the streets as the following vehicle tried to keep up in pursuit.

She could hear on the radio, the officer in the pursuit vehicle questioning her driver.

"Slow down, we cannot keep up. Has something happened? Why are you speeding? Advise your status."

Val was watching the pursuing vehicle from the back window. It was close behind and she could see the officer in it, trying to maintain visual contact by keeping pace.

Out of nowhere, another vehicle slammed into the pursuing vehicle, pushing it across the road. A man got out of the car as if to exchange information. As he approached the car, he pulled out a pistol and shot the officer in the chest two times as the car's window was wound down to exchange words.

Valentina's driver stopped the car and opened her door yelling for her to get out.

A red Audi had pulled up beside them and two men hopped out and grabbed Valentina, almost throwing her into their vehicle.

By now the team back at the compound had been alerted of the situation and were now rushing to vehicles to begin the chase.

Valentina was blind folded as one of the men sat next to her on the back seat. He told her to keep her head down and not make a sound.

She did as she was told and lay down on the back seat, making sure that her ear pods were securely still in place as her hands were not at this stage bound. Daniel had provided her with some sort of plasticene, which was holding them nicely in position.

Sometime later, the noises of cars seemed to disappear and all she could hear were birds chirping.

The car changed direction once again as they began to drive down a dirt road, until they came to a stop. She could hear the noise of gravel beneath their tyres.

Valentina was pulled from the car and was walked by the two men along what she guessed was a pebbled footpath. Eventually coming to a door, she could hear it being opened as they told her to step inside.

They walked down what seemed like a couple of hallways, until she was taken into a room and sat down.

The blindfold was removed and there sitting in front of her were four people.

The two thugs that she had made their acquaintance back at the hotel and the women that had slapped her in the face at her last kidnapping. The last person was the "insider" who was her driver and the connection with the federal agencies. She hoped that his loyalties would be on the right side of the law when the time came.

Her hands were still free, but her legs were now tied. She felt trapped and confused as none of this was going as per plan

The elite team of officers from the various agencies went into action as soon as they realised what had happened, and so did Daniel.

He grabbed Private Whittaker and asked him to go to the workshop as soon as possible.

Private Whittaker was given permission and the two headed out in a compound vehicle assigned to the soldier.

Upon arriving, the Private was encouraged to follow Daniel inside the garage. He watched as Daniel made his way to the vault that had been placed in the workshop some days before.

Daniel began to play with the combination, opening it up after spinning the handles a few times in different directions and hearing a clicking sound.

He yanked it back, to reveal what looked like a box. It was part metallic and part wood.

On the top seemed to have some type of funnel and on the side of it was a casing with levers and dials.

It was crude, but still solid.

Private Whittaker didn't dare ask what it was, but instead helped to carry it out as it was relatively heavy, even though it was only the size of a bread box.

They gently carried it to the car and placed it on the back seat as Daniel hopped in next to it to steady the contraption as they drove to where Valentina was being held captive. The tracking chip in Valentina's jacket gave the agencies the whereabouts of the hideout.

In the meantime, the agency teams were also heading out to the destination in a convoy, which would split up as they arrived at the building, covering all exits. It was a forty-minute drive from the embassy and situated in a rural setting.

The teams were instructed to be far enough out of sight until they were given their orders.

The agency team arrived before Daniel and Private Whittaker. The dwelling appeared to be an old abandoned commercial building. It was large, maybe a two-level building, but not derelict. It just seemed to be out of place in where it was situated. With no other buildings in sight.

The senior members of the team gathered to discuss a plan of action.

Posted on the front of the building were three-armed men from the gang. The agencies believed they could take these men out relatively easily with snipers. Without any idea of what 'eyes' the cartel had on the surrounding building, any move they made would be a risk. They kept their distance.

Just as they were assuming positions, a black SUV pulled up and two men hopped out. Both looked like they were of Thai descent. They stopped for a short period to talk to the guards and then continued inside the building.

It was not long before these men arrived in the inner sanctum of the building, where Valentina was being held captive.

Valentina's mind at first had been racing, but Daniel had spoken to her at length the previous night about how she may handle a situation like this.

He had told her pray for guidance from her guardians.

She knew by now that there are those that sit on the "other side" who are trusted with guiding us. We of course never see them, and many times we put it down to intuition when we are given insights by them.

Their job is to guide and protect. "You can tap into them, by focusing your intent on asking for assistance. They will hear you and come to your aid." Daniel informed her.

Valentina began this practice, knowing that the gang would be asking some heavy questions in a short period, in which she had no answers for any of them.

She closed her eyes, as they the others stopped to greet the new two visitors to the room. She began to focus on asking for protection and as she did so, she felt a presence that wasn't human, standing next to her. She was tuning into their energy. She opened her eyes and noticed two people right by her side, that were not standing there before. She wasn't sure if they were male or female, but she could feel the energy shift around her. She knew that they were not of this world as all she could see were blurred images. Images that are generally naked to the human eye.

A feeling of peace fell over her as she closed and then opened her eyes again. The group had now placed their focus back on her. One of the men was dressed in a jacket and denim jeans. He had a ponytail, a beard, and he was partially balding on top. It was obvious from his gestures and the way the others were reacting to him that he was the boss and the one they had been waiting for.

The women brought him over. He squatted down, to be at eye level with Valentina.

"Today you will give me the key and the location, yes?" he said in his broken English.

Valentina nodded. She knew she was safe but had no idea what she should say or what her guardians standing next to her may do.

The man pulled out a large knife and placed the blade near Valentina's eyes. The light was reflecting off the blade and back onto the ceiling.

"Talk, before I cut," he yelled. "I am a man of little patience."

Before anyone could speak another word, they heard a commotion from outside.

The agencies had chosen to take out the guards with the intention of breaking into the inner sanctum of the building. They had shot two of them, but the third they had been narrowly missed, and he was now firing back.

Agents had the front of the building surrounded and were intent in getting a team in to free Valentina and arrest the head of the gang in Asia.

The woman who was in the room with Valentina stepped outside, and you could hear her yelling to someone instructions about going out and attending to the situation.

Within minutes, heavily armed men were firing back at the agencies. Tom Watkins and his team were taken back as to the amount of manpower and firepower that had been residing within the building.

The gun fire reached the ears of those within the inner sanctum, and they became desperate to get answers.

The man who was the "inside" agent stood behind Valentina grabbing her hair and pulling her head up and back, as the blade came carefully close to her left eye. She could now see the black of the eyes of the man who was intent on cutting her, if she did not come forth with answers.

She closed her eyes and prayed.

Suddenly without warning, Valentina could hear a loud noise. It took her a second to realise it was an air raid siren. Daniel's warning, she thought to herself.

She knew that she had to get to the floor as instructed, but how was she to do that whilst her hair was being held tight by the man behind her, and the leader of the group was now holding a knife to her cheek.

The next thing she knew, she felt a hand pushing her down to the floor and onto her stomach, as she quickly checked her ear pods were still in place. The occupants of the room were now in a state of confusion. The women and the two bodyguards were ordered to go check where the noise was coming from.

Outside Daniel had arrived and started up the air raid siren that he had brought from the workshop. He then set up the bread box shaped machine he had been working on for the last few days with the help of Private Whittaker. They carefully took it out of the back seat and placed it directly in line with the building, with the large half shaped funnel facing the front doors.

He played with the knobs on its sides and began to turn up the dials. As if by magic, each of the men fighting the agencies at the front of the building, put their hands up to their ears and fell to the ground abruptly, shaking on the ground.

With the machine still on, Daniel and Private Whittaker picked it up and ran towards the front door. Agency officers followed in pursuit.

He was met by the Chinese woman and the two men, who had just come out from the back rooms. As the woman opened the front door to begin a gun battle. She too held her ears and fell to the ground with the two men also falling in a heap behind her.

Private Whittaker looked down as could see blood flowing out of their ears.

Whatever this machine is that Daniel had invented, it had devastating effects.

Although the team were cautious as they made their way down each hall. Daniel and Private Whittaker were running. They knew time was of the essence.

By the time he got to Valentina's room, he had to break down the locked door.

They kicked the door in, whilst still pointing the machine in the direction of the room.

Valentina looked up without raising her head.

All she could see were bodies strewn across the floors. Some were shaking violently with blood pouring from their ears.

Each of them appeared to be dying a slow death, and there was nothing anyone could do about it. She lay there waiting.

It was Daniel and Private Whittaker, followed shortly by a heavily armed team.

Daniel ran to her and gave her a hug. The machine has been turned off before they entered the room and now the arriving party surveyed the room of bodies. Checking each one for signs of life. Two of them were still alive, including the big Asian boss.

They untied Valentina's legs and took her away, passing Officer Watkins in the hallway who had arrived shortly behind the team.

No words were exchanged, but a thank you was mouthed by the officer.

Daniel placed Valentina in the back seat of their car and the machine was placed in the boot.

He took a seat next to her as the solider took the wheel.

Valentina was conscious, but weak. Daniel asked the driver to step on it and get them back to the compound asap.

It was too dangerous to take her to a hospital, as it was possible that these establishments may also have operatives loyal to these gangs.

Daniel already knew how to help. He just needed to get

her back to safety first.

He tried to keep her talking as she was nauseated and suffering from headaches. This was to be expected.

Valentina had her head on Daniel's shoulder. "How come I didn't die in there, like the others" she asked wearily.

"Well," Daniel started. "As we were driving over here, I chose to make connection with those from the other side. I went into a deep trance and requested your safety.

"I knew that if I could somehow reduce your exposure to the blast that we were sending, by getting you on the ground, then we had a chance of your survival. The headphones I gave you were extra thick and coated, so that it would give your eardrums some protection, but I knew that you would still have some aftereffects, like you are experiencing now.

"The agencies were intending to have a shootout until they got the main man, and I knew that this would be mean you would end up in the crossfire."

The driver sped up and was now only minutes from their destination.

Daniel continued. "When I made communication, I asked that you find a way to get to the ground and remain safe."

Valentina looked up and recalled that before the mayhem started, she remembered seeing two beings on each side of her, just as the main man was about to cut her cheek.

"Valentina, I don't think you were pushed by any human that was standing behind you. I think those that were sent to protect you intervened. I think those that are always there for you, were covering you with their wings."

Valentina sat up and looked at Daniel.

"You are right, something threw me to the ground. The person holding my hair was pulling me back, not pushing me forward. They would have had to have had very quick reflexes in order push me forward, instead of pulling me backwards.

"Wow, I'm not sure what to think about that, but I do believe it's true."

Valentina, then had a flashback. "I think I have seen these figures before. I mean the guardians that were beside me. I saw them when I had overdosed in LA. They must have been there also. They were the same figures I saw, thinking that they were Christiaan standing beside me. Instead, he had already left my apartment by that stage. My guardians were there and were sent to look over me."

The van pulled up to the gates of the embassy and waved them through.

Valentina was helped into the building by Daniel. Private Whittaker grabbed the machine out of the boot and brought it in with them.

Staff helped them back to their room, where they lay Valentina on the bed. She felt like she had been hit by a Mack truck.

The machine was brought in and placed on a table a few feet away from Valentina.

Daniel stood up and began to fiddle with the nobs. Turning left and then right, until he was satisfied with their positioning.

He instructed Valentina to lay still. He directed the machine towards her and turned it on. It made a small buzzing sound.

Valentina lay there, still feeling the thumping in her brain.

Daniel advised her that she would need to stay there for approximately forty-five minutes as the machine worked its way through her body. If she felt the need to sleep, to just do so.

Valentina did just that, dozing off as the machine did its magic. Other than a tingling Valentina felt no pain as the machine went to work.

Approximately fifty minutes later, she woke to find Daniel gently nudging her.

"How are you feeling?" he said as she gradually came around.

"Fine why do you ask?" she replied.

"Well, an hour ago you were suffering from massive headaches."

Valentina scratched her head and looked around the room as if Daniel had introduced her to some new information for the first time.

"That's right, but I feel absolutely fine. I thought that

machine caused destruction?" Valentina asked.

Daniel looked at Private Whittaker and smiled, high fiving each other.

Valentina was a little confused, but her mind was now clear. No headaches or pains through her body. It was as if nothing had happened.

She turned to Daniel, now remembering the events of the day. She pointed to the machine, sitting on the table and asked what its purpose was.

"Do remember all our conversations about everything vibrates at a frequency?" Daniel asked her.

Valentina nodded. "Yes, I remember everything you said."

"This machine I have made has a dual purpose. On the one hand it can be used to destroy or break down things through the alteration of frequencies. On the other hand, by producing this same alteration at a different frequency, it can realign a human being and bring them back into a healthy state.

"Have you heard of Nikola Tesla?" Daniel asked.

"The car guys?" Valentina replied.

"Not quite, that's Elon Musk's company, but the name comes from the same guy I am about to describe. Nikola Tesla was a brilliant inventor and scientist. He spent a lot of time working with electricity and he is one of the reasons that we have our electricity that we call alternating current today.

"An unusual man who kept to himself, but brilliant at the same time.

"Now one day he decided to test a machine he had built.

"He went out to a building site, that had already completed its steel frame. He put his machine against one of the steel pillars and turned it on, playing with the knobs and adjusting the frequencies.

"Nothing happened.

"He adjusted it again and after a couple of minutes the tower of metal began to vibrate. He said afterwards, that had he left it any longer, he could have easily brought down the whole thing, just with this little contraption.

"He understood that everything has a frequency of its

own and if you attune or alter the frequency, then you can change the structure of it. In this example, he found exactly what the frequency was, and he knew that hitting the right frequency would allow him to topple the structure if he chose to.

"This is the "weapon" element of frequencies. Today I used Tesla's principle to break you out of where you were being held. Military and police today around the world have been developing similar weapons that can attack enemies and subdue them. If I'm right, you can check some of these out on YouTube.

"Of course, on the flip side, you can use this technology to create harmony within humans. To bring their frequency back to a healthy state. A frequency that harmonises the human body, instead of harming it.

"Back in the 1930's a guy by the name of Royal Raymond Rife built a machine that the frequencies could be adjusted to heal people. Later another man by the name Dr James Bare did work on this field as well. Their results were tested with apparently amazing results, but the information was suppressed.

"What I did with yourself was bring your body back into its own equilibrium. When a person is not resonating at the frequency that it should, it will find that they suffer from maladies. For the last hour we have been bringing you back into the right frequency.

"If you take yourself back to indigenous people, they too used sound for healing. Take the original Australian people. They have the didgeridoo, a large wooden instrument that serves this purpose of using sound and frequency to assist with healing.

"So too the Tibetan people who use singing bowls. Metallic bowls in nature that come in different sizes to do the same thing."

Valentina thought back to when she saw a didgeridoo being played back in Australia and how she and Mia attempted to play one back at Uluru in the Northern Territory.

"I wish this type of technology was being researched more, than trying to find further drugs to poison the body." Said Daniel.

"You can only imagine someone arriving from an

advanced planet coming here and wondering why we choose to poison the body, then instead to cure it.

"So, what we have here is a doubled-edged sword. Used either for good or for bad, depending on the motives."

He motioned for Valentina to continue resting as the body was going through its recuperation phase.

"Time for you get rest for a little longer Val," Daniel said.

"Peter and I will go down and grab a coffee. It has been a long day for us too."

With that the men stepped out of the room, closing the door behind them and Valentina lay her head back on the pillow and immediately fell into a nice slumber.

The Power of Love

Later that evening Daniel and Valentina were visited by several members of the various Drug agencies, that had been working on the case. Besides Officer Watkins and Detective Squires was a small man, representing the US Drug Enforcement.

His name was Jack Kennedy, just like the president he told us. He was the commanding officer in charge of this operation and was honoured to be meeting Valentina and Daniel.

He was accompanied by Somsak Chen the representative from the Thai Department of Special Investigations. A short man whose English was limited but smiled a lot.

"All parties wished to thank Valentina for assisting them with the arrest. The main handler for Asia is now in custody, having survived the ordeal, and is to be interrogated and processed in the near future." Jack said to Valentina.

To date the group had little success in bringing down the leader of the global organisation, but they were in contact with Canadian authorities. It was just a matter of time. He explained to everyone.

In their eyes, today's events were seen as having been a successful operation as it broke the back of a major syndicate in Asia.

"We know that you have gone to great lengths to assist us. This has broken a chain that trails all the way back from Thailand to the top of the gang. We now must connect the dots to Canada," he said.

"Do not think we will forget your assistance in this matter and in appreciation, we have a surprise for you."

"A surprise, Valentina asked. What is it?"

"We will reveal this shortly. You will hear more in the next few days before your departure."

"I know that you have been through a lot lately, but if you are able to assist with one last favour, we would appreciate it."

Valentina looked at him, wondering what favour they now wanting from her.

"We were all wondering," Jack now continuing, "if you could reveal where the key was that the cartel kept talking about? If you could reveal anything you know that would assist the Thai police, as they are keen to retrieve the haul as evidence."

Detective Squires and Officer Watkins looked away embarrassed that Jack had brought this topic up once more.

"As I mentioned back in Australia, I have no idea where the drugs are or the key to retrieve them." Valentina advised the officer.

Jack Kennedy clapped his hands and said, "I think it is time for a celebratory drink."

They moved the party to a function room within the embassy, so that more of the team could join in and move around freely.

Everyone was given a drink of some description.

Jack Kennedy stood on a chair and made a speech.

"I would like to make a toast to our friends from Thailand and Australia for a job well done. There is still a lot more to do. I would like specially to thank Daniel for his assistance that he provided with his contraption, that we would like to take a better look at if he would allow us."

"A little too late," Daniel yelled back. "It has already been dismantled."

"And finally," Jack said. "I would like to thank the hero of this story, Valentina, who still proceeded with the mission, knowing the dangers that potentially lay ahead. God bless America.

"Please raise your glasses.

"To Valentina."

The room raised their drinks and clapped celebrating a win for one day in the fight against the drug cartels.

After about an hour Detective Squires pulled both Valentina and Daniel aside. Asking them to step out into the hallway.

He again congratulated them and then became a little more serious.

"We need you to do one more thing for us. Don't worry this one is not dangerous, and it may even bring you potentially some relief."

"So, what is it?" Valentina asked

"It's a surprise and all will be revealed tomorrow as Jack mentioned before. Both of you will need to be ready to travel, by 8.30am. Don't bother packing your luggage, you won't be leaving the country yet, but you will need to bring your passports."

Daniel and Valentina had no idea what to expect but agreed that they would be ready the next morning.

All returned to the room to celebrate with the different agencies and enjoy their time together discussing what had been a very successful day. Tomorrow would be different as apparently there was a surprise in store for them. Something to now look forward to.

The next morning both Daniel and Valentina were up early. They ate breakfast, wondering what today's surprise may entail. They thought that maybe they may get some sightseeing in before they were to depart. That would be good to see a little of Thailand before they needed to go home.

They were picked up promptly at 8.30 am, this time driven by Detective Squires. They were both excited and refreshed. Their energy levels were up, and they were pumped to go out of the compound without fear.

The drive only took around thirty minutes, as they turned in and toward the car park of the Bang Kwang Central Prison.

The Detective turned around to face the pair.

"As you may have realised, we are currently situated on the grounds of the Bang Kwang Central Prison, famously known as the Bangkok Hilton. Unlike any Hilton in the world, this is not one that you will find Paris Hilton, nor will you ever want to stay here. No luxury soaps found in their bathrooms.

"Locally the prison is known as "Big Tiger" because of its tendencies to eat and stalk its prisoners.

"It is notorious for its bad living conditions, where hundreds of people can be found in the same jail cell, sleeping on floors without mattresses in cramped environments. This jail is a men-only institution.

"I would like you to prepare yourself for what you are about to see, but I am sure you will find it educational."

They all stepped out of car, putting on their sunglasses

and hats.

"Do you think, he wants us to see what drug trafficking does to people?" Valentina whispered to Daniel.

"Maybe" Daniel replied, "but whatever we see I'm sure it will be interesting."

The three of them went through normal procedure of administration for admission and any declaring any belongings, including their wallets and phones were locked away in a safe, before they were taken to a waiting area. This only happened after a vigorous pat down by one of the guards.

Although Thailand has a hot climate, it seemed so much hotter, as they waited for their tour of the facilities.

Eventually a prison guard called everyone who was in the waiting area to follow him. They led them down a corridor, until they reached an area where there were several booths, that were all numbered. Detective Squires chose not to stay with them. Although he did stay with the group until they reached the booths, whispering something to one of the guards and pointing to Valentina and Daniel. The guard asked both of them to go to booth 3 and to wait as the Detective made his way back to the foyer at the front from where they had been waiting previously.

Valentina took a seat on an old wooden stool as Daniel stood next to her. There was a phone in front of them, as they stared at a weathered, plastic window. On the other side directly opposite was another booth also with a plastic shield, sitting this time behind bars.

They waited, expecting to get a presentation from the guards about what this room was all about, just like any other tourist information session.

Then from the corner of the room they heard some noise as prisoners began pouring into the booths on the others side of the barriers. They were of all shapes and sizes and nationalities. Mostly Thai, but some were Caucasian.

Daniel knew it was not uncommon for visitors to the country to go to their local embassy and gain a list of prisoners from their countries. Visiting them out of compassion to see if in some way they could help or provide some comfort to foreign prisoners far away from home. He gathered that this was what they were experiencing here. An understanding of prison life through the eyes of a prisoner.

The booths began to fill up one-by-one as each visitor would sit quietly waiting for a prisoner to sit opposite them and hear their story.

A tall man with a bandage across most of his face and hair walked slowly towards their opposing booth as a guard directed him to take a seat there. He was obviously Caucasian and worse for wear from his living conditions. He walked slowly, like a man without a reason to get up in the morning.

He sat down and picked up the phone, pointing for them to do the same.

Daniel chose to pick up before Valentina, as they had no idea what this person was like. His instinct was to protect her, even if they were behind barriers.

As Daniel put the phone to his ear, the man spoke.

"Daniel," said the man. "It's me."

Daniel was a little taken back and was trying to process how this prisoner could possibly know his name, unless of course they were given their details prior to this sit down, which was very possible. The authorities here had taken down enough details before allowing any of them into the complex.

"I guess you don't recognise me," the man continued, "maybe I have too much shit on my face."

The man slowly pulled back the bandage showing a Caucasian man with scars on the left-hand side of his face and head. This was a man who had been in the "wars".

Valentina and Daniel both looked carefully as something seemed familiar about his features.

Down the phone they could hear the man speak. "It's me Jacob guys, I am so happy to see you both, and together. I was told that you were here, but I can't believe that its actually true."

Luckily Valentina was sitting down as she felt faint on her rickety stool.

"Pass her the phone" Jacob said to Daniel, pointing to Valentina.

Valentina grabbed the receiver and put her mouth to the mouthpiece.

"Is it really you? ... But you are dead. We were told that you were dead." Valentina said in a low voice.

"Babe, I should be dead. For what I was contemplating to do, I should be dead, but I changed my mind. I thought of you and what you would think of me if I were to have gone ahead with it. Of course, my plan didn't quite work, and I ended up here."

"How many years do you have? We will get you the best lawyers, we will get you out." Valentina excitingly answered him.

"Babe, stop." Jacob insisted.

"I am on death row. I will most likely never leave here alive, but I am appealing my sentence, so who knows, maybe one day I will see the shores of Australia or the clubs in LA once again. God, I miss our life. I stuffed up really bad" he said as you could hear his voice falter.

Jacob when on to explain what had happened that day.

He was visited by the gang who had been instructed to retrieve their drugs and then "remove" him. Events of the day happened too fast, and some wrong decisions were made by all parties, resulting in the death of one of his colleagues, Robert Bastion.

"Somehow they knew I had no intention of making the delivery and they came after me. It was worth a lot of money to them, and I don't think they were intent on killing me at first. Well not until they got what they had come to the hotel for. It happened all too fast, and I got shot in the back of the head. It was just a flesh wound as it grazed my skull. Bloody painful, but not life threatening.

"I was taken away by police and was to be dumped or something, but one of them realised I was still alive, and told the other he would attend to my disposal.

"I'm not sure why he took pity on me, but he cleaned me up and instead of putting a bullet in my head, he brought me here. I'm not sure what is better, being dead or trying to survive in this hell hole.

"We pretty much eat maggots to survive and I'm not talking figuratively. Food is bad as you are expected to buy your own or eat the slop that is served out. Unfortunately, I didn't come with a bag of money, and I have been trying to lay low as I'm sure many of my cell mates could be employees of the drug gangs."

Valentina shed a tear. Both of happiness and of sadness.

They spoke a little longer promising to get money to provide him with food as it was obvious, he had lost a lot of weight, and that they would liaise with a lawyer for his defence.

Jacob held his hands against the plastic, that sat behind the bars looking at Valentina.

He stood up looking deep into her eyes.

"Please let me go..."

The phone clicked off as he was in mid-sentence.

The prisoners were all summoned back, and Jacob once again covered his face, strolling back to where he had come from, following the others down a narrow corridor.

Daniel and Valentina were ushered back with the other visitors back to the waiting area, where Detective Squires was waiting patiently.

Valentina felt mixed emotions. She wasn't sure if she should cry or yell with glee.

She was still in a state of shock from seeing Jacob.

She then turned to the Detective.

"How long have you known about him being alive?"

"We only found out about a week ago ourselves. We kept it from you until now as we needed you focused on the task at hand and to be honest, we weren't sure at first that it was really him. We also didn't want to put him in any more danger than he potentially is already.

"I mean it was the consulate that first told us that he was dead."

The three walked back out through the front gates and back to their vehicle.

"So, what now?" Daniel asked.

"How do we get him out?"

"Easier said than done" The Detective replied.

"This is Thailand, they don't take kindly to drug related offences. Especially from foreigners."

"So, we get good lawyers, and we appeal, Daniel retorted. Anyway, he was never caught with drugs in his possession."

"According to court records," said the detective, "it states that he did have drugs on his body. Most likely planted on him when he was admitted. He has an appeal in a couple of months, I believe. Proving your innocence in these types of cases, when apparently you have been caught red handed is difficult to fight in any country. Especially this one."

Daniel and Valentina spent another day in Thailand, before leaving the country to return home.

In that period, they organised money to go into Jacob's prison account to buy food and necessities, as well as liaising with his legal counsel to ensure that he would at least have a fighting chance in court.

They left early on their final day to get to the airport, travelling together talking about anything and everything. They had experienced more than most in such a short time frame.

They vowed to come back for Jacob's trial and keep in touch in the meantime.

Daniel saw Valentina off at her gate as she boarded her plane back to the states. She was tearful for so many reasons.

One was finding and potentially losing Jacob again. Another was saying goodbye to her friend Daniel, who had now become her protector and confidant.

They hugged and kissed each other goodbye.

"Talk soon," Valentina yelled back. "See you back here in a couple of months."

They never saw Detective Squires again, as he was to return home the next day after completing his work with the task force.

The plane trip home for Valentina was one of sadness, but also hope. She knew she had to return to work but wondered if it would ever really fulfill her again.

She had experienced so much in this period and had grown as a person. A spiritual awakening had taken place in her.

She now saw the world differently than ever before. Daniel had taught her to see it through spiritual eyes and for the first time, she was seeing it not through black coloured glasses as she used to see everything, but she now saw it as a much bigger universe of connected beings. Not in a bad way, but almost like a helicopter view of what *possibility* means.

Val arrived home and was greeted by Mia and family, who had not seen her for such a long time. She had so many stories to tell.

Life went back to some normality back at the hospital, but she no longer felt that it was for her. She kept up her spiritual practices, she was taught and even with the worry of Jacob, she was at peace, but not totally content.

Valentina quit her job after six weeks, thanking all those that had supported her.

She booked her tickets to go to Thailand to go to Jacob's hearing that was only weeks away.

Everything was packed and ready to go when she received a phone call from Daniel.

"Hey Val, how are you?"

"I'm great, she replied. Looking forward to seeing you again and of course Jacob. I have so much to ask him."

"That's why I am ringing. There have been some issues in Thailand."

"Problems with his trial?" she asked.

"Take a seat Valentina, I need to tell you what has happened."

Valentina sat down as instructed, fearing the worst.

"I have received a call from the Australian consulate in Thailand. It appears that Jacob has been in a fight."

"Is he ok?" Val asked concerned as to Jacob's well-being.

"Jails in Thailand are very hard; Val. Foreigners can get picked on by the locals in these establishments and eventually these lead to organised fights.

"Jacob was challenged and to survive he had to accept a challenge. He had no choice, but to defend himself. He had never really recovered from the injuries he had sustained from prior to being admitted into the jail system. Eventually like many Caucasians he became a target for stronger inmates.

"I believe he was challenged to fight, and he accepted to not appear weak. From third party accounts, it is believed he put up a good show. Fought hard, but the man he was up against was an experienced Thai boxer and injured Jacob badly.

"He didn't die from his injuries in the fight, but that night, someone had a homemade shiv. A makeshift knife from something like a toothbrush ground down to a point and he was stabbed while he was resting. Unfortunately, there was no assistance that came to his aid. There are never any witnesses in these places, even when you have two hundred people in the same cell.

"We are not sure if it was just an internal conflict within the jail or if the gang caught up with him and paid someone to do the job. The consulate suspects it may be the latter.

"Valentina, Jacob is dead. He didn't survive his injuries that night."

Val went quiet.

She composed herself and spoke again.

"Love you Daniel, thank you for informing me, but I have a bit to process."

"Me too," said Daniel. "I know we can talk about this later, but I would like you to come back to Australia for a break. We could both go to the Gold Coast, and you could see where Jacob was brought up."

"I'll think about." she said.

Valentina howled. She knew that she may never have touched Jacob again, but she had hope. She knew that he was on death row, but there is always part of you, that thinks that a path may change, even when the individual has chosen it.

She knew that Jacob had followed his path and that his decisions and choices had led him to this point. What she knew even better was that he was now free. That he had a chance to have his own "Review" and one day he would return with another opportunity to make things right and gain his learnings.

He wasn't gone, he had just transcended.

Valentina took Daniel up on his offer and arrived six weeks later. Rebooking her Thailand airfares to the Gold Coast in Queensland Australia. The birthplace of Jacob Spriggs.

The flight was long and tiring and again she had to

pass through Sydney airport and catch a local carrier up to Queensland on the Gold Coast.

Daniel had arrived a few days earlier and had hired a car to pick her up from the airport.

The plane arrived and unlike many airports she had been through in her life, she was required to depart on the actual tarmac. She stepped out of the plane to lots of sunlight and humidity.

She walked down the winding ramp, until she hit ground and took the short walk from plane to the airport terminal. She followed the signs that took her through a large food court, past the toilets, until she went through the security doors, manned by a sole woman.

She entered the doors and saw Daniel, running to him and giving him a big hug. It felt like two souls reconnecting.

She gave him a big kiss on the lips, which took him back, but he accepted her enthusiasm without fuss.

He grabbed her carry-on bag, and they went to the baggage carousals to wait for her bags to come out. They headed out the doors with bags in tow and headed across the road to the short-term car park, where Daniel's hire car was now waiting.

He popped the boot and put her luggage in as Valentina got out her sunglasses and hopped into the car, stretching her legs out, whilst she put on her seat belt.

"Ok, welcome to the Gold Coast. It should take us approximately an hour to get to our hotel, depending on traffic." Daniel said as if he was a tour director.

"The suburb we are going to is called Surfers Paradise and it is very popular with the tourists, so I'm sure you will enjoy."

The drive was a pleasant one as Valentina looked out at the small shopping strips along the highway as they travelled. People were dressed in their shorts, swimwear and flipflops. It was very different to Alice Springs and the weather made her think of Florida.

They eventually hit Surfers Paradise, and she could see the ocean as they drove along the Esplanade. It was beautiful, with people sprawled all over the beaches. Some tanning, others playing beach volleyball, and many were in the water enjoying the beautiful Pacific Ocean.

"Here we are" announced Daniel, as they turned into a large high-rise hotel.

Valentina looked up and saw the name. On the front it spelt the words SOUL.

"Are you kidding me?" she yelled. "This place is called Soul?"

"Sure is, and I thought it was appropriate. Probably the best hotel on the Gold Coast with seventy-six floors of luxury and ocean views straight from your balcony."

Obviously, Daniel had money.

They parked below the building and took the lift to their room. Level 55, as Daniel had already checked in some days earlier.

When they entered the room, Valentina was hit by a beautiful view of the ocean and she could feel the sea breeze flowing through, hitting her face. It was a large two-bedroom apartment with all amenities, including a kitchen.

Daniel led her to her room, which was on the opposite side of the apartment to his. He gave her the master bedroom, which had its own bathroom.

She began to do some unpacking but was exhausted from her flights and instead asked Daniel if it was ok, that she got some sleep to refresh.

He naturally agreed and said that he would head over to the supermarket nearby and grab some snacks, drinks etc for them.

Valentina hopped into bed and fell asleep immediately, taking in the serenity of the room, whilst she could hear the splashing from the pool below.

When she woke, she hopped into the shower and changed clothes before re-entering the loungeroom where Daniel was sitting sipping a red wine. He offered her one and she asked if they could go explore their surroundings instead.

They headed down back to ground level and walked out through the arcades into Surfers Paradise.

There were many people around and it was obviously a tourist destination. People were in all types of summer attire. There were couples, singles, and families all enjoying this beach haven.

The main street was called Cavill Avenue and it was

lined with shops and restaurants on each side. No cars were allowed in this area and on the side was a mid-sized undercover shopping centre.

There were people of all nationalities, Japanese, Indian, Arab speaking countries and of course Australians.

They chose to sit down at one of the iconic restaurants called 'Charlies', to grab something to eat and drink, whilst watching all the people heading back and forth. To and from the beach.

Daniel went up to order and returned saying, "Check out the thong on that guy."

Valentina looked over the railing to see what he was talking about, trying to find a man wearing a thong.

Daniel laughed, pointing out the guy in the near distance to her left. Wearing big, large flipflops.

He pointed down to the guy's feet and Val could see he was wearing oversized pink flipflops.

"A thong in Australia means two things." Daniel said. "One meaning is that it is another word for flipflops. We call them "thongs" and the other one is the same as in the States, and we call that a "thong" in the singular. The one between your legs" he laughed, as he watched Val's confusion.

"What a confusing country" Valentina quipped.

The place was bustling, and the people were relaxed. She saw tourists walking up to two beautiful girls wearing gold bikinis with a sash across their chests. Maybe they had just won a local beauty contest she thought to herself.

"They are Meter Maids," Daniel informed her.

"Many years ago, they introduced coin operated car parking meters on the streets to stop people leaving their cars all day and hogging the carparks, whilst spending the day at the beach. Instead, it stopped people wanting to come into Surfers and do their shopping. So, they came up with the idea of having these girls go put coins in the meters, so people wouldn't get a fine and then spend their money, hopefully at the traders.

"I'm not sure if they still do this, but today they raise money for charities, by walking around and having their photo taken with tourists. Lots of people get their photo taken with them."

Valentina took a sip of her strawberry milkshake that

she had ordered and smiled. "So, this is where you and Jacob lived?"

"Well not exactly here, but I'll show you tomorrow. Surfers Paradise was a special place for us when we were younger. I taught Jacob to ride a surfboard here when he was still very young. Surfing is popular with Gold Coast kids, and so is the water, as it has a connection to those that live up here.

"If people, don't live on the water, they love to go to it. Most kids can swim and many of them join the lifesaving clubs and become what they call "nippers". Young surf lifesaving guards in training.

"The Gold Coast literally has water everywhere. Ocean, canals, swimming pools. It's part of life for those that live in this part of the world."

"I love that," Valentina replied. "So, water has an affinity for you?"

"I guess it has, just as it does with Australian indigenous people."

They spent the day walking around, even heading over to the Q1 building where Daniel once lived.

That night they walked out near the night clubs on Orchid Avenue and people watched, as young adults came out in their clubbing gear. There were people of all ages out for a night's entertainment.

Valentina loved the atmosphere, but deep down felt something was missing.

The next day they travelled down to the suburb of Robina. Today famous for its large shopping centre. Daniel drove her past the old home, pointing out where Jacob's bedroom was situated at the front of the wooden dwelling.

It was a basic three-bedroom home with a large carport on the side.

They spent the next few days seeing the sites, attending the theme parks, like Sea World and Movie World and on the second last evening of their stay, they headed to the suburb of Main Beach.

Daniel pulled up in a side street and stopped in a carpark near a shop called Peter's Fish Market. It was just a stone's throw away from the Versace hotel.

They both got out and walked into a nice shop with all

types of fish caught that day. Fish that they either sold fresh or cooked for you, whilst you waited.

They each ordered some hot chips, flake, and a couple of potato scallops or what some in Australia call, potato cakes. A thin sliced piece of potato battered and deep-fried.

When their order was ready, they took the food and headed back to the car. Even though there were available tables outside that they could sit at. Daniel said, "let's go somewhere else. I have a special place we can sit."

They drove for a short while until they hit another carpark that was near the water. Grabbing their food, they headed out towards a walkway. Until they reached the end to sit and eat their dinner.

"This area is called "The Spit" Daniel informed her. The Spit extends into the seaway and is the gateway between the Gold Coast Broadwater and the open ocean. I have always found it a special place to reflect."

They enjoyed their meal chatting about life and sometimes reminiscing about Jacob.

The Glue

The week was enjoyable, relaxing, and peaceful. Valentina was even given some surf lessons by Daniel, in which surprisingly she did well for a beginner.

Alas her stay was to end in a couple of days, but she was glad she had made the trip. It was Jacob's hometown and she felt she had honoured him.

She was sitting on the balcony with her feet stretched out just relaxing, before Daniel and her were to head downstairs to have breakfast.

Daniel came out to join her and placed his hand gently on her shoulder in order not to startle her. He smiled as he took a seat. Also looking out to the water.

"Today, I have something special for us to do."

"What did you have in mind?" Valentina asked.

"You will have to wait for it, but it will bring completion."

Valentina laid back on her chair and looked out to the beach, where many people had begun their daily ritual of walking along the sand.

The two of them had a brunch, after walking around on the beach themselves, feeling the sand between their toes and watching kids making sandcastles as pretty girls were taking selfies, for Instagram.

Eventually they made their way further down the beach to a quieter area. As they approached, they found a large group of people waiting near the water's edge. Many of them recognised Daniel, hugging him, high-fiving and shaking hands.

Daniel turned to Valentina with a big grin on his face.

"Come meet some friends, Valentina. Come and meet Jacob's friends."

Jacob had been part of the surfing community on the Gold Coast and many people remembered him.

"Today," Daniel said, "we will remember Jacob."

He pointed out to the ocean and told her that we were all going to paddle out.

He yelled to everyone to get on their boards and begin the paddling. They all grabbed a board and ran into the ocean. Friends has brought boards for both Valentina and Daniel to use that day.

Not a lot of noise was made as they moved quickly to get onto the water.

Valentina did the same and paddled out with the group until they reached an area that they agreed was appropriate for them to stop and form a large circle of boards.

Daniel lagged a little behind the group and could be seen paddling with an object on his board that was glittering in the sun.

As he neared the group, he paddled to be next to Valentina. She looked down at his board and saw a small metal vase. She guessed that it was an urn and Daniel caught her eye and nodded. It was Jacob's ashes. Daniel had arranged to have them sent to him after Jacob's death. Today was the most appropriate day to let him be given back to the living water.

Each surfer held hands to make up the circle. They were around fifty strong, both male and female.

Daniel grabbed Valentina's hand and said, "This is your last lesson today, Valentina. I want you to absorb it and make it part of you."

"What's the lesson?" she whispered back.

Some of Jacobs friends made speeches, talked about Jacob as a boy who was sometimes known as the wild child. Others talked about his good heart and how he would do anything for a mate.

No one spoke for a while, and you could hear the splashing of water against the surf boards as the group continued to hold hands.

Daniel, then paddled to the middle of the circle with the urn in one hand.

He looked around the group and spoke loudly.

"Jacob meant a lot to all of you, and you also meant a lot to him. I didn't spend as much time with him as he became a man, but I knew him as he was growing up. I taught him to ride a bike and to surf.

"Jacob had his faults, there is no doubt about that, but then he was no different to all of us. We all carry our failures with us every single day of our lives.

"He had it tough. His old man wasn't the easiest person to get along with and Jacob copped the brunt of it along with our mother. In all honesty, it was at times, a hell for him. One that no child should experience. He unfortunately felt the back of a hand or a full clenched fist on more than one occasion.

"He rarely complained, he just got on with it. Jacob will be remembered for his ability to become one with a person. To have this innate ability to listen and turn any day that was black into sunshine."

Daniel turned to look directly at Valentina.

"What Jacob had, which I am sure most of you here know, is that Jacob related to people. When you met him, you liked him. When you spoke to him, you wanted to listen to him.

"When you touched him, you knew that he would pass on a part of himself that you needed to get through the day."

Daniel motioned for Valentina to paddle out in the middle with him as the circle got that little bit smaller, as the group again joined hands.

You could hear tears from both men and women.

"Jacob understood instinctively that he was connected to others and that connection spread further than just the sands of the Gold Coast. He would never say he was spiritual, as many of his demons controlled him at times, but Jacob knew that we were all connected, and that love is what was that glue. The glue that makes humans transcend humanity to become God-like.

Like a spider's web, his energy was able to spread across to others, encasing them.

"I ask that you never forget my brother. You carry him in your heart as a fellow traveller of the waves.

"For those of you that haven't met Valentina yet, she was Jacob's partner. Their connection was this love that carried them through several countries.

"We celebrate your life Jacob because you are like us. Someone trying to find purpose on a journey, whilst honouring your human connection to the spiritual world. We know you have now journeyed home, without pain or suffering that you endured here."

He then handed the urn to Valentina and asked that she now empty it back into the ocean.

As she did so, the group put their hands in the water

splashing them around. Some threw flowers that they had brought with them in their teeth, as they paddled their way out.

As the ashes were caught by the gentle wind, hitting the water, Valentina felt at that very moment, something passing through her. She was never able to explain or describe the sensation, but she knew that it was Jacob. Holding her hand, like he always did.

At that point, she knew her last lesson was understanding that our connection to loved ones do not stop because the physical does. The energy of love can always be felt if we choose to continue to connect to it.

Daniel explained later that many of us still try to connect to the dense physical energy of the body after someone has died. We visit graves because it makes us feel better. The spirit was never there. Of course, it is there when you call upon it.

Connection never stops because of physical departure. It's always connected, you just focus your intent, and they will hear you.

The group yelled as the final ashes fell from the urn. They held hands again and in their own way prayed for their brother that his journey would be a safe one.

Both Daniel and Valentina knew he would be back.

The group spent the afternoon on the beach and into the night. They kept the noise down as the beach was close to nearby apartments.

Daniel had a small group around him as they sat enjoying the warm night's air.

Valentina sat by his side, crossed legged on the sand as Daniel began to talk to the small group around him.

"You know when I was a boy back in Alice, I sometimes felt that I was an outsider. I didn't come from the town. Maybe in some ways I was different. It took me a while to connect to people.

"In time I changed, and when I changed, so did my experiences. My relationships and barriers melted into a different wavelength.

"What I want to do is help you understand the final phase of your reason for being here."

Those that had known Daniel for a long time, were keen to hear his thoughts. Many knew his story about his near-death experience and his teachings. They were always keen to gain more knowledge from his wisdom.

"I want you to imagine a pond" he said. "A body of water that each droplet is connected to the next. When you look upon it, it makes up a mass of water.

"Together it is quiet and still. The water that is sitting at your feet is distant and separated to the water on the other side of the pond.

"Then you grab a stone and like when you were young, you skim it across the top of the water, creating ripples, as one droplet affects the next, well beyond where the stone touched it originally.

"Now we know that the ripple will never make its way to the other side. As its force is not affected by such a small stone, and the interruption to the pond is minor.

"Now imagine if we dropped in a much larger stone or at least a larger composition of dirt. A massive boulder or even a meteorite into the same pond.

"Would the ripple be larger or smaller?" he asked them.

They all agreed it would naturally have to be larger.

"See even though we can now see the ripple across all of the pond, it is still the same composition of water, is it not? When we use the larger stone, the ripple is far more powerful as it travels now further. In other words, as a separate stone, it causes some waves, but as a large mass it has the power to create a change in the dynamics of the water."

The group sat quietly trying to grasp where he was going with this.

"As an individual Soul, you are able to create a ripple effect. It will affect those generally around you and a little beyond. But Souls were not meant to be separate stones. They are meant to be part of a larger composition.

"Not a pond, but an ocean.

"You are not meant to be separated from each other; you are meant to be like separate consciousness that connects as if it were one. Like in a concert, which makes up a choir. Not just a soloist.

"This is what we call a "Unity Consciousness", whereby the one spirit moves through everything. The only way to be disconnected from it, is to make a conscious decision to not be part of something greater. To push it away and make your spirit lesser. To take on a vibration that is so dense that you become weaker by your very thoughts. Yet even with this disconnection, you are still part of the ONE.

"To allow vibration to enhance, you need to learn to surrender to the thinking that you are following a path back to the source and that each person you experience on earth is part of the ultimate fabric.

"Many of you think, you have been separated from Jacob by his passing, but that is never the case. Spirit transcends any physical barriers. To become one, Souls will travel together through incarnations. I may have mentioned this before, but it is an important point to understand.

"As you take on physical manifestations, your soul "group" will regroup and come back to learn lessons together, until eventually, over many lives, you resonate or vibrate at the same levels, so that you can move closer to the source.

"You have many names for the source. Some of you scall this source God, others say the Universe. No matter what way you articulate it to be, it is the same thing. The highest vibrating consciousness that we aim to go back to. It is where we came from.

"To connect, we need to learn how to change our frequency. Like changing a radio or TV channel. If we transmit at a different frequency, then we do not usually pick up the station we want. We do pick up something, but not necessarily a station with images and audio.

"Connection with others isn't always easy, especially if their frequency is at a different level.

So here is the challenge for humanity. To learn to change it and to gain a spiritual view of the world we have created. To become one with the Unity Consciousness and raise our vibration.

"The physical view is easy. Just open your eyes, it's all around you. The spiritual world is not through these physical eyes. It comes by reconnecting back to a higher YOU. One that exists elsewhere. One that your physical eyes will never see. A vibration so high that we humans call it love. Love is the Universe's vibration and is the glue to everything.

"If you were to imagine the spiritual world of a never-ending piece of patch quilt. You make up part of that quilt, once you are at the same frequency as the rest of it.

"Together as one, you create the "Face of God."

"You create the fabric of The Universe."

Daniel looked around the group of six sitting around him and reached out for a bottle of beer to cleanse his parched throat.

Daniel sat back and put his legs out to give himself a stretch.

"So, none of us are disconnected from Jacob. I guarantee you Jacob was sitting in the middle of that ring on the water we formed. Why? Because we called him."

Daniel, then stopped talking. He let everything that he had just spoken about to the small group gathered sink in. To integrate it with their model of the world. He knew he was repeating himself but was hoping that new perspectives were beginning to form.

No one spoke for a while. They all understood the final part of why we are all here.

Reconnection with the Source, by connection with each other.

"This is why you can create change by putting together large groups of people who focus their intent and pray on the same thing. Even if these people are separated across the world, they are connected and can push a combined vibration to get a result."

The group had been so engrossed in their learnings that they had not realised that the larger party was pretty much dispersing. Everyone knew not to interrupt a teaching by Daniel as it usually meant a lot to the listener.

Finally, this small group decided it was time to go their separate ways. They all hugged each other, and each went to Valentina, as someone who was now one of them.

Daniel and Valentina decided to head into the suburb of Broadbeach and have a late supper.

They held hands like they had known each other forever.

Wandering the main street of Broadbeach, they found a nice restaurant and took a seat.

It was busy and people were still sitting in restaurants

and bars or walking along the street eating ice cream.

Valentina and Daniel ordered some drinks and some desserts.

"You know Daniel, only a few months ago, I thought my life was over. It has been a hell of a ride, but somehow I survived."

"You are here," Daniel replied, "because it is part of your path, to be here. Luckily you followed it in the end. You weren't meant to die on the floor of your apartment. Your guardians ensured that to be the case.

"Trying to understand our existence on this planet is difficult. We come with no road map. No instructions. We take one step in front of other and hope we are making the right decisions. When we live within a certain vibration, your life will change. If you remember it is still following a path for you to learn something. So don't expect struggle to be removed. It is how you perceive it and react to other energies, that will determine your improvement.

"Expect setbacks and live always through a spiritual perspective.

"....and learn to surrender to it. We tend to fight the path that we are travelling. You can't find your "way", if you struggle to let it become."

"Can you clarify that a little more?" Valentina asked.

"Most of our lives we fight to become more human. We search for the things that make us human. New cars, toys, jobs, or people that make us feel worthy. Instead, you can still have your ambitions and wants, but realise that trying to force energy into that square peg, when it should be a round hole is a fruitless exercise.

"Learn to 'allow'. Let your path unfold and realise that your intentions will help you to create your reality. As long as it is aligned with your higher purpose then it will become so."

"So how will I know if it aligned?" said Valentina.

"You will feel it. You will notice when things you do, are no longer forced. When people around you are also aligned and you are not with them for what they give you, materially, physically, or emotionally, then you are in the spirit of alignment. Your creativity, which is a part of all of us is finally unleashed.

"When I say creativity, I don't necessarily mean that you can now paint or draw, I am referring to the ability to create a fuller, more enriched life on earth, because it is one that is aligned with the higher YOU. The real you, that has chosen to have a human experience."

They both looked at each other and smiled spending the rest of the night laughing, telling stories, and remembering their ordeal over the last few months.

Recalibration

Eventually it was time for Valentina and Daniel to part ways and to each to fly back home. Daniel back to the Alice Springs and Valentina to Los Angeles.

Upon Valentina's arrival into the States, she was greeted by family and friends at the airport when she returned. It had been a long trip, but she was glad to finally be home with loved ones.

The following Sunday, there was a big lunch to be held and everybody, including the neighbours turned up. Everybody wanted to know about what had happened in her life. From her trip to Australia, kidnappings, bikies, and prisons in Asia.

"Most importantly" Valentina told the group, I learned how to live.

"I made deep friendships and lost deep relationships. I suffered, but I grew. I understood the Universe point of view, rather than the human point of view.

"I am eternally grateful to all of you and those on the other side of the world that helped me understand that I am more than what you *see* in front of you. I have purpose and today I want to announce that I intend following my purpose" Valentina said to her captive audience.

Turning to her mother and sister, "I'm sorry mama, but I still wish to heal people and I think I can do that in a different capacity. I have just been accepted to work with the indigenous people in Australia. I know that they need good doctors, and I want to reconnect with the earth and make a difference. There is so much for me to learn, which I cannot gain here.

"Please don't be mad, but for now, this is my calling. Some of their communities have problems that I think I can relate to and understand."

Her mother put Valentina's face in her hands and lovingly looked in her eyes.

"My dear Valentina, I could not be happier than to hear you are finding a new life and still using what you studied and trained for. Of course, I would have preferred, it was here near me, but our hearts are never far from each other. Your sister and I will talk to you regularly online, and you must promise to come home from time-to time."

"Of course, mama, Australia is safe, and I already have friends over there."

Everybody clapped and a good time was had by all that day, and well into the evening as they ate and danced to the music.

Her friends all wanted to know the whole story. What was it like in Australia and Thailand and dealing with drug gangs?

She did her best to give some detail around what she had seen, but she struggled to explain what had taken place within herself.

Over the next few weeks, Valentina put her affairs into order and prepared to move to the land down under. There was a lot to pull together, but her family and Daniel guided her as to what she would need to make such a transition across the water.

She sold all her furniture and her car, giving away some of her belongings to local charities.

She made sure to catch up with old colleagues, who had helped her in hospital and thanked those that had contributed to her recovery, including Dr Riley who had been kind enough to hold her job for a period before her resignation.

Eventually, she had a girl's day out with her best friend Mia, which included a day of shopping and a nice sit-down lunch for just the two of them.

"There is something different about you Val," Mia said. "I just can't pinpoint what it is. It's like you are more confident. Like something in you has been ignited, I will say."

"I think you are onto something," Valentina replied. "Something has been ignited. For such a long time, I thought my life had been extinguished. Something not worth living.

"Funny isn't it, my job was to save lives, but it was my life that needed saving. Even with Jacob, I didn't understand the true meaning of why I was here on this planet. Jacob was good for me to forget my demons, so I thought.

"I think we both brought each other's demons out, and together we both needed to release them. He will have to repeat his journey, potentially back on earth. Maybe somewhere else, but I think it will be back here. I'm guessing, I'll make a trip back with him too. Who knows what that will look like?

"What I do know is, he is my soul mate, and I'll travel with him forever.

"You know something Mia. I don't fear death now. I used to a little when I would see people badly injured in the emergency ward. Sometimes on reflection afterwards, I would wonder about my own mortality. Now I think that is a silly concept. "My mortality". I have the opportunity and the knowledge to live forever. In a place that is so different, yet so familiar.

"Daniel told me once that when he died, he was amazed by all the colours that he could now see. He said that there are colours on the other side that we have yet been exposed to. It's almost like our world is dull and when we do move on, our eyes are finally opened. The veil is lifted.

"I am eternally grateful to know that when my journey here finishes, that it just gets better."

The two finished their lunch and made their way back to Mia's car. They hopped in after placing their bags in the boot and Mia turned up the radio.

They sat back and listened; it was a song by Alicia Keys called No One.

It was her and Jacob's favourite song.

For the first time, Valentina really listened to the words as she lay back on her seat with the sunroof open and the sun beaming down on her face.

It talked about nothing, and no one can get in the way of how you feel for someone you love, no matter how bad it gets. Even when you are in pain, your love will come through and things will work out.

Valentina thought of Jacob and how it didn't matter where he was in the universe, their love would last forever.

She sat back, right against the headrest and then almost jumped from her seat, as she mumbled to herself.

"The Key.... *Alicia Keys*. The singer, that was what he was talking about."

"Who was talking about honey?" said Mia.

"It was a message from Jacob. He wasn't trying to tell me about where there was a drug stash or sending me a physical key. He knew that his time was coming. He wanted to express his love from the beyond, through music that we both loved. He wanted me to know that he would always be there for me.

Then some of the words of the song replayed back in her head about everything was "gonna to be alright".

Valentina smiled knowing that she was going to be fine. She lay back in her seat tapping to the music in her head. Jacob's wish of bringing her back to Australia to live was to now be fulfilled.

She had found her WAY and was never again alone in this world.... or the next.

Author's Note

Many centuries ago, the world was more aware of its roots. Older civilizations and indigenous people were exposed to our true creation story. To our true spirituality. Somewhere along the way we have lost it to a modern world, where "things" have replaced interaction. Where people choose to talk to the person next to them if only, they have a phone in their hand.

In order to regain our true selves and move towards the Source, we need to begin to see who and what we really are. Spiritual beings that have chosen to gain new Wisdoms on a planet that provides challenges for our own growth.

In order to change consciousness on this planet, you need to firstly understand origins of spirit and why soul chooses paths of difficulty. That coupled with a mindset of understanding and removing old thinking and barriers that hold back not only our own well-being, but the well-being of the Unity Consciousness of all spiritual beings that reside on this planet.

If you wish to begin to the first step towards change, then you need to work on yourself. To understand your origins and then live life through that lens of connection to something greater than you.

The world is currently falling asleep. There has always been hope that humans would begin raising their consciousness to a level that would transform our very existence.

With an ebb and a flow, we have seen it rise and then fall back, as we have entered an age that we now have begun to drug our children and turn on our backs on anything that cannot be proven.

All is not lost for humanity, because we are not humanity. We are spirituality.

Manny Fiteni

About the Author

Manny Fiteni is an author and educator of people around the world who choose to transform their minds and begin a journey of understanding their human and spiritual connections.

Through his D.R.E.A.M Methodology he can bring about change in both adults, teenagers and the business community.

Manny's path started in the corporate world of finance and investing, requiring him to work at optimum levels for long periods. His interest in self-development and spirituality has taken him on a journey of self-discovery, which now translates into his teachings and books.

Today he is a leader in helping individuals and businesses create their own transformational journeys.

www.mannyfiteni.com